Wolf's mouth lingered upon Dara's, his tongue testing and seeking entrance to the sweet cavern beyond her lips. Humiliated by her own perfidy, Dara began to push against his chest. She could stand no more torture. She wanted him to kill her and be done with it before she further betrayed what honor she had left.

"Have you no heart? Do you have to torture me before you end my life?"

Wolf looked down at Dara, bewildered. "End your life? I know in the past my kisses have made some women swoon, but they have yet to be proven fatal."

"You mean you don't intend to drown me?"

"I meant only for us to bathe, but since you prefer other sport, I am more than willing to oblige your wishes."

"You mean you only brought me here to seduce me?"

Also by Cordia Byers
Published by Fawcett Books:

CALLISTA
NICOLE LA BELLE
SILK AND STEEL
LOVE STORM
PIRATE ROYALE
STAR OF THE WEST
RYAN'S GOLD
HEATHER
DESIRE AND DECEIVE
EDEN
DEVON
THE BLACK ANGEL

MIDNIGHT SURRENDER

Cordia Byers

FAWCETT GOLD MEDAL • NEW YORK

A Fawcett Gold Medal Book
Published by Ballantine Books
Copyright © 1994 by Cordia Byers

All rights reserved under International and Pan-American Copyright Conventions. Published in the United States of America by Ballantine Books, a division of Random House, Inc., New York, and simultaneously in Canada by Random House of Canada Limited, Toronto.

Library of Congress Catalog Card Number: 94-94409

ISBN 0-449-14782-7

Manufactured in the United States of America

First Edition: October 1994

10 9 8 7 6 5 4 3 2 1

Chapter 1

Thunder seemed to shake the eight-foot-thick granite walls of Castle Phelan. The sound jerked Wolfram into a sitting position. His abrupt motion sent waves rippling across the hot bathwater and over the sides of the large brass-bound tub in which he soaked his aching body. He'd just drifted off into a light, relaxing doze when the loud commotion from the main hall interrupted his rest. A frown chiseled a path across his wide brow as another roar came from below. Giving an angry swipe, he rid his face of the steamy moisture that had condensed upon his skin and came to his feet, again sloshing the water over the sides of the tub onto the wide, rough-hewn floorboards.

Ignoring the puddle he'd made, Wolfram stepped from the tub wearing only the amulet he'd been given at birth by the woman he considered his mother. In his thirty-two years of life, he'd never taken off the aged medallion. Made of brass, and of no value to anyone but himself, it had long ago turned blue-green, leaving the strange symbols carved into its tarnished surface barely visible to the eye. However, the master of Castle Phelan treasured the small object as he treasured all of his possessions. It was all he had to remind him of the woman who'd raised him until her death, when he was ten years of age. Upon her deathbed, Ada revealed the secret that had changed how he viewed all women. She

1

also made him swear never to take off her gift, telling him that it would bring him luck.

Wolfram had never believed the medallion held any magical power, as his mother seemed to have thought, but he still wore the amulet in memory of her and the sacrifices she'd made for him.

Wolfram's hard-planed body gleamed golden in the torchlight as he stalked across the chamber to the door and threw it open with such force that the heavy oak portal crashed back against the gray stone wall. Splinters of shattered wood flew through the air as he strode out into the dimly lit corridor and down the passageway to the stairs that led below.

Exhausted from the long day he'd spent going over Phelan's lands and the disaster left by Phelan's last steward, he was in no mood to put up with his men's raucous behavior on this eve. He wanted to enjoy a few hours of peace and quiet before he once more had to face the problems he'd assumed when he accepted King Edward's beneficence.

The thought made Wolfram's lips quirk into a sarcastic grin. He wasn't so addlepated that he was foolish enough to believe Phelan a charitable gift. Wolf knew exactly the reason King Edward had bestowed the castle and the land upon him. At a time when every pence counted in England's coffers, the king could ill afford to pay for Wolf's services in any other manner. Edward III, the tall, energetic, pleasure-loving warrior king, was also a shrewd politician who knew how to manipulate people to do his bidding. He had found a way to reward Wolfram without it costing him money or a rift between himself and his nobles. He had granted his bastard mercenary the gift of knighthood and Castle Phelan. The knighthood ensured Wolfram's continued loyalty, and Castle Phelan's dilapidated condition staved off the jealousy of Edward's nobles. None of them wanted the responsibility of trying to make the impoverished estate prosper. It would put too much of a drain upon their own finances at a time when the taxes to feed Edward's war against France were already putting a strain upon their purses.

The thought of the problems Edward's gift had created in his life wiped away what might have been construed as a slight smile. His expression turned even darker as his bare feet took the last worn stone step and he came face-to-face with the chaos that had erupted in his hall.

"Sean, Seamus, enough! Or I'll have you both put in the dungeon!" Wolfram ordered upon seeing two of his best men wrestling in the circle of onlookers.

Like a bucket of cold water upon a fire, Wolfram's stern command drowned the spectators' enthusiasm for the skirmish going on between the two men. Their cheers of encouragement died in the air as they turned to find the master of Castle Phelan standing naked and furious like an ancient bronze deity. His hard, muscular body seemed to exude power, making everyone aware of the strength the new master of Phelan possessed.

Several of the serving wenches made the sign of the cross and shyly turned away after a quick, furtive inspection of the battle-hardened body of the man who had only recently come to claim the improvised domain that overlooked the cold waters of the North Sea. His male beauty awed them and set their hearts pounding against their ribs, yet they couldn't stop the sensation of fear that also accompanied Wolfram's sudden appearance. Excitement and apprehension mingled and made them shiver at the prospect of being under the same roof with the handsome man whom people called the Lone Wolf.

Those who couldn't explain his prowess in battle had accused him of being part man and part beast. However, after close inspection, none who viewed the master of Castle Phelan in his naked glory could find any sign of the wolf in the sinewy body. It wasn't until they looked into his black, fathomless eyes that they realized why others were wary of Wolfram of Phelan. There, in the shining depths, they saw the untamed forces within; there, in the onyx pools shadowed by thick, curling, sooty lashes, lay the fire that drove him, the ambition that made the world fear him as they did his namesake.

A blanket of silence settled over the hall, with the exception of the blows and grunts still coming from Sean and Seamus MacDonald.

"Hold, I say!" Wolfram ordered again. His eyes moved over the assembly surrounding the fight. He mentally noted the provocative looks and smiles he received from the more brazen women who served in his household, and he stored the information away for later use, when his tired body was in a more amicable mood.

Wolfram wasn't surprised by the open flirtation. He well knew his own appeal to the opposite sex and accepted it as his due. Since his first woman at the age of twelve, he'd known the effect his large body and sex had upon women of all stations in life. Be they lady or maid, he had no problem keeping his bed filled and his body satisfied. Women had spoiled him by throwing themselves in his path. They had also engendered a certain amount of contempt for their sex by their willingness to surrender everything they possessed to have the famed Wolf in their beds.

Wolfram loved the female body and the satisfaction it gave him. However, he considered women weak, brainless creatures who needed a man's firm hand to guide and protect them from themselves.

Phelan's priest said women were afflicted with a weakness for sin, their bodies serving as vessels for the devil to tempt man's flesh. And he urged all men to resist their demon's way, saying it was up to men, who had the strength and courage that their weaker counterparts did not possess, to save the sinners, or all women were doomed to suffer in hell for being such abominations in the eyes of God and the Church.

Wolfram didn't agree entirely with the priest's views about women being vessels of the devil, but he had as yet to meet a woman who had the strength to resist his seduction. He drew his thoughts back to the struggle that continued between the two men.

Disgusted, his temper sorely vexed, he strode across the hall to where a long stave had been carelessly left by one of the men-at-arms. Gripping the long wooden pike with both hands, his expression unaltered, he turned and purposely entered the circle of spectators. The powerful muscles that thickened his arms and banded his wide chest flexed smoothly beneath his bronzed skin as he raised the weapon and brought it down across the two men's dark heads. The blow echoed across the hall as the two jerked and then spun about to defend themselves against this outside attack. Bull-necked and ox-chested, the two giants stared at the naked man, ready to give assault until they realized whom they faced. Each handsome face mirrored a sheepish expression as they glanced back at each other. Standing shoulder to shoulder, ready to defend each other as they had done since they were old enough to remember, their identical features reflected their dismay at having the master of Castle Phelan's anger directed upon them. Twins in face and form, Seamus and Sean MacDonald waited for Wolfram to speak.

Wolfram tossed the stave back across the hall, ordered one of his men to see that it was taken to the armory, and then turned back to eye the twins critically. His exasperation mounted. They would never change. The rogues were two of his best men, and their love of battle had often seen him victorious. However, their love of a good fight often led them to fight each other when they couldn't find anyone else.

Wolfram drew in a deep, determined breath. He wouldn't allow them to continually disrupt his household with their squabbles. If they wanted to fight each other, they would have to settle their disagreements outside the castle walls. Phelan was old and far too dilapidated to withstand two giants battling within its halls. And though he himself made his living fighting other men's wars, he wanted peace within his own home, and he would have it if he had to throttle the MacDonald brothers with his own bare hands.

Dark brows knitting over his straight narrow nose, he eyed the twins grimly. "What is the meaning of this?"

Again the two, who had become known as Ox and Bull because of their size and temperament, glanced at each other and shrugged good-naturedly. Grins spread across their craggy faces. "We had a minor disagreement over a wench."

Wolfram's dark brows lowered. "Your minor disagreement has nearly taken the roof off the place."

Sean the Ox's grin deepened as he glanced overhead and then back to the man feared by so many. "It would seem we're losing our touch."

His attempt at levity didn't succeed with the master of Castle Phelan. "I've warned you two before. I'll have no more fighting. This is my home now, and I'll have peace here. Do you understand?"

Another sheepish look passed over the MacDonald twins' faces and they nodded. "Aye, my lord. We do get carried away at times."

"Then it's settled," Wolf said, and turned to go back up the stairs and finish his bath before the water grew any colder. The tension of the last few minutes had done little to ease his aching muscles.

To the dismay and shock of a man dressed in the king's livery, Wolf nearly tread upon him. The man jumped back to avoid a collision with the naked giant who towered over him by several inches.

"What do you want here?" Wolf asked, unperturbed by the man's sudden appearance or his own state of undress.

"I—I—" the messenger stuttered, turning beet-red before clearing his throat and attempting to speak again. His gaze swept down Wolf's naked frame, resting momentarily on the narrow hips and the masculinity cradled in the dark glen of curls before he jerked his eyes back to Wolf's face. "I'm sorry, my lord. I'm not used to coming upon such a scene."

Wolf smiled. "Have you never seen a naked man before?"

"Ah, yes . . . but a naked man separating two identical giants is not oft' seen. 'Twas a sight to behold. Like two Atlases battling for Thor's world." Again the messenger's gaze swept down over the hard planes of Wolfram's well-hewn body. He moistened his lips and again cleared his throat.

Wolf's expression darkened. He'd seen men like this one before, and cared not for them. Perhaps sodomites had their place in the scheme of things, but he preferred they keep their desires to themselves. "Again I ask what you do here."

The messenger, realizing his error, jerked his gaze back to Wolf's face once more and determinedly kept it above the wide, strong shoulders that looked carved from granite by a master sculptor. His decision didn't help quell his sudden desire to touch and taste the man. He suppressed a yearning sigh that threatened as he took in the pure beauty nature had wrought in the man's face. His voice mirrored his admiration as he said, "I came with a message from King Edward to his knight, Wolfram of Castle Phelan."

"Then I am the man you seek," Wolfram said. "Make yourself comfortable at my table while I clothe myself. Then we will speak in my chamber."

The messenger bowed courteously, but could not stop the sigh that escaped as he watched the bronzed god ascend the stairs.

The messenger reined in his desire. He knew he could lust after Sir Wolfram until the end of his days. The look he'd received from the man left little doubt in his mind to which sex he preferred. The master of Castle Phelan did not welcome his attentions. Again the messenger sighed and gave a mental shrug as he glanced toward the long table set up near the huge fireplace. He scanned the assembly, hopefully searching for a man who might understand his interest and be willing to sympathize with his plight.

The messenger nearly squealed aloud when he turned and came face-to-face with two thick bodies. He moistened his lips as he slowly looked up at the two giants who had been doing battle when he arrived. He gave them a wobbly smile and swallowed uneasily as they stood assessing him through eyes as blue as the morning sky.

Ox returned the messenger's smile and slapped the smaller man companionably on the shoulder. "You've nothing to fear here. The wolf only eats his enemies."

"Come sup with us, little one," Bull said. "Then tell us the news from London. Is there word from France? Does the king send for us? Are we going to fight again?"

Suddenly feeling as if he'd escaped the executioner, the messenger nodded, though he couldn't divulge his reason for journeying to Phelan. However, he'd not chance insulting the two giants by refusing to sup with them. If necessary to stay in their good graces, he'd fabricate gossip from Edward's court.

Wolfram cast a regretful look at the tepid bathwater and then shrugged into his velvet dressing robe. It seemed of late he could find no time to himself. Everyone and everything was demanding his attention since he'd become a landed knight of the realm. He brushed back a raven curl that fell over his brow. He was beginning to believe that war was a far easier way of life than that of a man responsible for the land over which men fought.

Wolfram crossed to the table, which held a flagon of ale and several stacks of documents that needed his attention. He ignored the pile of parchment and poured himself a goblet of the dark, rich brew. He was now wealthy enough from the booty taken during his campaigns to have servants attend his every need, but after so many years of seeing to his own welfare, he felt uncomfortable at summoning a servant to pour a simple goblet of ale.

Wolfram crossed the chamber and settled himself in the leather monk's chair in front of the hearth. He stretched out his long, shapely legs to warm his feet by the fire, slowly sipped the ale and savored the warmth it created within his belly as he wondered what message the king's man had brought. It had been his understanding at his last meeting with Edward that he was now free to retire to the property the king had given him. His services would no longer be required.

Wolfram let out a long breath and dropped his gaze to the flames devouring the thick logs. He was tired of fighting, tired of intrigue. All he wanted now was to settle down and put all his energies into making Phelan prosper so that his children would never have to live as he had.

The chiseled planes of his face hardened with the memories. His eyes narrowed as he watched the past rise through the flames. His first years hadn't been easy, but Ada had seen that he never went hungry. From the pittance she earned selling her herbs and pigs at market, she'd kept him clothed and fed and had seen him educated by the monks at St. Andrew's priory. He'd never questioned why he had been one of the privileged few to be taught his letters and to cipher numbers. Like all children, he'd taken his life for granted, never expecting it to change.

However, it had altered drastically when Ada died. But before she took her last breath, she revealed the truth of their relationship, explaining to him that his true birth mother had been a noble lady who left monies for his upkeep during the months Ada was to wet-nurse him. Ada explained that she'd used the coins for his education at the priory, wanting him to have a small part of what he truly deserved.

Ada also told him that after the first year, when he was weaned and it was time for him to be returned to his real mother, she had not come to claim him. Ada had tried to find her, but to no avail, learning that the lady had given a fictitious name when she'd taken Wolf to the village. Having no recourse unless she, too, wanted to abandon him, Ada had raised him as her own. Now, with her death imminent, knowing she was leaving him defenseless, she told him the story of his past, with the hope that he might in some way find his real family.

Wolfram's brow furrowed at the bitterness that rose at the memory of the years that had followed Ada's death. Absently, his hand closed about the amulet on the leather thong about his neck. Ada's hopes had never been realized. After her death, he'd had no time to consider anything but his own survival. The breath had barely left Ada's lifeless body before he'd been cast out of the tiny thatched cottage. He then turned to the only people who he thought might offer him aid. But alone and possessing no coin to pay for their benevolence, the monks had turned him away when he'd gone to the priory.

It had taken only a few hours for the ten-year-old Wolfram to realize he'd find no charity in the world in which he lived. Without wealth or a family name, he and those like him were considered a bane upon society, and everyone did their best to see them wiped off the face of the earth.

Wolfram had been too stubborn to meekly surrender to such a fate. He refused to just lie down and die. He had begged, stolen, and fought to eat, and had learned early that the strongest survived. He also learned any show of gentleness could be construed as weakness, and leave him open to attack. As the years passed and his body matured, he'd realized his strength and courage were commodities that he could sell to those who hired men to fight their wars.

That knowledge had come on the day he'd saved Lord Sidney's life against a band of thieves. Out of gratitude, Lord Sidney had taken him under his wing, polishing the rough-hewn, half-grown man until he became a man to be reckoned with. Swift and proficient with the weapons of war, Wolfram served his benefactor loyally until Lord Sidney's death. However, Lord Sidney's attention had also made him enemies, such as Nigel Sidney, the lord's elder son and heir. He'd hated Wolf from the moment of their first meeting, and had tried often through the years to make his father hate Wolf. His lack of success only added to his hatred, and as soon as Nigel claimed Lord Sidney's title and lands, he turned upon Wolf, ordering him from his home and off his land forever.

Having no home nor any other way to make his living, Wolf began to hire out his talents to the highest bidder. A reckless young man who lived on the edge of danger, heedless to the consequences in love or war, Wolf's boldness and skill at both made him the victor and gained him the reputation of a man to be feared.

"Papa? Is Ox and Bull fighting again?" a small voice said from the doorway.

Dragging his thoughts from the past, Wolfram looked toward the door where a small, dark-haired girl stood timidly looking at him. He sighed mentally, accepting the fact that if he had any weakness, it was for the tiny bit of a person who looked at him through large brown, worshipful eyes. She was the only female he'd ever allowed to touch his heart after Ada's death. He viewed all others with an eye jaundiced by the memory of his birth mother's abandonment and the misery he'd endured because she'd not wanted to claim him.

A slow smile tugged up the corners of his mouth. "Aye. But they've now called a truce for a moment. Isn't it far past the time that you should be in your bed?"

The little girl's smile lit her cherubic face. She glanced down the passageway to make sure her nursemaid was nowhere in sight before she bounded toward the tall man seated in front of the fire. A giggle escaped her as she clambered into his lap and settled herself firmly against his hard middle. As had become her habit since she was old enough to notice the medallion about her father's neck, she reached for it and smoothed her small fingers over the blue-green surface as she answered him honestly and with as much dignity as she could muster in her five-year-old body. "Aye, but I couldn't sleep with all the commotion going on downstairs. Ox and Bull are worse than the stable boys."

Wolfram's smile deepened as he arched a brow at his

daughter. "What do you know of stable boys, pet?" He wound his fingers in the dark curls that were as gossamer fine as newly spun silk.

"Enough to know they fight and roll over and over in the mire." She wrinkled her small nose. "I don't know how anyone could like a boy. They're all nasty creatures."

Wolfram chuckled. "Pet, I hope you still feel that way in ten years. It would save me much worry." Wolfram set the child from his lap and stood. "Now, my sweet Ellice. It's time for you to get back to your bed. I have business to attend this eve."

Ellice looked up at her father and took his strong brown hand. "Will you tuck me in, Papa? Nurse is snoring so loud, I'll never be able to wake her."

Wolfram lifted his daughter into his arms, mentally making a note to speak with Ellice's nurse. If the woman could sleep through the ruckus that had taken place earlier, something untold could happen to his child and the nurse would never be aware of it. His arms tightened about Ellice. If the nurse wasn't always vigilant, it would be easy for his enemies to steal his daughter.

Wolfram's soft expression faded with the thought. Should anyone attempt to ever harm his child, they would pay with their lives. He protected those he loved and what he owned.

After tucking Ellice safely back into her bed, he kissed her and started to turn away. "Are you going away again?"

Her soft question made him pause and look back at his daughter. Wolfram attempted a reassuring smile. "I know not, pet. At the moment I don't intend to ever leave you again, but I must do as my king bids."

Ellice seemed to accept her father's answer far better than he did. She nodded her understanding and then curled on her side, her small hands cradling her rosy cheek. "Good night, Papa. I love you."

"Good night, pet. May the angels bring you sweet dreams," Wolfram whispered as he bent and brushed his lips against her brow. "And I love you. Always remember that."

Wolfram returned to his chamber to find the king's messenger awaiting him with Ox and Bull. His questioning look was like an unspoken command. Without a word, they shrugged good-naturedly and left him to discuss his business in private.

"Now, sir. What message do you deliver from our good King Edward?" Wolfram asked, striding behind the table. With a wave of a hand he indicated the messenger to take the chair in front of it. After the man was seated, Wolfram settled himself in his chair and braced his elbows on the table's rough surface, awaiting the man's answer.

The messenger dug into the small leather satchel at his belt and withdrew a rolled parchment. He started to hand it to Wolfram and then paused, wondering if his host could read. Though beautiful in face and form, he knew the man was of low birth and had only gained knighthood as payment for his services to the king.

Accurately reading the man's hesitation, Wolfram reached for the document and once more silently thanked his mother for her forethought in seeing to his education. The look of surprise that flicked across the messenger's face was his reward as he unrolled the parchment and perused its contents. A moment later he looked up, his dark eyes unreadable. He stared at the small man sitting across the table from him for a long moment before he came to his feet and walked to the fireplace. He stood with hands clasped behind his back. The firelight danced across the wide expanse of chest, exposed by the deep vee opening of his dressing gown, and drenched his features in gold as he stared into the flames as if searching for an answer to send to his king. Finally he turned his head to look once more at the messenger. "Can Edward find no other for this mission?"

The messenger came to his feet and shook his head. "You and the prince are friends. He knows you would not betray him."

"How odd for Edward to trust a mercenary and not his own nobles," Wolfram mused aloud, still undecided.

"King Edward also told me to tell you in private that he understands the expense Phelan has been upon your purse, and that you may keep all the plunder and ransom you gain instead of dividing it with the crown."

"Is the prince aware of Edward's decision?"

"Aye. The prince is the one who encouraged his father to ask you to join in the campaign."

Wolfram let out a long breath. "Then I have no other choice but to honor King Edward's invitation to join the Black Prince in France."

The messenger smiled his relief. "King Edward will be well pleased when I inform him of your decision."

"I will begin to gather my men and supplies tomorrow," Wolfram said, already mentally distancing himself from hearth and home and the image he'd built for himself as a landed knight of the realm. He drew in a long breath and seemed to grow even larger in size as he shed any semblance of a gentleman and once more became the warrior who fought and killed and thrived upon battle.

His raven hair fell in thick blue-black curls about his shoulders as he threw back his head and bellowed for the twins. In the distant recesses of the castle his call sounded like the howl of a wild animal. The servants who heard it made the sign of the cross and muttered among themselves about curses and devils. Sean's and Seamus's reaction was to smile at each other and bound up the stairs toward Wolfram's chamber. They had hoped the messenger had brought orders for Wolfram that would free them all of the drudgery of turning into farmers. War was far more exciting and adventurous than watching peasants till the soil.

The sound echoed through the granite halls, out over the crenellated towers, and into the moonlit night. The king's messenger shivered as he looked at the man whom Edward considered his fiercest warrior, and understood the king's reasoning. The Lone Wolf was returning to the hunt.

Chapter 2

France 1355

The silk standards displaying the colors and arms of the Rochambeau family swayed gently in the draft that moved through the great hall. The whitewashed granite walls were immaculate, showing no sign of soot from the large hooded fireplace that had been added to the castle less than a century earlier. Wealth and family pride had kept the stone fortress from becoming coldly militaristic through the two hundred years that it had stood in defense of the generations of the Rochambeaus.

The air held no scent of spoiled food or animal excrement, which often reigned in castles where numerous people slept, ate, and lived under the same slate roof. The Lady Dara of Castle Rochambeau saw to it that the servants sprinkled herbs over the fresh rushes covering the stone floors. Their minty fragrance shielded the senses against any of the offensive odors that often accompanied the men-at-arms and the servants who failed to bathe as frequently as their masters.

Torches burned from the rod-iron brackets along the walls supporting the arched ceiling of the main hall. Their light sent wavering shadows across the floors and ceiling, while sweetly scented beeswax candles in silver candelabra graced the white-linen-covered table upon the dais where the lady of the castle and her guest sat partaking of their meal of roasted pheasant, venison, and wild boar.

Dressed in the burgundy Rochambeau colors, a page stood close at hand, ready to respond to his lady's smallest request to refill her cup or silver plate. Other servants moved among the long trestle tables that had been set up below the dais. They served the lesser-ranked members of the Rochambeau household as well as the guests who did not merit eating at the table with Lady Rochambeau. They all dined on the same feast, heartily consuming the repast from trenchers of wood and tankards instead of the silver reserved for use by the Rochambeau family. The fine wine from the winery loosened tongues that were ordinarily staid, and the merriment increased as appetites waned for the food of the stomach and turned toward more lusty menus. The meal progressed, as did the noise, blocking out all conversation of the two people who sat upon the dais, away from those who might want to pry into the affairs of the mistress of Rochambeau Castle.

The joviality below the dais didn't penetrate the shock of the young ebony-haired, blue-eyed woman who sat looking at her guest as if he'd suddenly turned into a leper.

He gave her a smug smile and casually steepled his long, bejeweled fingers beneath his chin. His beard, as ebony as her hair, had been trimmed neatly into a point. Its color contrasted sharply with his pale skin, giving his appearance a satanic air as he narrowed his blue eyes and said, "I'm afraid you have no other choice."

"Charles, you must be mad to even contemplate such a thing," Dara Rochambeau said incredulously. She couldn't believe her cousin could come to her home and propose such a preposterous thing to her.

"No, my dear. I'm not mad. But I am your only living male relative, and it is my responsibility to see to your welfare. As the Count of Evreux and the King of Navarre, I understand the necessity to protect our family through strong marriages."

"I fear you forget Paul. He will be returning soon."

"I forget nothing, sweet cousin. I understand your need to still believe that your brother is alive, but I must think of your future." Charles released a long breath and sadly shook his head. " 'Tis a shame. Paul was a good man, and I, as his cousin and longtime friend, am only trying to do what I know he would do for you."

Unable to sit calmly and listen to his mad rantings any longer, Dara pushed back her chair and stood. He and Paul had never been friends. Charles of Navarre had never befriended anyone. He thought only of himself and what he could gain from his intrigues. He often pretended friendship to further his aims, but in truth, he was like a great black spider that lured its victim into its beautiful web to dine upon their flesh. Dara had no desire to have the Rochambeau fortune, or herself, be his next feast.

Navarre worked his wiles on those unwary souls who were gullible to his wealth and heritage. Through his mother, the daughter of Louis X, he was directly descended from the Capets, but his parents had renounced any claim to the throne of France. Believing himself denied his birthright, Navarre had become a jealous and scheming man who would do anything to reclaim the power he felt was his due. He'd even married King John's daughter, who had only been eight years of age when her father had tried to gain Charles's loyalty and influence in Normandy by attaching him to the Valois family with his own flesh and blood.

Charles of Navarre hadn't been satisfied with the king's favor, especially when no dowry was forthcoming. No matter what he gained, he had to have more.

"I truly don't know what you hope to gain by this,

Charles. But I won't do your bidding. You are not my legal guardian. Paul is. And until the time when the king decides to make me his ward, I have the right to do as I see fit with my life. That doesn't include marrying a man nearly thrice my age. Now if you will excuse me, I shall retire for the night. You and your men are welcome to stay at Rochambeau until tomorrow."

Charles's pale features flushed a dull pink. His congenial expression faded. He'd be obeyed or the girl would suffer the consequences. His eyes glowed with an icy blue light that reflected his cold, heartless resolve to force Dara to his will if necessary. "Dara, I would reconsider your decision, were I you."

Dara paused and looked back at the man sitting at the table. His velvet gipon with its fine linen undertunic and glittering buttons, and the fine cut of his close-fitting hose, reflected the man's riches. She didn't understand what more he could want. He was already the King of Navarre, the Count of Evreux of Normandy, and the son-in-law to the King of France. He possessed wealth and influence. What would he gain by forcing her to marry?

"But you aren't me, Charles. Now I would thank you to desist from this plan of yours, or I shall be forced to ask you to leave Rochambeau."

Charles came to his feet. "I had wanted to make this easy on you, cousin. But I see you are determined to force my hand."

"You have no power over me. Since father's death at Crécy, Paul has been my guardian and heir of Rochambeau."

"Paul was your guardian, but he is dead. Our good King John has granted my petition to make you my ward since I am your only living male relative."

Dara felt her world tremble, but she stood her ground. She inched her small chin up defiantly. "I don't believe you. King John would never place Rochambeau's welfare in the hands of a man whom he cannot himself trust."

Charles's expression turned harsh. "Lady, you test my patience and my good nature. I have done what I think is best for my family, and you will obey."

Dara shook her head. "No. I will not. Desist in this pretense. What you are trying to do is not for the Rochambeau family. It is for your own gain that you hope to marry me to the Marquise Duress."

Charles looked at Dara, his eyes cold and malevolent. He smiled grimly. "Do not say I did not try to be kind."

He raised a hand. The diamond rings flashed with a fire of their own in the candlelight as he snapped his fingers. In what seemed less than a blink of an eye, the hall filled with Navarre men-at-arms. He calmly glanced back to his ashen-faced hostess. "Now, my dear. Have your servants pack a few of your things. You will be staying at the Convent St. Marie until you decide to come to your senses."

Dara glanced at the stunned group sitting below the dais. Uncertainty, bewilderment, fear, and anger could clearly be seen upon their faces. She didn't know what to do. Her people would fight until their last breaths to defend her, should she ask it of them, but she knew they were outnumbered by Navarre's followers. His men-at-arms would fall upon them, slaughtering the Rochambeau people like sheep to the market. She shuddered at the horrible thought. She was responsible for these people and couldn't allow them to sacrifice their lives for her. Dara's shoulders sagged. Until she could find a way to thwart Charles's plans, she had no other choice but to allow herself to be sent to the convent.

Charles chuckled, astutely reading her thoughts. He confirmed her fears. "You're wise to decide not to put up any resistance. My men are well trained, and they would massacre your people were I to order it. Paul was foolish to take all of Rochambeau's best men with him. It left his home and his family vulnerable to attack. So you see why I now feel it is in your best interest that I intervene. You need someone to take care of you."

"Keep my brother's name from your foul lips. He went to fight for his Christ. Paul, in his good heart, believed that he left no enemies behind who would betray his family as you are doing."

A look of disgust flickered across the King of Navarre's narrow face. "More the fool was he if he thought he had no enemies in France. He should have stayed here to protect what was his. Now, Lady. Ready yourself for St. Marie. The Reverend Mother is expecting you."

"King John will know of your treachery," Dara threatened, grasping at anything to deter her cousin.

He merely smiled at her as if she were a simpleton. "Our good king is already aware that you may be guilty of treason, Lady. He is leaving it up to me to find out the truth. I am your judge and jury. And it is only through my generosity of spirit that you are allowed to go to the convent. You could be sent directly to the Bastille until I have either proven you innocent or guilty of the charges against you."

"You're lying. King John would never believe a Rochambeau disloyal."

"Perhaps at one time," he said, eyeing Dara calmly. He had things well in hand and wouldn't allow her shrewish behavior to rile his temper beyond his control. She would suffer for her insult once she was in the marquise's bed and his aged, withered flesh invaded her tender body.

Charles felt his sex stir at the thought of Dara naked beneath male flesh, and shifted in his seat to relieve the discomfort. He had to get a grip on his own desire.

Dara's virginity was far too valuable a commodity to even consider taking her, as he'd wanted since meeting her upon her twelfth birthday.

Putting his thoughts back to his plans, he regarded Dara calmly as he continued to destroy any hope she had of receiving help from France's king. "You see, my dear Dara, things are not going well for our monarch. The defeats his troops have suffered at the hands of the English, and the ravages to France's finances from the labor shortages left by the plague, have made our good King John distrustful. In the past he has foolishly allowed himself to be led astray by his father's advisers, de Lorris and de Bucy. That in itself was enough of a mistake to gain him only hostility from his subjects."

Satisfied that she could do nothing to thwart his plans for her, he continued, "So you see, dear cousin. You may decry me to my father-in-law, but it will do you no good. He has faith in me."

"Then I fear for France and our king," Dara said, unable to curb her wayward tongue. She had inherited the stubborn spirit that all preceding generations of Rochambeaus had been known to possess. The mountain goat had been her family symbol since the year 1000, when King Robert II had honored her ancestor by proclaiming that the Rochambeaus possessed the same qualities of the ram. Like the fine beast of the Alps, they were strong, fierce, and stubborn to a flaw. The standards hanging along the walls now bore the image of the ram ready to butt heads with the enemy. For more than three centuries her family had fought and died for France. And she'd not meekly surrender Rochambeau to this man whose intrigues were a disgrace upon the family name.

"Cousin, you do tempt fate. The marquise would not mind if his new bride came to him without a tongue. All he's interested in is what's between your legs."

"You are vile," Dara ground out, her voice filled with all the loathing she felt for Charles of Navarre.

Charles's thin control upon his temper finally snapped. He came to his feet and slammed a fist down on the white-linen-draped table. "Enough of your shrewish tongue. You have not heeded my warning, and now you must suffer the consequences." He cast a black look over his shoulder at the stunned audience, and then turned his gaze back to Dara, standing pale and defiant. An evil little smile tugged up the corners of his thin lips as he raised a bejeweled finger and pointed at one of the men seated at the lower table. "Take him and strip him bare. Then tie him to the whipping post in the bailey and lash him fifty times so all can see what happens to those who serve a traitor such as the Lady of Rochambeau."

What little color was left in Dara's cheeks drained away. She shook her head, unable to bear the thought of one of her people suffering because of her. She crossed to where Charles stood smugly watching two of his men capture their victim. They clubbed the man over the head with the hilt of a sword and carried him unconscious from the hall. "Charles, you can't do this. The man has done nothing."

The point of Charles's beard seemed to tremble as he snarled, "The man's suffering is on your shoulders, cousin. It is the price you pay for disobedience. Fortunately for your man, I am in a lenient mood tonight, or your serpent's tongue would have surely been the death of him. Now all he'll receive is a good whipping." His eyes narrowed as he placed both hands on the table and leaned forward. "I've endured enough of your belligerence, Lady Dara. If you do not do as I bid, the next man I choose will die."

Dara accepted her defeat as graciously as possible under the circumstances. "I will summon my maid to pack my things for St. Marie." The King of Navarre did not attempt to stop her as she turned away.

Dara stared out the narrow embrasure overlooking the gardens where the nuns grew vegetables to supply the convent and the few peasants who lived nearby. She'd been at St. Marie for nearly a month, but she had as yet to find a way to get a message out of the convent to King John.

Perplexed, Dara's brow furrowed and she thoughtfully chewed at her lower lip. She had tried to convince the Reverend Mother to send word to the king that she was innocent of the charges made against her. Unfortunately, her pleas had fallen on deaf ears. Though a good woman at heart, St. Marie's Reverend Mother had been taken in by Charles's charm as well as his power and wealth. She had told Dara that she should be grateful to her cousin. He was doing what was best for a young woman without the guidance of a father or brother to keep her out of trouble.

Though the Reverend Mother was a woman with authority, she found nothing wrong with Charles's actions, believing, like so many others, that a woman was too weak of mind to survive without a man's firm hand to help guide her in the righteous direction. She ruled a convent filled with women, but she had closed off her mind and heart to anything beyond the realm of the Church.

"Humph!" Dara snorted, disgruntled by her thoughts. "I need no man to guide me. I've proven that at Rochambeau." She was proud of what she had accomplished. Had she not taken on the responsibilities of the family estate when her brother decided to chase his dreams in the East, Rochambeau would now lay in shambles.

It annoyed her to be considered as something too

helpless to breathe without the dictates of a man. Having overseen the welfare of the Rochambeau lands and people, as she well knew other women did when their husbands and fathers were called to war, Dara didn't understand how women could be considered the weaker sex. They labored to bring life into the world in the field as well as in the bed.

Dara wasn't used to others looking at her as something too feeble-brained to think for herself. She'd been independent far too long. She'd been blessed with male relatives who had always treated her as an equal. Perhaps things would have been different had her mother lived. But Dara seriously doubted it. Her father had often bragged that his daughter was a match for any man. He'd prided himself on the fact that Dara could read and write and keep his accounts better than his male steward.

Dara had loved her father and brother deeply for the faith they placed in her. And she hadn't felt deserted or neglected when they went off to fight. She was proud of them and the courage it took to do battle for their beliefs, whether on the land of their birth or far away in the land of the Saracens.

Her father had given his life for France, and now, if what Charles said was true, Paul had also died for his country and religion. Dara drew in a shaky breath. It was too painful to contemplate. She didn't want to think that she had lost both her father and brother. They were all the family she had. Without Paul, she would be alone and at the mercy of men who only wanted to use her for their own gain.

Dara glanced up at the darkening sky and turned away from the window, determined not to dwell upon the things she couldn't change. It was nearly time for vespers, and she couldn't afford to be late or Reverend Mother would have her scrubbing the chapel floor again. Her knees still ached from the last time she failed to be on time for prayers.

Dara adjusted the soft white woolen wimple that floated like soft wings at the sides of her cap. Since coming to the convent, she'd been denied her own clothing. According to the Reverend Mother, they were the clothes of the devil. They had been stitched by women who sinned with the flesh, and she'd not have the lush velvets or brilliantly colored silks under St. Marie's roof. Dara had been given the mantle of a novice, and her own garments were stored in the leaky shed near the garden wall.

Her sandaled feet made little sound upon the timeworn stones as she hurried along the quiet corridors toward the sound of voices raised in prayer.

Dara paused to listen outside the tall, intricately carved chapel doors. She thoroughly disliked being held captive, yet couldn't stop herself from appreciating the sweet voices praising God. Were it not for the condition in which she was held, she could come to enjoy the peace and solitude found in St. Marie. She understood the comfort it gave the women who had decided to take the vows of the Church.

However, Dara recognized the fact that her own temperament was not suited for such an atmosphere. Too many more weeks behind the thick convent walls and she knew she'd go completely mad.

She rested her hand on the cold iron latch, but didn't enter the chapel, as was expected of everyone who lived beneath St. Marie's roof. She knew the only thing that had saved her sanity in the past weeks was her need to prove Charles of Navarre a liar to his king. She might have to wait to exact her revenge for what he had done to her, but sooner or later her time would come. She would prove her loyalty to King John and make him realize the treacherous snake he held to his bosom.

It had become her habit each night after the candles were extinguished and the convent's inhabitants found their rest in their tiny, barren cells, to lay plotting her revenge. She had sworn that King Charles of Navarre would suffer for every broken nail she'd received digging in the vegetable garden, every inch of red itchy skin she'd gained from washing the cooking utensils, and for all the sore muscles and bruised knees she'd received from scrubbing St. Marie's corridors.

"I see you are again attempting to thwart my orders, Lady Dara," Reverend Mother said quietly at her side.

Dara jumped with a start of surprise at the sound of the soft but firm voice. Her insides clenched into a tight knot as she recognized the voice she'd come to dread. Her cheeks flushed crimson with guilt, and she glanced uneasily away from the dark, assessing eyes. "I did not mean to be late, Reverend Mother."

"I seriously doubt any sinner sins on purpose, but they still have to suffer for the acts they commit," Reverend Mother said. Her voice mirrored none of the angry resentment she felt for the young woman who had been placed in her charge. The girl had shown no subservience since her arrival. Her spirit remained unbroken and undaunted by all the humbling chores assigned to her. She remained the Lady Rochambeau even when she'd had to lug buckets of manure from the stables for the garden.

Reverend Mother's eyes narrowed, and the chin band of her cap pressed into her skin as she pursed her lips. "Go to your cell. I will decide in the morning what punishment you deserve for this latest infraction. You are to have nothing to eat tonight."

Dara squared her shoulders, proudly defiant. "Mother, I have done nothing wrong. I was present at vespers, though I was on the other side of the chapel door."

"My decision is made. You cannot digress your way around the fact that you didn't attend vespers as directed. Since the King of Navarre brought you here, you have been determined to show all of us that you do not have to obey our rules. But in that you are wrong. I will see that you do, one way or the other."

"Mother, I don't wish to cause you any more trouble. If you will allow me to send a messenger to the king, I am sure he will understand that I am being kept here against my will and that I am not guilty of treason."

Reverend Mother's expression didn't alter. "Do not expect me to help you thwart your cousin as you've tried to do with me. The King of Navarre told me about your wicked tongue. I'll hear no more lies or pleas from you, demoiselle. Now go to your cell and await your punishment for disobeying me."

Dara acquiesced without further argument. For now, she'd hold her tongue. She didn't want to rouse Mother Superior's ire to such an extent that she'd be sent to the tiny cubicle beneath the chapel floor.

Dara shivered at the thought. She had learned of the punishment box from one of the young nuns. The box served as a place for the novices who had broken their vows to contemplate their sins. Several, it was rumored, had even died in the cramped little hold from suffocation.

Dara's old fear crept up her spine with prickly claws. She couldn't abide being confined in a small space, unable to move about freely. Even the thought of being locked in a room was a horror to her; being confined in a place like the penance box was unthinkable. She knew she would die should she ever suffer such a fate.

Dawn had just begun to lighten the eastern sky when Dara received her summons from the Reverend Mother. She'd slept little, and the black circles rimming her eyes mirrored her tortured night. Her knees quaked from lack of food, but she forced herself to remain standing in front of the older woman, who had seated herself in a thronelike chair behind a large, intricately crafted table with spooled legs that ended upon clawed feet.

Reverend Mother saw the strain upon the younger woman's face and nodded sagely. "I see from your eyes that you have already begun your punishment. However, I can't allow you to get by with such impertinence no matter how much sleep you lose. I have to set an example for the others. You are to scrub the corridors and empty the slops for the next week. If you disobey me again, I will have no choice but to put you in the penance box to contemplate the error of your ways."

"Thank you, Reverend Mother. I will do as you bid," Dara said, nearly sagging with relief.

"Now, you are excused."

Eager to be about her punishment, Dara turned away, but the Reverend Mother's softly spoken words made her halt and look back at the older woman.

"But, Lady Dara, I warn you. This is my last time. You will receive no more leniency from my hand."

Dara nodded mutely. There was nothing else to be said. While she was at St. Marie, she'd have to obey the rules. She quickly opened the door and closed it quietly behind her. She smiled as she started off to find a bit of cheese or bread to quell her hunger until the midmorning meal. She'd agreed to obey, but she hadn't agreed to quit trying to find a way to prove herself innocent of Navarre's charges.

Dara had just managed to choke down the dry crust of bread she'd cajoled the cook into giving her when the bell over the gate sounded a warning. Surprise and fear mingled within the sisters and novices who rushed from their daily chores and made their way to the top of the stone wall surrounding the convent.

In the distance the sound of horses and the clang of armor could be clearly heard. A peasant from the village came running up the narrow lane, waving his arms overhead as he cut across the cultivated fields and pasture where the convent's plump heifers grazed contentedly upon the lush green grass.

"They're coming!" he shouted up at the Reverend Mother as he skidded to a halt in the inner courtyard. Sweat streamed down his pale, fear-stricken face, and his breath came in short pants as he said again, "Hide, sisters. They're coming."

Before the Reverend Mother could ask who, she saw the dark line forming at the edge of the clearing. Her heart seemed to still in her breast as she recognized the English banners waving in the morning breeze. At the head of the procession rode three giants; two sat black destriers, while the one in the center rode a pure white horse. A red standard with the emblem of a black wolf flew overhead.

Reverend Mother made the sign of the cross. "God have mercy. It's the horsemen of the apocalypse." Her voice wavered. " 'Behold a pale horse and he that sat upon him his name is Death . . .' " Again she made the sign of the cross and glanced at the frightened faces of the women surrounding her. They had all heard the stories of the uncivilized English. They were said to be half beasts who slaughtered without mercy, raping and pillaging at will. Nothing was sacred to the monsters. 'Twas said they spitted and ate their victims' babes to appease the devil they worshiped.

Reverend Mother seemed to age within the moments she stood watching the English troops trample the newly sprouted crops. "What are we do to?" she asked no one in particular.

"We must close the gates, Reverend Mother," Dara said, taking charge of the frightened females, though her own heart felt none too brave within her breast. It began to pound against her ribs like a drummer set to a march when she saw the archers advancing behind the mounted men. Unstrung, the longbows they carried were as tall as the archers. It was the weapon that had felled her father at Crécy and had given the English the advantage.

"Yes, yes. At once!" Reverend Mother said, nodding her agreement before calling out, "Close the gates. This is a place of God and not of war. But we will not meekly lie down and die. They will have to take St. Marie by force if they do not give us amnesty."

The thick iron-bound portals swung closed and the bar clanged into place. The sound was nearly inaudible over the din coming from the English troops.

Reverend Mother glanced toward Dara and felt comforted by her presence. Less than an hour ago she'd censured the girl for her lack of humility and discipline. And until this moment she'd considered the Lady Dara far too worldly for a young woman of good name. Her spirit and easy laughter seemed to be ripe for the devil's purposes. However, the Reverend Mother was quickly changing her opinion. The inhabitants of St. Marie needed the girl's strength of character to see them through this trying time.

Reverend Mother reached out and took Dara's hand. She looked into her sapphire eyes as she spoke earnestly. "Lady Dara, you must tell us what is to be done. We have lived in peace even when war has raged around us. I can pray for my sisters' souls, but I lack the knowledge of how to deal with men who would harm them."

"Take the sisters back inside, Mother. I will wait here to learn the English soldiers' intentions."

"You are brave, Lady Dara," Reverend Mother said

gratefully. "We will go to the chapel and pray for God's mercy upon us."

"I'm not brave, Mother," Dara whispered as she watched the sisters hurry down the steps to the chapel like a flock of white doves. She didn't feel at all courageous standing alone on the convent wall to face an enemy that made her knees tremble. However, there was no one else who could negotiate an agreement that would see the convent and its inhabitants left in peace. She was the only person at St. Marie who had any experience in dealing with the world outside the convent walls. And she prayed she had learned enough from overseeing Rochambeau to keep the Reverend Mother and the sisters safe.

When the last sister fled into the chapel and closed the heavy doors, Dara turned to stare at the men approaching the convent. She couldn't suppress her reaction to the sight, and instinctively made the sign of the cross as she watched them drawing near.

The knight in the forefront left no room for equanimity. He looked ferocious, clad in silver and black armor, with the standard of a wolf flying nearby. He rode a magnificent destrier. Its iron-shod hoofs ate up the yards and sprayed dirt behind him. The knight controlled the beast with a strong hand as the animal jerked his fine head up and down and snorted as if eager to do battle.

Dara squared her shoulders and raised her chin at a haughty angle. She'd stand her ground, no matter how badly her feet wanted to run. She cleared her throat as the silver knight reined the great beast to a halt at the convent gates. He raised the visor of his helm and looked up at her.

"Open in the name of King Edward of England," the silver knight said in perfect French.

Dara didn't move. "St. Marie is a place of God. Go

your own way, Englishman, and leave us to our prayers."

The knight reached up and removed his helm. He brushed a stray raven curl from his brow before placing the helm in front of him on the saddle. He crossed his arms over the shining metal and once more looked up at Dara. He eyed her grimly. "Sister, we mean no harm to anyone within St. Marie's walls, nor do we seek to take what belongs to the Church. However, I will know if you are trying to shield our enemies from us. Now open your gates or I will order them breached."

Dara glanced uncertainly toward the chapel. The knight had promised no one would be hurt, but could she trust an Englishman's word? "We shield only those who have taken the vows of the Church. Now, leave here. Do not desecrate this holy place with men who lust for the blood of our countrymen."

"Mademoiselle, you try my patience. I have come to take St. Marie for the Prince of Wales in the name of his father, and I will take it either by force or your surrender. The decision is up to you."

"Please, monsieur, we ask that you leave us in peace to do God's work and to pray for the souls of those who die in your battles."

"I am sorry, mademoiselle, but I must insist that you open the gates. I will give you my word as a knight in the service of King Edward the Third of England that none within your walls will be harmed if they have not raised arms against us."

"This is a sacred place for the women who wish to serve God. We can't allow your men to profane it."

What little patience Wolfram possessed now came to an abrupt end. He'd done his best to convince the young nun that he'd not allow his men to harm the sisters of St. Marie. He had been ordered to secure the boundaries of the Black Prince's holdings, and he would do it whether a few nuns approved of his methods or not. He looked once more at the white-mantled young woman.

"Mademoiselle. I give you one last opportunity to open your gates to me before I have them broken down."

Stalwartly, Dara held her ground. "Monsieur. I will open the gates if you will promise that only three of your men will be allowed inside to search for your enemies."

Wolfram's dark eyes narrowed upon the slim form on the wall. His brow furrowed and another errant strand of blue-black hair blew across his forehead. He absently brushed it aside. "Ten, mademoiselle."

"Four," came her reply from the wall.

Deep lines etched Wolfram's shapely mouth. "Seven."

Dara folded her arms over her chest and glared down at the silver knight. "Five."

Something akin to a smile briefly touched Wolfram's lips before he gave a curt nod. "Five of my men will enter, but be warned, Sister. Should anything happen to any of them while within St. Marie, no prayers will save you from my wrath. I will brook no treachery from man or woman. I will level this place and execute everyone who resides here."

Dara stiffened, refusing to let him see her fear. She nodded. "Then we are in agreement. You will grant St. Marie and those within her walls amnesty once your men ascertain there are no enemies hidden here. And then you will leave us to return to our prayers."

"I have given you my word that no one will be harmed, but I fear I can't tell you we'll leave after the search. We make camp here for a fortnight or more."

"But—" Dara began, but Wolfram raised a silencing hand.

"Try my patience no more, Sister. Open your gates or rue the day you saw the Black Prince's forces approach St. Marie."

Knowing she had no other recourse, Dara called for the convent gates to be opened. Wolfram signaled for four men, and with them, he rode into St. Marie.

Chapter 3

Wolfram reined his destrier to a halt in the quiet inner courtyard and dismounted. He watched the young nun who had negotiated with him scurry down the narrow flight of steps that led to the courtyard. He involuntarily caught his breath when, in her haste, she nearly stumbled over the hem of her white mantle. With the grace of a gazelle she recovered her balance without a break in her stride and crossed to where he stood.

Wolfram felt his heart still as he looked down into the face of the young nun. He had seen many a beautiful face before, but never one that took his breath away as did this young woman dedicated to God. She possessed the face of a defiant angel, desirable, yet unattainable to man.

Wolfram's blood heated. He felt himself drowning in the sapphire depths of the large, thickly fringed eyes that stared bravely back at him, daring him to do his worst. Wolfram tore his gaze away from the intriguing eyes only to find it snared by the heart-shaped mouth that had been touched with the sweet hue of summer roses. Held in a firm, determined line, her luscious lips gave no indication that she could be easily conquered. Wolfram's blood heated anew, and he wondered how her perfect mouth would taste. Would it be as sweet as the soul she had given to God or as fiery as the look in her beautiful eyes? He was tempted to find out.

Suddenly realizing the impropriety of his thoughts, he jerked his gaze back to her eyes and was startled to see the first flicker of uncertainty within their fathomless depths. He smiled to himself, admiring the girl's courage, though he knew now that she wasn't as brave as she pretended.

"Sister, we are here on behalf of Edward the Third, King of England, Duke of Guienne, and the rightful King of France. If you harbor any enemies of his, I suggest you turn them over now or suffer the consequences."

Dara drew in a deep, steadying breath and prayed the English knight would not hear her heart slamming against her ribs like a rabbit caught in a cage. She feigned a bravery she did not feel and glared up into the dark eyes that watched her as if she were a mouse to be toyed with before being devoured. Dara squared her shoulders and resolutely ignored the tiny claws of fear that pricked their way up her spine. She'd not surrender to the urge that kept making her feet want to flee as far and as fast as they could carry her away from the imposing man. She couldn't leave the sisters unprotected to this silver-armored beast. She raised her chin. "Monsieur, I have already told you we harbor no one here who wishes anyone harm. And I would plead with you again to be merciful and leave us in peace."

Expecting no other answer, Wolfram ordered his men to dismount and start searching the cloister. He had not lied when he'd said that everyone at St. Marie would rue the day if they were concealing the enemy. No matter how attractive he found the young nun, or how sacred the convent, he would level it to the ground. He had been hired to secure and increase the boundaries of the prince's holdings when possible, and he would do it no matter who stood in his way. The Lone Wolf did not fail when he was sent out to hunt.

Wolfram turned toward the chapel, his long strides eating up the distance across the courtyard. Dara had to take three steps to his one as she raced to try to prevent him from entering. She threw herself against the intricately carved doors. Arms spread out, she shook her head. "*Non*. You cannot enter here."

"Step aside, Sister. I wish you no harm, but if you insist, I will physically remove your presence from my path," Wolfram said, undeterred by the nun's dramatic attempt to stop him. The young woman was beginning to annoy him. He had given his word no one would be harmed, but she kept acting as if he intended to slaughter everyone in sight.

Again Dara shook her head. "*Non*. You may search the rest of the cloister, but you may not trespass upon the sisters at their prayers."

Unable to stop himself from once again feeling the prick of admiration for her show of courage, but determined to finish what he'd come to do, Wolfram reached out with both hands and took Dara by the shoulders. He set her away from the door as if she were no more than a bit of eiderdown. Without a glance back at her stunned face, he opened the door and strode into the softly lit chapel.

The murmur of prayers slowly ebbed into silence as he made his way down the aisle to where the Reverend Mother knelt before the sepulcher that contained the bones of the convent's patron saint.

A man whose faith in the Church had been shattered when the priests turned him away from their door as a child, Wolfram believed in God but felt no need to link himself with a church. He felt as close to God mounted on his horse as he did in a place of worship. God to Wolfram was the earth, the trees, the air, the beauty of life, and the goodness within each. God was not the rules set by men in black robes. Perhaps he was a heathen in the eyes of Phelan's priest and those like him, but Wolfram wouldn't change to please the man or anyone else. Nor would he allow anything to come between him and his duties, be it the soft prayers of nuns or the hard battle cries of his enemy.

Hearing the jingle of steel mail behind her even before the last prayer dwindled into an uneasy silence, the Reverend Mother made the sign of the cross and clutched her rosary to her breasts as she slowly came to her feet and turned to face the man she'd seen from the distance. Expecting the pale, fleshless countenance of death, a gasp of surprise escaped her as she bent her head back and looked up into the knight's handsome face. She instinctively made the sign of the cross again. The man was the embodiment of everything evil. He exuded power, sex, dominance. His features had been carved by the devil's own hand to entice and weaken the spirit of those who might try to deny him.

God help their souls, the Reverend Mother prayed. The man was devastating to look upon. His eyes, as black as the devil's, held her bound in place, unable to move to defend her helpless charges. And his mouth, structured with firm, hard lips, crinkled slightly at the corners as if he mocked her inability to withstand his beauty.

The Reverend Mother tried in vain to speak, but no words came to renounce the devil's messenger who held her mesmerized and intimidated. Understanding the shock and fear his troops' arrival would have created among the cloister's inhabitants, Wolfram said, "You nor any of the sisters have anything to fear, Reverend Mother. I do only what my duty to King Edward of England and France requires. We don't war against women or the Church."

The Reverend Mother moistened her dry lips and swallowed uneasily. In the twenty years of her rule at

St. Marie, she had faced plague, pestilence, and famine, but nothing had ever terrified her as much as the Englishman who had already defiled the sanctum of the cloister. Until this day, war had raged around the convent, but never had it entered the gates.

"This place is a sanctuary," Reverend Mother said, finally finding her voice.

"There is no sanctuary for those who go against Edward," Wolfram said, sweeping the chapel with his dark, assessing gaze. From the vaulted ceiling, where a gold chandelier gleamed in the light spilling through the stained-glass windows over the altar, to the religious relics made of precious gems and metals, the vast riches of St. Marie were displayed with pride. The ransom for them would be great.

A flash of light streaked down the chapel aisle as his men trooped inside. They paused to appraise the chapel as Wolfram had only moments before. Ox came forward to where Wolfram still stood. "We searched every nook and cranny of the place and found no one."

Wolfram glanced over Ox's wide shoulders to see the young nun standing at the end of one of the pews, surrounded by her fellow sisters. She nervously chewed at her lower lip, unaware that her youthfully innocent gesture once more belied the brave front she'd displayed earlier.

Wolfram again felt his blood stir and forcibly drew his gaze back to the woman at his side. "Reverend Mother, I will require a portion of your stock and flour to feed my men. Our animals will also need grain."

"We don't have enough to feed your army. We have only enough for ourselves and the people we serve," Dara said, his words bringing her out of the trance that had held her still since the Englishman had entered the chapel. She fought down the feeling of terror that careened through her as the English knight's black gaze swept over her and then back to the Reverend Mother.

Wolfram cocked a brow at the Reverend Mother, wondering not for the first time why the woman allowed the young nun to speak for her. Seeing he'd receive no answer from the older woman, he directed his words toward Dara. "I do not ask for your charity. I demand your obedience. This place now belongs to King Edward the Third, and I hold it in his name. It is your duty to serve my men as you would serve him."

"Non," Dara said, pushing her way past the huge man who had come with the English knight. "If we allow you to take the stock and flour, our people will starve until the crops are harvested."

Wolfram's face hardened. "They are Edward's people now, Sister. And they will comply with my orders, as will you."

Putting aside her fear, Dara faced Wolfram. "If these lands now belong to your king, then it is his responsibility to see that his people do not starve."

"We do not ask them to starve, Sister, only to share," Wolfram said, approving the girl's spirit. It was a shame that she'd taken her vows. She would have been an interesting diversion while he completed his mission here.

"How do you share with thieves and robbers?" Dara said. "You English have ravaged this land, burning and pillaging until we have nothing left to share with our own children."

Dara's remark echoed through the silent chamber. All eyes riveted upon her before they moved to the face of the tall knight whose bronzed features seemed suddenly hewn from stone. His dark eyes reflected his anger as they pinned Dara to the floor. A despairing groan slipped from the nun standing behind Dara, but she quickly slapped a hand over her mouth to silence herself. Wide-eyed, she backed away from the center of the knight's fury.

"It is fortunate for you, Sister, that we do not war upon those who serve the Church."

"You do not war upon those who serve the Church because there is no need when you can starve them to death without wasting the effort to slay them with your sword."

"Enough," Wolfram growled, taking an involuntary step toward the young woman who dared to malign him to his face. No one had been so foolhardy since his first tourney, when he'd slain the man who had called him a bastard and a liar who did not deserve to participate with men of honor.

"Please, Sir Knight," Reverend Mother said, forced to intervene before Dara's wayward tongue saw her slain. "She is young and doesn't know of what she speaks. Please forgive her. You are welcome to share what we have."

Wolfram's dark gaze never left Dara's resolute little face. His words were laced with menace as he said, "Bite the hand of my generosity no more, Sister, or suffer the consequences."

Dara suppressed the shudder created by the chill of terror racing down her spine. The look in the knight's eyes bespoke no mercy should she rouse his anger again. Determinedly, she held her ground. She'd not cower. No Rochambeau would bow down to an Englishman.

"She will trespass no more upon your good graces, Sir Knight," Reverend Mother said, moving past Wolfram and taking Dara by the arm. She glanced back to the silver knight. "With your permission I will see her to her chamber."

"You are all free to return to your prayers, Reverend Mother. We have finished what we came here to do and now will bid you good day. This afternoon I will send several of my men here to collect what is our due. They will oversee the division of your stores as well as the stock animals."

The Reverend Mother nodded and quickly led Dara out of the chapel and down the tiled corridor to the narrow little cell. She closed the door behind her and then turned on the younger woman. Her voice was filled with nervous exasperation and apprehension as she said, "Your continued stubbornness would have seen you dead."

Dara crossed to the window and looked out at the garden that would soon help fill their enemies' stomachs. She nodded, fully aware that she'd allowed her tongue free rein while locking reason in the dungeon of her brain. She'd been foolish to argue with the knight, but no matter how she tried, she couldn't forget it was men like him who had slain her father at Crécy. It was men like him who were responsible for the suffering that now lay across France. It was men like him that made the hearts of young French maids take to flights of fantasy.

Dara abruptly stiffened as she realized the direction of her thoughts. How could she allow herself even to think about the man's beauty when in truth he was nothing but a monster clothed in silver and black?

Dara flashed the Reverend Mother a guilty look before looking down at her hands. "I'm sorry, Reverend Mother. It was unwise of me to challenge the devil's henchmen, yet I couldn't just meekly surrender everything you and the sisters have worked for. I know I have been here only a few weeks, but I have seen the good work that you do."

"Yes. We do good deeds, but we must temper even those, Dara. As you must temper your tongue. No life is worth a few bags of grain or pigs and chickens. You have done well by St. Marie today, and I would see you keep your stubborn little pate, no matter how exasperating you are."

Dara's face lit as she smiled at the Reverend Mother. For the first time she felt she could befriend the older woman. "Thank you for your intervention. In the future I will do everything in my power to give you no further cause for complaint."

"Your courage today has wiped away your past indiscretions. Now we must decide what is to be done."

Dara bit down on her lower lip and glanced once more toward the garden that she'd helped weed. The carrots and potatoes were now ready to pick. It wasn't right for them to have to give up everything to their enemies. She glanced back to the Reverend Mother and arched a questioning brow. "Is there anyplace that we might hide a portion of our goods, so that when they are divided, the Englishmen will receive far less than they expect?"

Reverend Mother's face lit and she nodded vigorously. "Yes. There is the old root cellar beneath the storage shed. It hasn't been used in years."

"Then that's where we'll hide the flour and grain," Dara said, dusting her hands together matter-of-factly.

Reverend Mother smiled. "If I'm not careful, child, I could come to appreciate your rebellious spirit."

Dara raised her chin proudly in the air. "I am a Rochambeau, Reverend Mother. We have never been a family to meekly surrender to anyone who thinks to conquer us."

"As I've found by experience," Reverend Mother said, her smile deepening before she turned serious once more. "Now, what is to be done?"

Like so many times on her own estate, Dara took charge. She quickly had the nuns scurrying from one cellar to another, hiding bags of flour, grain, potatoes, carrots, honey, fruit, and anything she thought the Englishmen would find useful.

It was well past the noonday hour when she paused to consider the consequences of her own actions. She hated to think what might happen to the inhabitants of St. Marie should the Englishmen suspect what they'd done. As the knight had said, he'd show mercy to no one. Dara shuddered visibly and suddenly felt like praying. She needed to reassure herself that she'd made the right decision, because her actions had now endangered everyone within St. Marie.

Unaware that a pair of ebony eyes watched her, Dara crossed the courtyard and entered the chapel. Silently she made her way down the aisle and knelt at the altar. She looked up at the stained window that depicted the story of Christ's life, and made the sign of the cross as she prayed for God's help in keeping the English knight oblivious to their ruse.

Wolfram quietly closed the chapel door and stepped out into the sunlit courtyard. He took a long deep breath of cooling air into his lungs and sought to put the young nun from his mind. It wasn't an easy feat to achieve. Unaware that she'd been observed in her prayers, the young nun had knelt at the altar, her beautiful face lifted to the window, her large blue eyes raised toward heaven. The soft afternoon light made her appear as an angel from the God to which she prayed.

Wolfram's heart slammed against his ribs and he shifted to ease the tightness that pressed against his braies. Damn! He was in a bad way for a woman if he was lusting after a nun. He hadn't meant to come back to the cloister with his men, but he couldn't get the young, defiant beauty out of his mind. From her reaction that morning, he'd suspected that she would try to convince the Reverend Mother to hide their supplies, but as far as he could discern, nothing had been disturbed. His men were now in the cellars dividing up the provisions.

Wolfram glanced once more at the chapel door and shook his head. Tonight he'd find a peasant wench who would be willing to help ease his problem. Satisfied with his decision, he crossed the courtyard and mounted his destrier. He guided the powerful animal toward the convent gate. There was still much to be done before he could turn his efforts to easing his body's craving. He needed to make sure his men had secured the area and to see what news the scouting parties had brought back.

Confident that the men he left behind would see to the supplies, Wolfram urged his mount into a gallop across the open fields.

From atop the convent wall Dara watched the last ox-cart roll through the convent gate on its way to the English camp. It was well past time for vespers, but in her present state of mind, she couldn't abide the thought of being cloistered away in the chapel while the convent's livelihood was being stolen by the English. Dara moved into the deepening shadows and stared at the flickering light of the campfires in the distance.

How she would love to alert King John to the Englishmen's activities. Such proof of her loyalty would be all she needed to convince the king that a Rochambeau would never consider treason, much less attempt it.

Dara's eyes widened as an idea began to glimmer at the edge of her mind. Her face lit with excitement. She could aid France as well as thwart Charles's scheme. She would learn all she could of the Englishmen's plans and then take the information to the king. Such an action would prove her loyalty completely.

Dara cast a quick glance over the courtyard below.

Should the Reverend Mother suspect her intentions, she would find herself locked in the penance box.

The thought made Dara shudder, but didn't deter her from the course she'd set only a moment before. She'd be back before anyone discovered that she'd left the convent. Once she had the information she needed for the king, she'd manage to convince the Reverend Mother to allow her to take it to Paris herself.

Secure her plan would work, Dara glanced down at the courtyard. Seeing no one, she quickly descended the flight of steps and hurried along the path that led to the garden. To guarantee her success, she had to retrieve her own clothing from the shed. She couldn't venture out at night wearing her wimple. The white mantle would bring her notice as soon as she stepped a foot outside the convent walls. She couldn't risk that happening. She had to get as close to the Englishmen as possible to learn of their plans.

Dara passed the garden that the soldiers had trampled in their haste to pluck the fresh vegetables to fill their own bellies. She kept a close watch on the cloister as she opened the shed's squeaky door and stepped inside. Her trunks had been stacked haphazardly against the back wall, under the hole in the slate roof. Dara made a moue of disgust as she slid her hands over the slippery mildewed leather in search of the latch. Already rusting, she had to prize the hasp open and then force back the lid.

The clothing within was a disaster. The rain of the previous weeks had soaked the material, and the mice had enjoyed chewing corridors through the thick velvets and brocades. The silks were completely ruined by water and mildew and gave off an offensive odor. Dara rubbed her nose and tried to prevent the sneeze that followed as the scent reached her nostrils. Sickened by the waste of her lovely gowns, she tossed several mantles to the floor before pulling a dark burgundy velvet from the trunk. She held it up in the moonlight that now spilled through the hole in the roof. The mantle looked little more than a peasant's rag, but there was nothing she could do about it. She couldn't go to the English camp dressed as a nun.

Resolutely, Dara took off the wimple and chin-band cap before she shrugged out of the white mantle. She laid all the garments carefully atop a trunk before she pulled her own clothing over her head. She ran her fingers through her dark hair, allowing herself the luxury of feeling the thick curls fall freely about her shoulders and down her back in a wild mass of silk for the first time since coming to St. Marie.

Without the inhibiting costume she'd been forced to wear, Dara suddenly felt alive and ready to undertake the mission she'd set for herself. Peeking around the shed, she saw that the cloister now lay in darkness. She breathed a sigh of relief.

Wasting no more time, she hurried toward the small postern gate near the rear of the convent wall. It was the gate where alms were given to those who could not enter the convent walls. Dara had previously considered using it as a means to leave the convent, but the right moment had never presented itself until this evening, when everyone was still too upset over the arrival of the English troops to worry about any of the nuns leaving St. Marie.

The well-oiled latch slid open easily. Dara was quickly free of the convent walls and running across one of the open fields toward the army encampment. Her feet sank into a newly plowed furrow, and she sprawled facedown across the rows. She hit the soft earth with a hard thump. She gasped her surprise and found her mouth filled by freshly churned soil.

Dara let out a grunt of disgust and spluttered, spitting

out dirt and grass as she clambered to her knees and then pushed herself to her feet. With a swipe of the back of her hand, she brushed her hair out of her eyes, smudging her cheeks and brow with dirt. Unnerved, she glanced about to see if she'd been spotted by anyone from the English camp or the convent. It would not do for her to be caught spying on the English dogs. They'd cut her down without a thought.

A tingle of fear spurred Dara forward before she could change her mind and retreat in the opposite direction. She hurried toward the trees bordering the English camps. She'd maneuver around the outside encampment and make her way to the knight's camp. He would have the information that she would need to take to King John.

The murmur of voices grew louder as Dara neared the encampment. Situated in the middle of dozens of small camps, a large tent had been erected. She surmised it belonged to the silver knight. Dara stealthily edged her way through the underbrush and trees toward her destination. She recognized the camp of the yeomen. They relaxed around their fires, joking and telling stories or talking about their families in England. At another camp the knights sat drinking wine and enjoying themselves with tales of great exploits while their squires cleaned armor and weapons, readying them for the next battle. The infantry made up another camp. They, too, sought to conserve their strength, since much of the hand-to-hand combat would be left to them. Their lives depended upon strong, well-rested arms.

Dara saw the standard of the wolf swaying gently in the evening breeze over the large tent and smiled. She had found what she sought. Now all she had to do was to get close enough to hear what was being said. Keeping herself in the shadows at the forest's edge, she crept nearer and nearer until she could see the campfire where the large man called Ox stood. He raised his tankard above his head and said, "To the Lone Wolf. May he never hunt in vain."

Dara gaped in awe as she saw another large figure stand and raise his tankard in the air. "For Edward, England, and the Black Prince." She blinked to clear her vision, unable to believe what she was seeing. The double image didn't vanish. She shook her head again in an effort to dispel the two identical apparitions. It did no good. They remained, dark and fearsome.

Dara swallowed uneasily as she realized that they were the two riders who had flanked the silver knight that morning. She shivered and began to ease back into the deeper shadows behind her. She was beginning to believe she might have made a mistake by coming to the English camp. It seemed filled with giants. Perhaps it wasn't too late for her to turn around and retrace her steps to the convent gate. She'd find another way to get the information she needed for the king.

"Where do ye think yer a'goin?" a heavily accented voice said in a mixture of French and English. He clamped a meaty hand down upon her shoulder and spun her around. The Wolf had required all his men to learn at least some French for their own protection should they be taken captive by the enemy.

Dara stiffened as she looked up into the beefy face of an English yeoman. She moistened her suddenly dry lips and opened her mouth to speak, but no words would pass the lump that had lodged in her throat.

"I asked ye a question, wench. What are ye doin' here? Spying?"

Dara rapidly shook her head and finally managed to squeak, "*Non.* I was merely passing by on my way to the village." She couldn't tell them she was from the convent. It would bring the silver knight's wrath down upon the Reverend Mother and the other sisters, for he'd never believe she had come without their knowledge.

The thick fingers bit into Dara's shoulder, making her wince. "Ye don't expect me to believe ye were just out taking a breath of air, do ye? I know a spy when I see one."

"I'm not a spy. Please, let me go. I'll trouble you no more," Dara whispered, nearly whimpering from the pain his heavy fingers were inflicting upon her.

"I'll let ye go after I've turned ye over to the Wolf. He'll get the truth out of ye one way or the other." The yeomen's eyes moved over Dara and his thick lips broke into a semblance of a smile. "Aye. He'll get something out of ye or in ye before this night is done, I'd be willing to bet." He chuckled and turned her toward the glow of the campfire.

Dara stumbled as he shoved her along in front of him. She wanted to run but knew it would be useless to even attempt an escape when she was surrounded on all sides by her enemies. When Dara nearly tumbled to her knees from the yeoman's shove, the soldiers sitting about the fire, enjoying their few hours of rest, came to their feet. All eyes riveted upon the peasant woman with the mass of raven hair flowing wildly down her back.

"Well, Henry? What have ye found in yon woods? A wood sprite?"

"A spy more like it," the yeomen growled, pushing Dara closer to the roaring fire. "I brought her here for the Wolf."

Ox and Bull glanced at each other. Deviltry flickered in their thickly fringed eyes, and their lips quivered from withholding their laughter. They couldn't wait to see Wolf's reaction when he returned to camp to find this bit of flesh just waiting to be had. Wolf had been on the prowl for just such a prey since he'd returned

from the convent all heated up and chomping at the bit
to find a wench to ease his aching loins.

"Even the devil does his bidding," Ox said at last, a
grin curling up one side of his mouth.

Bull shook his head. " 'Tis not the devil's work,
brother. Look at her. She's an angel." His gaze swept
over Dara. "Although, I admit, a dirty one. But in
Wolf's present state, I seriously doubt he'll object to a
little bit of grime."

"I'd have to agree with you, Bull. The soil that
smudges her skin will only add spice to the taste of her.
And knowing Wolf's present state of mind, he'll devour
her so quickly that he'll not even note that she lacks a
bath."

"I know not of what he'll taste or not. Or if she's
devil or angel," the yeoman said. "I know only that I
found this wench spying on you and I'll leave her here
for ye to decide her fate. I've done me duty."

"Aye. You've done your duty fairly, Henry. And Wolf
will be grateful," Bull said, allowing the yeoman to
know his loyalty would be rewarded.

The yeoman nodded curtly and left the clearing and
his prisoner behind. He knew the Lone Wolf never forgot those who served him well. He'd receive extra coin
for this night's work.

Dara looked from one darkly handsome face to the
other, unable to tell the difference in them. Both men
possessed black, curling hair that had been cropped
close to their heads, as well as arched brows that rose
over mischievous thick-lashed eyes. Their high cheekbones and narrow noses didn't take away from the
mouths that were full-lipped, yet not unappealing. In all,
the two identical faces were very handsome indeed.
However, that did little to reassure her as the two stood
looking down at her like something they'd won at the
fair.

At last Ox stepped forward and tipped up Dara's chin with a long-fingered hand. He scrutinized her smudged face, assessing her finely sculpted features before he nodded his satisfaction. "Methinks you'll do well this night, wench. Tomorrow will be soon enough to hang you if Wolf thinks yer guilty, as the yeomen believes."

"But I'm not a spy. I was merely on my way to my home in the village. Please let me go," Dara said in halting English. She was now grateful to her father for his insistence upon her learning English as well as German.

"You need not trouble yourself by begging us, wench. Wolf is the one who will decide your fate when he returns," Bull said, thinking little of the fact that she had answered him in English. The war had lasted so many years that even French peasants had learned a smattering of English. Intrigued by the beauty beneath the grime, he failed to note that her accent was far too cultivated for her to be a peasant.

Ox glanced at his brother. "Should he not be pleased, I think I will take the wench as me own."

Bull's congenial expression dimmed. "Nay. She belongs to me should Wolf not want her."

The brothers glowered at each other as Dara stood too bewildered and frightened of being hanged for spying to realize that they were about to fight over her like dogs over a bone.

"The devil take it!" Wolf exploded as he strode into camp, his face a mask of exasperation. "One more word from either of you and I'll have you in chains. I'm in no mood for your childish squabbles."

The two giants seemed to wilt before Dara's eyes as the knight they called Wolf entered the circle of light surrounding the campfire. The play of night shadows and golden firelight over his face only heightened his beauty. Dressed now in a white undertunic that peeped through the slashes in the short leather gipon that hugged his strong body and emphasized the strength of his wide shoulders, he was just as imposing without his silver armor.

Bull was the first to regain his composure. "Yeoman Henry brought something for you."

Wolf arched a quizzical brow at the brothers. They smiled at him and moved out of his path of vision. Wolf's expression didn't alter as his dark gaze swept over Dara from head to toe.

"It would seem he found this wench spying on us," Bull continued.

"I wasn't spying," Dara burst out, suddenly shaken by the heat flaring in the silver knight's eyes. She knew it was her imagination, but she could nearly see flames dancing in the onyx orbs.

Ox and Bull stepped out of Wolf's path as he approached the girl and calmly asked, "Then what do you here?"

"I was on my way to my home in the village," Dara said, holding firm to her lie.

"You are on your way home, yet you find it easier to circle around our encampment near the woods than to take the direct route by the road."

"I was afraid," Dara stuttered, almost groaning aloud with frustration. He was right. No one in their right mind would get close to an army encampment when they could easily avoid it by taking the road.

"Afraid, wench? Or spying, as the yeomen suspects?"

Dara shook her head rapidly from side to side. She had to make him believe her, or she'd find herself hanged on the morrow. "Please, I am no spy. I was merely curious. I had never seen Englishmen before."

Wolf's grim expression didn't change. "What did you expect to find? That we cook and eat babies?"

Before realizing her mistake, Dara nodded.

Instead of taking offense at her gesture, Wolf's lips began to twitch and then broke into a smile before he threw back his head and laughed. The sound seemed to silence the entire camp.

"Damn me," he said at last, wiping the mirth from his eyes. "I needed that." Wolf sobered as suddenly as he had laughed. He swept Dara with another assessing gaze, and then nodded his satisfaction. He glanced at Ox. "Take her to my tent and guard her well until I decide her fate."

Chapter 4

Dara tensed as Ox took her by the arm, but she didn't resist as he urged her toward the large tent. She didn't know what else to do. For the second time in her life she found herself confronted by a situation she couldn't alter with an order or an objection.

A few minutes later she stood bewildered in the middle of the English knight's spartan quarters, wondering how to extricate herself from this latest dilemma and manage to keep her head on her shoulders at the same time.

Dara's gaze moved over the tent, seeking any avenue of escape. Finding none, she sank down on the fur pallet that took up much of the floor space. Drawing her legs up, she buried her face against her knees. She'd come here to free herself from Charles's scheme and now found herself in worse trouble. Dara felt the hot sting of tears burn the backs of her lids. She squeezed her eyes tightly shut. She couldn't allow herself to cry. She'd not feel sorry for herself and give in to the fear chewing away at her insides.

Dara's head came up, and she squared her shoulders resolutely. She was a Rochambeau, not a coward. The enemies of France would not conquer her before the battle even took place. She would stand her ground against the English knight known as the Lone Wolf.

She'd not surrender her life meekly. She'd fight for every breath until her soul left her body.

As Wolf opened the tent flap and walked inside, a streak of firelight momentarily illuminated the tent's shadowy interior and jerked Dara from her musings. The flap fell back into place behind the knight. Shadows once more reigned as she looked up at the powerful man who stood with feet spread and arms akimbo. Dara swallowed hard. It was easy to make battle plans when she wasn't facing the enemy. However, he now stood towering over her, a mountain of stone, hard and impenetrable.

Dara's gaze swept down over Wolf's sinewy form, taking in the wide expanse of chest, his lean waist, the rock-hard thighs and shapely calves. She shuddered, unable to contain the involuntary shiver of apprehension that passed along her spine. He could snap her in half with a flick of his fingers.

Noting her reaction, Wolf frowned and arched a quizzical brow. "Does my appearance not please you, wench?"

Dara could have laughed at the incongruity of his question had she not been too terrified. How could this man even think his appearance pleased her when in truth she despised everything about him? He was her enemy: a man whose very presence meant death and destruction to the people of France. She eyed him belligerently but remained mute.

Wolf reached down and jerked the short gipon over his head and tossed it aside. A moment later his undertunic followed. The medallion fell back into place, swaying gently in the middle of his bronzed chest. Wolf absently touched the metal as he said, "Since you do not choose to voice your objections, I assume you are pleased with what your eyes devour so greedily. Disrobe and let us be done with it. The hour grows late and I need my rest."

Dara's shocked gaze flew to Wolf's face. Shielded by the muted shadows, the expression in his dark eyes was unfathomable, but she sensed it boded her no good. She'd naively believed he wanted to interrogate her further. Jolted with harsh reality, she realized she should have known what the knight truly intended from the remarks made by his men. The Wolf had far more devious plans for her. Before the thought had fully formed, Dara shot to her feet as if struck by lightning. She bolted toward the only avenue of escape. Her fingers had just touched the flap when a strong arm encircled her waist and lifted her off her feet. She struggled, squirming and kicking, against the hard muscles banding her body. She squealed in frustrated protest as she tried to pry his arm free with her fingers. She heard as well as felt the deep chuckle that rumbled through her captor's chest before she found herself falling backward.

Wolf tumbled them both onto the pile of furs. The breath left Dara upon impact with the hard earth and his heavy body. Staggered momentarily, she gasped to pull air back into her burning lungs. Her senses clearing, she renewed her struggle for freedom. She twisted and bucked beneath his crushing weight.

"Cease, wench!" Wolf bellowed as he sought to subdue the vicious vixen. His skin already burned and bled from the deep grooves she'd dug into his forearms with her fingernails.

Panic-stricken, Dara paid no heed to his command. She squealed again and found a new burst of energy for the fight. When she felt him shift his weight to hold her down with his leg, she thrust her knees upward in an effort to find enough leverage to twist herself from beneath him. Her knees came in contact with his groin.

His breath left him in a great rush, and his fingers bit into her flesh as he tensed and fell away from her. Wolf doubled over and drew in a ragged breath as incapacitating pain washed over him.

Giving no thought to her captor's agony, Dara quickly took advantage of her freedom. She rolled away from Wolf and sprang to her feet in nearly the same moment. Without a backward glance at the man who by now had managed to raise himself to his knees, she burst through the tent flap and ran, heedless of the direction. She was too terrified to realize that each step she took carried her deeper into the enemy camp.

"Stop her!" came Wolf's angry command from behind her. Her feet flying on wings of panic, Dara raced on, frantic now to reach the safety of the darkness edging the encampment. She ignored the sound of the men who scurried to obey their master. Like hounds on the scent of the fox, they bellowed and hooted, making a game of the chase as she fled like an animal being run to ground.

Several pairs of hands snared her at the same time, dragging her to a halt, disguising their pawing and probing under the veil of holding her captive for Wolf. The deteriorating material of her gown gave under the stress of all the grappling fingers. It ripped at the seams and fell away from her shoulders as if cut by an invisible dagger.

Stunned to find herself almost naked in the middle of the baying crowd, Dara froze. Left with only her thin chemise to protect her modesty, she crossed her arms over her breasts and lowered her head to hide her humiliation. Her dark hair fell about her shoulders, shielding her to the waist from the lascivious eyes of the men surrounding her. She sensed rather than saw their leader's presence before his large hand clamped down on her arm and jerked her against his rock-hard chest.

Dara's head snapped back, and she was forced to look up into his angry face.

"Wench, you deserve a good beating," Wolf growled.

His comment roused hoots of approval from the men. They winked and poked each other in the ribs before whistling their encouragement. Others loudly offered their advice upon how to deal with such a recalcitrant wench, urging Wolf to put her over his knee and give her a good trouncing to show her that an Englishman was now her master.

Wolf didn't seem to hear any of the ribald comments as he stood looking down into Dara's fathomless sapphire eyes. The blood drumming in his temples and the heart slamming against his ribs blocked out all sound and logic. Suddenly oblivious to everything except his own needs, Wolf swept an arm down Dara's body and lifted her off her feet. He ignored her struggles as he turned back toward his tent, his prey firmly secured within his arms.

Dara's dark hair spilled about them like a curtain of fine silk as she shook her head from side to side and pushed against the wide chest, to no avail. She could no more escape the powerful arms that held her than she could bands of steel.

The tent flap fell into place behind them, separating them from the noisy crowd outside. Wolf didn't release Dara until he had her once more flat on her back upon the furs. He placed one leg over her abdomen to hold her still as he propped himself up on one elbow to observe his captive. Though only a sliver of light from the campfire illuminated the tent's interior, it provided enough brightness for him to inspect his hostage's features. His dark gaze drifted over her dirt-smudged face, taking in the fine lines of her cheekbones, the sweetly molded lips, and the tiny tilted nose, before he looked once more into her arresting sapphire eyes.

Wolf felt the prick of recognition but could not place where he'd seen the wench before. He shrugged the feeling aside. He was in no mood for guessing games, or for that matter, any kind of games the wench thought to play. He lowered his face to within inches of Dara's. He could feel her warm breath against his lips as he said, "Wench, you gave me a merry chase this eve. But I am now weary of such sport. I wish to play at other games."

Dara's lower lip trembled as she drew in a shaky breath and whispered, "I am innocent."

Wolf leaned back and arched a dubious brow. "Innocent of spying, or—" He ran the tip of his finger down the front of the thin chemise that covered the soft mounds of her breasts. "—of man's touch? Which is it to be wench?"

"Of both."

Her answer made Wolf hesitate. As a man who sold his services to the highest bidder, he'd never been plagued with an overabundance of righteous ethics upon the field of battle. Trained as a mercenary from early in life, he took what the conquered land provided for his needs—be it food, treasure, or women.

In war there were only the codes of honor set by the warriors. Chivalry existed in the minds of the nobles and upon the tournament fields, not on the battlefields where men like himself as well as common yeomen and infantrymen shed their blood like sheep to the slaughter.

However, Wolf had no great desire to rape any woman, much less a virgin. There had never been a reason to rape. He'd always had enough women to appease his lust. Even in the heat of battle his blood had never stirred with the need to punish the women of the vanquished with rape. As victor, he'd claimed the spoils of war, but he had never taken a woman who didn't want him. Many considered him an uncivilized heathen for selling his sword arm to the highest bidder, but he did have certain standards he set for himself. He preferred his women warm, moist, and willing. It made it much more pleasurable for all parties involved, especially after a grueling battle.

"Do you speak the truth?" Wolf queried.

Cheeks flooding with color, Dara looked away from Wolf's penetrating eyes and nodded.

Wolf released a long breath in disgust. He believed the wench. Shaking his head at his own misfortune, he moved his imprisoning leg off Dara before he flopped over onto his back. He laced his fingers behind his head and stared up at the ceiling. A muscle worked in his craggy cheek. " 'Tis the devil's own luck. I find two beauties in the same day and can bed neither."

Afraid to move or say anything that might renew Wolf's attack, Dara lay mute at his side.

Slowly, Wolf turned his head to look at his silent companion. She was just the opposite of the angelic little spitfire at the convent. This wench was of the earth, not of heaven. The soil that besmirched her skin was like a brand that told of her heritage. Though innocent now, her earthy beauty would soon see her tossed into a haystack and deflowered by some healthy, overeager peasant who wouldn't have any qualms about taking her virginity. Unlike Wolf, he'd throw up her skirts and sink himself into her sweetness, giving no thought to her innocence.

Wolf's gaze lingered on Dara's tempting lips. He felt himself swell once more against the tight material of his braies. The girl was his chattel by right of war. Edward had given him the liberty to keep anything he chose as his men made their way across Guienne. He was to pillage as he saw fit.

Wolf's expression darkened and he looked away from the temptation. It would be so easy to take her, but he couldn't. Wolf released a long, resigned breath. It was growing late and he needed his rest. He'd decide the girl's fate tomorrow. For tonight she'd remain with him.

Wolf turned his back to Dara and pulled a fur up over his shoulders to ward off the chill of the late evening air. "Sleep now. Tomorrow will be soon enough to decide what is to be done with you."

When Dara didn't respond, Wolf rolled to his stomach and raised himself up on his elbows. The medallion dangled in the air as he looked down at her. "Don't attempt to escape again. I promise you'll live to regret it." With that, he once more settled himself down for the night, and within minutes the sound of his soft snores filled the tent.

The peal of the convent bells awoke Dara. She yawned, gave a languorous stretch and slowly opened her eyes, to find herself staring into a pair of thickly fringed ebony eyes. Her own eyes widening in shock, she gasped and bolted upright. She looked about the tent, desperately trying to orient herself to her strange surroundings.

"Good morning, wench," Wolf said, stretching his arms over his head. Like a great cat awakening from a nap, he flexed his muscles and then sat up. The furs fell away from him, baring his nakedness to Dara.

Unable to stop herself, Dara gaped at him. She'd seen naked men before, but none built of nothing but pure muscle and power like Wolf. Though still unwed, Dara had assumed the role of Lady Rochambeau and the duties that went with the title. It had been her responsibility to attend the male guests when they accepted her father's hospitality. She showed them the way to the steam baths her father had built to imitate those he'd once seen in the city of Baden on the Rhine River. She also oversaw the servants who helped the visitors bathe.

Dara's stomach quivered with an unusual sensation that made her feel like she'd eaten butterflies. She couldn't stop herself from admiring Wolf's lean body. Until this moment she'd thought all men were alike. Now she knew they definitely were not. This man had been hewn of granite and then sculpted by the hand of a master craftsman.

Dara jerked her gaze away from Wolf and felt her cheeks crimson with heat. Her unladylike thoughts about a man who was her enemy shocked her. She should see only his faults, not his beauty. Her discomfort surged ever higher when she realized with a start that she had slept at his side all night, completely unaware that he'd stripped off his braies.

Unnerved by such intimacy, her skin flaming from head to toe, Dara fidgeted with the furs that lay heaped about her. This man unsettled her as no one else had ever done. There was something about him that seemed to touch an unknown and unexplored part of herself that she didn't truly understand. In a time when she should be worrying about her fate at Wolf's hand, she had been acting like a moonstruck maid, admiring his physique. It was total madness.

For hours after Wolf had fallen asleep, she'd lain awake, seeking any means to be free of the Englishman. She now realized the urgency she'd felt to get away from Wolf didn't stem entirely from the fact that he held her captive. She was physically attracted to the man. Dara found the thought unconscionable, especially since he was her enemy. However, she couldn't deny it. And she feared him even more for being able to rouse the demons inside of her. Demons that could make her forget everything else but the man who had come to conquer France.

Wolf ran a hand through his tousled hair and glanced back to the girl sitting in the middle of his bed. She looked like a wild thing sitting there with her long dark hair cascading down her back to the furs lying about her. His hand itched to reach out and run his fingers through the glistening mane, but he resolutely ignored the urge to touch her. Throughout the long night, it hadn't been easy having her so near. Especially near dawn when the morning chill had invaded the tent and the girl had innocently sought out his warmth. She'd snuggled like a tiny kitten searching for a comfortable spot, until her head lay cradled against his shoulder and one arm draped his middle.

Wolf had felt like a man trapped between heaven and hell. His body responded to the scent and feel of the female pressed so tantalizingly close. It throbbed and ached, demanding a release that he could not give it. It hadn't helped to know that he had fostered the misery upon himself because of his own set of morals.

Wolf's gaze moved over Dara. The muted light spilling in through the slit in the tent fully illuminated her features for the first time. A frown furrowed his brow as he studied her face for a long, thoughtful moment. A look of amazement crossed his own features. Unable to believe what he saw, Wolf reached out and captured Dara's wrist, drawing her near. Again his gaze moved over her features, branding each one into his brain and comparing them to the face of the young, defiant nun at the convent. Denied his quest because of the lack of light, Wolf came to his feet, and giving no thought to his state of undress, dragged Dara out of the tent and into the damp dawn air.

"Damn me, but you are her," Wolf said as he captured Dara's chin and forced her to look up at him.

Seeing recognition in his eyes, Dara tried to shake her head in denial. "I know not of what you speak."

"Lies will send your soul to hell, Sister," Wolf said grimly. The wench had played him for a fool. She'd smudged her face with dirt and dressed herself as a peasant to disguise herself in order to spy upon them.

"I know not of what you speak," Dara repeated again. She had to convince him that he was mistaken about her identity.

Wolf's fingers pressed into her skin as he queried, "Did the good Reverend Mother send you here? Or is King John so weakened that he has to use nuns to fight his battles?"

Flinching under the pressure upon her skin, Dara again tried to shake her head. "Nay. You are wrong. I am but a peasant from the village."

The gesture that curled Wolf's lips up at the corners could not be misconstrued as a smile. He released his hold upon Dara. "Then wench, we will go to the village. One way or the other, I will know your identity before the sun reaches its zenith this day."

Taking her by the arm, he thrust her toward the guard who had stood sentinel outside the tent all night. "Watch her well." He turned and began bellowing orders, sending the camp into a flurry of activity.

A half hour later Wolf again stood before Dara, dressed once more in the leather gipon he'd worn the previous night. However, he also wore his long sword and an eighteen-inch dagger at his side. His men had scoured the area the previous day for any sign of the enemy, but one never knew what to expect in enemy territory. Nor had Wolf lived for thirty-two years by being foolhardy. He wore no armor, but he and his guard would be well armed and ready to defend themselves should events require it.

"Find the wench's mantle and a horse," he ordered without a glance at Dara. Before she had time to invent another logical reason for Wolf to allow her to go to the village alone, Dara found herself draped in her mantle and plucked from the ground as if she weighed no more than a feather. She was set upon the back of a huge horse. The saddle, one meant for a man suited in armor, was like a great box that rose on a high ridge above the horse's back in order to give a warrior enough leverage to use his weapons. Swallowed by the size of the saddle, Dara felt like a child. Her feet dangled helplessly above the stirrups that hung so low, a mounted knight could virtually stand upright to deliver blows from side to side. Dara clung to the pommel and prayed she'd not fall to her death from the back of the great beast. Her teeth chattered from fear or from the vibration of the horse's gait. She couldn't be sure of which as the animal moved forward.

Wolf glanced at the young woman who rode at his side, pale and silent. A new wave of fury washed over him. Yesterday he had seen her at her prayers and had castigated himself for his licentious thoughts about a woman dedicated to serve God. But no matter how much guilt his lusty thoughts created, he still hadn't been able to get her innocent beauty out of his mind. It had tortured him throughout the day and into the evening.

His eyes narrowed upon the face that had plagued him since he'd first seen her in the convent courtyard. And he wondered how anything so beautiful could house such deceit behind it.

Wolf took the bridle of Dara's mount and turned the animal toward the convent. He'd get to the bottom of this mystery far sooner by going straight to the Reverend Mother.

Seeing the direction they traveled, Dara nearly toppled from the saddle as she jerked around to look at Wolf. "This is not the direction to the village."

Wolf smiled grimly. "We go to the convent."

"Nay. You said you were taking me to the village."

Again the grim smile touched Wolf's lips. "I changed my mind."

Panicking anew, Dara stuttered, "You—You can't do that."

"I beg to differ, wench. I can and will do exactly as I please."

"Nay. I want to go to the village. It is my home."

Wolf arched a questioning brow. "You seem unduly upset at the thought of going to the convent. Are you such a sinner that you fear a place of God, or do you have other reasons for not wanting to go to St. Marie?"

"I just want to return to my home," Dara said honestly. Her shoulders sagged in defeat. In truth, that was all she had wanted since the day Charles forced her to leave Rochambeau. She had involved herself in this situation to try to make King John realize that he had erred in ordering her sent to the convent. Now she doubted she'd ever see Rochambeau again. Once they reached the convent and Wolf learned her identity, he'd have her hanged for spying.

Dara glanced at the knight riding silently at her side. She honestly couldn't blame him for her situation. He was doing his duty to his king, as she'd tried to do for hers. He thought her a spy, and he was right. And as such, as an enemy who sought to do him harm, he had treated her far more kindly then she deserved.

Dara's gaze swept over Wolf's perfect profile. She could not deny that the man intrigued her far more today than when she'd first set eyes upon him. She was not naive to the barbarity of war. War and rumors of war had surrounded her life since the day of her birth. She knew that unprotected females like herself often became the spoils to be used by the victor. Yet Wolf had not taken advantage of her. He possessed the power to do with her as he pleased, yet he had not seen fit to abuse her. When peasant women often suffered the brunt of the soldier's brutality, he had left her untouched.

Dara's gaze drifted along the line of his full lips to the hard plane of Wolf's square jaw. The man had shown her humane treatment, though she knew that the warrior within him wouldn't allow her to escape punishment once he proved her guilt. Had she succeeded in her quest, she could well have caused the death of many of his men. And as a warrior, he had to put the welfare of his troops before anything else. A chill of fear zigzagged its way up Dara's spine and raised the hair at the nape of her neck. She could nearly feel the noose about her throat.

Dara jerked her gaze away from Wolf's features as he reined his mount to a halt in front of St. Marie's gates and ordered them opened. A loud squeal of protest came from the rusty hinges as the heavy portals yawned wide like a toothless mouth. Iron shod, the destriers clattered into the courtyard where the Reverend Mother stood waiting. Her tense face as pale as the white wimple that fluttered about her shoulders in the morning breeze, the long sleeve of her habit concealing the hands she clasped tightly in front of her, she looked sculpted of alabaster.

Wolf reined his mount to a halt and drew Dara's alongside. He glanced at his captive before looking down at the Reverend Mother. Folding his arms over the pommel of his saddle, he leaned forward. "Reverend Mother, do you know this wench?"

Reverend Mother flashed Dara a helpless look and then nodded.

"Then be so good as to tell me who she is?" Wolf ordered, noting the look that passed between the two women.

Again the Reverend Mother looked at Dara and saw her give a furtive shake of the head. A frown creased the older woman's brow. She didn't know what Dara wanted her to say. She looked once more at the English knight who watched her with his dark, devil's eyes. She swallowed uneasily and managed to whisper, "She is the Lady Dara de Rochambeau."

Wolf's head snapped around, and he stared at Dara as if she'd suddenly grown warts. His eyes narrowed. "Is what she says true?"

Determined not to cower even in her last minutes upon earth, Dara lifted her chin and squared her shoulders. She had hoped the Reverend Mother would understand her silent plea for anonymity, but she should have realized the older woman would be too terrified of Wolf to keep her identity from him. "Yes. 'Tis true."

Wolf's face flushed a dull red with anger. He looked once more to the Reverend Mother. "And has the Lady Rochambeau taken her vows?"

"*Non.* She is here by the request of the King of Navarre."

Dara could have groaned aloud as Wolf's black gaze shot back to her. She could nearly hear his mind working as his eyes moved slowly over her, assessing her value to him, alive or dead.

The smile that tugged up the corners of his shapely lips didn't reach his eyes. "Mademoiselle, it seems your neck has been spared for a short while, or at least until I can ascertain how much I can gain by your ransom."

"Sir Knight," the Reverend Mother said, taking a tentative step forward. "I will pay her ransom."

Wolf cocked a dark brow. "How so, Reverend Mother? Do you offer the church's coin and gold plate?"

The Reverend Mother shook her head. "Nay. I can give only what is ours, nothing of St. Marie's."

Knowing that the nuns had little of value that belonged to them personally, Wolf said, "What do you offer, Reverend Mother?"

"We have the foodstuffs and grain that we hid yesterday. They are ours to do with as we please because we worked for them with our own hands."

Wolf's face darkened and he looked once more at Dara. He knew the culprit responsible for the nun's devious attempt to thwart his demands. "Like all of your kind, your treachery only deepens, mademoiselle."

Dara glared back at him, unashamed and defiant. "I do what I must for France."

"We shall see what you will do for France when I'm through with you, wench," Wolf growled.

"Please, Sir Knight. Allow Lady Dara to remain here with us. She is young and undisciplined at times, but she wishes no one any harm," Reverend Mother pleaded.

"I fear you don't have enough grain or gold in all of St. Marie to ransom this wench, Reverend Mother. She is my prisoner, and as such, she will remain with me until I have the ransom I request. Send word to the King of Navarre that he may have her back for fifty thousand crowns."

" 'Tis unreasonable. Charles will never pay it," Dara blurted as a chill of alarm raced up her spine. It would be far more profitable for Charles to have her die. He then would inherit the Rochambeau lands, since he was her only living relative.

Wolf's expression didn't alter as he said, "You had best hope he does. It will not go easy on you if he does not. You are a spy and will be treated accordingly."

"May I bid the Reverend Mother and the sisters good-bye?" Dara asked quietly. She'd keep her dignity all the way to the scaffold.

Wolf gave a curt nod. "Aye. You may make your

farewells and then gather your belongings. Enough time has been wasted this morn."

Wolf made no move to dismount or assist Dara from the huge destrier. After much twisting and turning that tugged up the hem of her mantle to reveal much of her shapely legs to Wolf's ebony gaze, she finally managed the feat. Once her feet touched the ground, she flashed Wolf a triumphant look and walked toward the chapel where the Reverend Mother and the sisters awaited her. The look she gave Wolf before closing the chapel door behind her seemed to dare him to have the nerve to interrupt their prayers.

Wolf didn't accept the dare. He didn't need to prove his power over the girl who had suddenly metamorphosed from peasant to lady. Her fate now lay in his hands. Let her have her last minutes at St. Marie in prayer. The treacherous little wench would need all the help God and man could give her if the King of Navarre refused to pay her ransom.

Chapter 5

It seemed the island across the Channel bred nothing but giants, Dara mused as she watched Wolf and a tall fair-haired man stride across the encampment. Dara glanced at the MacDonald twins Wolf had left to guard her. All Englishmen seemed to have one thing in common: size.

Dara looked back to the man at Wolf's side. Nearly as strongly built as her captor, he stood of the same height as Wolf, but where Wolf seemed made of onyx with his dark hair, ebony eyes, and sun-bronzed skin, the visitor was smithed of gold. His hair and full mustache gleamed like newly minted coins in the afternoon sunlight. Even from the distance, she could see the flash of his blue eyes as he and Wolf stopped to speak with one of the yeomen. He held himself with such proud bearing, he seemed to rule over all he surveyed. A charismatic smile touched his full lips as he bent his bright head to listen to the man. He nodded sagely and made a comment that made the yeoman's weathered features split into a proud grin before he bobbed an awkward bow.

Watching the yeoman's deference to the newcomer, Dara knew the golden visitor was no ordinary knight. And as the two handsome men made their way through the smaller camps to Wolf's, Ox and Bull uncoiled their large bodies and came to their feet, their identical faces alight with excitement. Dara watched the giant twins curiously. Their actions only served to confirm her suspicions. She'd never seen them show such respect to the man they served. When Wolf and the newcomer approached, Ox and Bull each gave the golden giant a gracious bow.

The newcomer's easy smile again touched his full lips. He slapped each brother companionably on the shoulder. " 'Tis good to see you two rogues again. I had feared you both might have decided you'd had enough of war and let Wolf come back to Guienne alone."

Ox and Bull shook their curly heads simultaneously and denied in unison, "Nay, sire."

Wolf laughed at the incredulous looks that passed over the twins' faces. "I think Ox and Bull would rather be put on the rack than forced to remain at Phelan. They seem to find farming a bit tedious for their more adventurous natures. I honestly believe they would rather fight than do anything else."

Ox flashed Wolf a wry grin before looking once more to the fair-haired man. "Your Highness, there is one thing we like to do better, but a good battle comes in a close second, especially when there's not a comely wench to be found."

The light blue eyes passed over the twins to come to rest upon the young woman standing quietly a few feet away. His appreciative gaze moved over her before he looked back to the MacDonald brothers. A knowing smile spread his full mouth. "It would seem you've found a comely wench to entertain you until the next battle."

It took a moment for the twins to comprehend the prince's meaning. Again they shook their heads in unison. "Nay, sire," Ox answered. "She's Wolf's, not ours. We only guard her to keep her from escaping."

"Ho! What can this mean, old friend?" the prince

said, deviltry twinkling in his blue gaze. He arched a golden brow. "Are you losing your touch or did my ears just deceive me when Ox said they were guarding the wench for you? 'Tis a strange turn of events if you now have to put guards on your women to keep them. After all these years of having every female in sight throw herself at your feet, it must be quite a shock to find one who can withstand that face of yours."

Wolf's swarthy features deepened in hue. "She is my prisoner, sire. They guard her to keep her from escaping, nothing more."

"Then introduce me to the maid," Edward, the Prince of Wales, said, his eyes lighting with interest. The wench was far too beautiful to waste if she wasn't warming Wolf's pallet.

A tiny crease knit Wolf's brows as his dark eyes found Dara. He didn't like the unusual twinge that pricked him at the prince's command. If he didn't know better, he could believe it was something akin to jealousy. But that was impossible. He'd never experienced such an emotion about a woman in his life. He could imagine such feelings over a suit of fine armor or a good destrier, but never over a female. There were far too many for the taking to worry over just one.

However, Wolf's frown deepened at the thought of his friend's interest settling upon Dara. He told himself that he was not personally involved with the girl. She was a deceitful wench all told, but she was also an innocent. And Wolf knew the Black Prince too well. Should his friend decide to have her, he would. Like his father, Edward III, the prince loved women, especially beautiful women like Dara of Rochambeau. The Black Prince hadn't earned his nickname because of the color of his armor. He had a wife and children awaiting him in England, but he enjoyed other females at will whenever one piqued his interest.

"Lady Dara, come here," Wolf said, his thoughts making his command far more brusque than he'd intended.

Dara swallowed uneasily and stepped forward, wondering what she'd done to incur Wolf's anger. She raised her chin and glared up at him, determined not to allow the knight to see that he frightened her when he was in one of his black moods.

"Sire, this is the Lady Dara of Rochambeau," Wolf said, taking Dara by the arm and drawing her forward. The pressure of his hand silently bid her to curtsy, but Dara resisted. "Lady Dara, a curtsy is customary when you have the honor of being presented to a royal prince," Wolf ground out, his annoyance with himself and Dara mounting by the moment.

"In England, courteous behavior may differ, but here in France a man does not treat a lady like a sack of potatoes when presenting her," Dara snapped. She jerked her eyes away from Wolf's darkening face and looked at the golden prince. She immediately executed a graceful curtsy. "I beg your pardon, Your Highness. Please forgive me, but I fear that being held captive has done little to improve my own behavior."

The Black Prince stepped forward and took Dara by the hand, drawing her to her feet. He smiled down at her. " 'Tis easy to forgive someone with your beauty, Lady Dara of Rochambeau."

Edward paused, studying Dara's features as if conjuring up some distant memory. At last he said, "Ah. Now I remember. I once met your father when my father brought me with him to pay homage to King John."

Dara's face froze and she stiffened. "My father died at Crécy."

Edward's smile faded. " 'Tis sad. But many good men have died because of John of Valois's foolishness."

"King John is no fool," Dara returned, steadfastly defending her king and country.

Edward glanced once more at Wolf and shrugged. He released Dara's hand resignedly. Though he often said he valued a spirited wench as much as a spirited destrier, he enjoyed a more docile female than the Lady Dara. "Now, I understand the problem you have, my friend. She is a bit testy." He looked back to Dara, his expression cool and unreadable. "But 'tis still a shame to waste such beauty."

"Your Highness, I waste nothing. Her ransom should arrive before we set off to Poitiers. I have already had a messenger sent to the King of Navarre."

"Navarre," Prince Edward said, his lips crinkling up at the corners as he fought to suppress his mirth. He lost the battle and burst into laughter.

Wolf frowned, fully aware that the prince's mirth was at his expense, but not understanding exactly how he'd brought it about.

At last Edward wiped his eyes and sought to collect himself. " 'Tis unfair to enjoy myself at your expense without an explanation, but I couldn't help it when you said you'd contacted the King of Navarre for the girl's ransom."

Wolf's frown didn't lighten. "He is her kin."

The Black Prince nodded. "Aye. But Navarre has decided if he can't have the throne, then neither should his father-in-law. He is working to help *us*."

Dara's involuntary gasp drew all eyes to her shocked face. She looked from gold to ebony and felt herself go numb. She had known from the beginning that Charles would not ransom her from Wolf. But she had hoped to gain her freedom. Now she would never be allowed to leave because of what she'd just learned of her cousin's intrigues. He truly played with treason. And by divulging that bit of information, the Black Prince had just sealed her fate.

Dara paled as she saw the look in Wolf's eyes. He also understood that she could not go free without jeopardizing everything they had worked to achieve.

"Take her to my tent," Wolf ordered. Neither Wolf nor the prince spoke until Ox and Bull had escorted the shaken Dara away. Wolf's expression was grim as he looked back to his friend. " 'Tis true I can expect no ransom from Navarre?"

The prince nodded and seated himself on the leather camp stool beside a small table where Wolf took his hurried meals. "Aye. Navarre is to meet Lancaster in Normandy."

" 'Tis also true then that the girl knows far too much about what we do for me to allow her to go free?"

The prince nodded again. "Unless you have other plans for her, 'tis best that you keep her until you return to England. There she can't hurt our cause, and when this affair is done, you can ransom her to King John. Her family has always served the monarchy, and he should be willing to ransom her for their loyalty in the past." A smile again touched Edward's lips. "And look at the bright side of this, Wolf. You now have time to conquer the headstrong wench. Once that's done, she'll be a prize well worth the effort."

Edward's head swiveled toward the tent where Dara had been taken. He drew in another resigned breath and looked back at Wolf with something akin to envy. "I only wish I had the time, but alas, I have too many other things to expend my energy upon. I bring with me one thousand knights, squires, and men-at-arms; two thousand archers, and a great number of Welsh foot soldiers. I'm determined to make the rebels of Guienne rue the day they turned against their lord, the King of England."

Edward reached down and took up a handful of the dark soil. He held it out to Wolf. "This earth belongs to the Plantagenets by right of the blood of my grandmother, Queen Isabel. And I intend to make those who have forgotten their loyalty pay for their foolishness. I will have every inch of their land laid to waste before their eyes. And when their children cry out with hunger, they shall weep for what had once been."

"Can nothing stop this horror?" Dara said as she watched the smoke plumes rise over the hill. The smell of destruction traveled on the wind, carrying the message that the Black Prince had intended when he'd arrived in Bordeaux. Dara squeezed her eyes closed, unable to endure the sight of another town burned to the ground. During the past month, the English army had moved across the once beautiful and rich land of Armagnac. Nothing had been spared. After looting the villages and towns for anything of value that could be carted away, the English troops had set granaries, mills, and haystacks ablaze. What stock they didn't steal, they slaughtered and left to rot in the hot sun. They'd smashed wine vats, destroying the wine before moving out to the vineyards and orchards where they cut down the vines and fruit trees heavy with their ripening crop.

Dara shuddered and turned away. She could take no more of the savage plunder against innocent men, women, and children. She had to get away. She had to get back to Rochambeau before she lost what little sanity she still possessed.

Dara glanced at the sooty, sweaty faces of the foot soldiers who had already returned from the burning village. Sitting beneath the shady trees, they relaxed, speaking among themselves as if they had only gone for a morning stroll instead of on a mission to devastate her homeland. They cared not one whit that those who survived the attack would eventually starve.

The men paid little heed to the dark-haired girl held prisoner by their leader. After the first few days of her captivity, their curiosity about her had waned. Without being told, they knew the boundaries had been set by the Wolf himself, and her ever-vigilant guards ensured those limits. No man under Wolf's command was foolish enough to accost his beautiful hostage and chance incurring the wrath of the MacDonald twins as well as their leader.

"Where do you go in such a rush, Lady?" Ox asked, hurrying to keep up with Dara's rapid steps.

"I don't know," Dara answered honestly, her voice tight with emotion. "I just know I can take no more of this."

A large hand on her arm drew Dara to a halt. "Lady, 'tis war, not a tournament to be enjoyed by spectators."

"And I want no more of it. I'm tired of seeing France laid to waste for the pleasure of Englishmen. I'm tired of hate and destruction," Dara said, and tried to jerk her arm free of the imprisoning hand.

Ox frowned down at the petite brunette. He'd begun to like the girl, but he felt no guilt for the mission they'd been sent to accomplish. War was war, and there was nothing sweet or pretty about it. " 'Tis our job. We do only what we must to guarantee our victory."

Dara glared up at the giant, rebellion sparkling in her sapphire eyes. "Does killing innocent villagers guarantee your victory? Does burning their houses and fields ensure their loyalty to you? *Non*. It does not. You win no war by terrorizing the people who can't fight against you. You are all brutes, cowards and murderers."

"Nay, Lady. We murder no one. By Wolf's order we take no life unless it is in defense of our own. We have orders to harry and waste the countryside but not to kill the people who work it. Dead Frenchmen can pay no taxes to fill the Black Prince's coffers."

Dara didn't believe a word Ox was saying. She'd seen what Wolf's troops had done. The number of baggage wagons grew each time a raiding party went out and came back laden with loot. The blackened earth where villages had once stood also multiplied with each sortie into the countryside.

Giving Ox's shin a sharp kick, Dara jerked her arm free from his hand when he jumped to avoid another blow from her slippers. Taking advantage of his moment of weakness, she fled back to the tent that had become her prison.

Dara threw herself down on the pile of furs where Wolf slept so soundly each night and burst into tears. She wept for her country and for herself. She cried out all the fears that had germinated within her since the prince had informed Wolf that he'd receive no ransom for her. The knowledge that she possessed the power to ruin the intrigues of Navarre and the Black Prince only served to make her fears take deeper root.

Each day for the past month, she'd expected it to be her last. Captivity and worry over her precarious situation had sapped her spirit like a leech set to a fresh vein. She'd become lethargic, showing little interest in anything, as if anesthetized by laudanum. She'd lost sight of the girl who had been so audacious that she'd schemed to cheat the Englishmen of their spoils. Unfortunately, her plan had been for naught. Out of concern for her, the Reverend Mother had revealed her ploy and Wolf had taken the rest of his portion.

When there were no tears left, Dara lay for a long time sniffling into the furs like a small child, yet she felt cleansed. Her tears had melted the invisible shackles that had held her bound far more securely than those made of iron. The thought seemed to give her new impetus. She sat up and wiped her nose. Using the hem of her sleeve, she rubbed the last moisture from her lashes and cheeks. Squaring her shoulders, she looked about her prison, determined to find a means of escape. She wouldn't allow herself to surrender, or she would become like the French countryside, wasted and of no use to anyone. She had to think of Rochambeau and the honor of her family. She had to survive to prove that she had committed no treason against France or her king. And she had to tell King John that Navarre was the viper within his household.

Engrossed in her musings, Dara jumped with a start when the tent flap opened and Wolf strode in. He dropped his sword and belt to the floor and pulled his gipon over his head. As in the weeks past, he paid little heed to the woman who had become a frightened mouse that scurried out of his path whenever he came near.

At first Wolf had been puzzled by the change that had come over the girl after the prince's visit to his camp. But as the days and weeks passed and the campaign progressed past the borders of Guienne, he'd become too busy to concern himself with the girl's moods. He had far more important things upon his mind. It was becoming harder by the day to keep his men in line where the populace was concerned. He feared soon they would ignore his orders to leave the peasants and villagers unharmed. One more day like today, and he himself might just break his own orders. He and Bull had been surprised near dawn by a bunch of peasants set to start their day skewering Englishmen. He'd had to leave several unconscious in the dirt from the flat side of his blade. They'd awake with pounding headaches and bloody pates. But in Wolf's view, he'd been very lenient. An aching brow was better than death.

Wolf glanced once more at Dara. Perhaps it would only be a few short months until he was rid of her. He'd received a message from the prince that King Edward and the Duke of Lancaster would take up the northern campaign when they arrived in Normandy. Upon their arrival, Wolf and his troops were to return to Bordeaux, where the Black Prince would take command. The prince's order freed him to return to England with his hostage.

Wolf jerked his undertunic over his head and ran his hand across his chest, wiping away the sweat that beaded his bronze skin. The medallion about his corded neck swung in the air as he bent to retrieve a clean undertunic from the leather-bound chest that contained his clothing. It would be good to go home.

After so many months away, he longed to see Ellice. Since her birth, he'd spent little time with the child. He'd had to make a living with his sword in order to have the money to care for his daughter. However, he now had a hearth to call his own, and he wanted to settle down and watch her grow. She needed the stability of a parent to give her the love and protection that every child craves and deserves. Sadly, she didn't have a mother who could be with her when he was away. Jeanine had died giving birth to their daughter.

Wolf pushed the thought of Ellice's mother from his mind. He didn't want to remember her sweetness nor the guilt he still carried for not making her his wife before their time together ran out. He'd been on campaign in France when he learned she was to have his child. Though he'd cared for Jeanine, he never loved her, but intended to make her his wife for the sake of their child when he returned to England. However, as he sought to muster together every gold noble possible to support his new family, fate had cruelly intervened, taking Jeanine away before he could set things right, leaving him to raise his child as best a warrior knew how.

Running a hand through his sweaty hair, he turned

once more toward the doorway. After a morning in full armor under the blazing sun, he needed a bath to rid himself of the stench of his own body.

Catching another glimpse of Dara from the corner of his eye, he turned his attention fully upon her. Her gaze didn't waver, but met his directly as she sat glaring up at him, her eyes glassy, her dark hair streaming about her, her face red and splotchy from the heat. She, too, looked as if she could use a good scrubbing. "Come wench. 'Tis time to bathe."

Dara made no move to obey. She would not meekly do as he bid ever again. She'd submitted to an Englishman's orders for the last time. Her loyalty to her country and her family wouldn't allow it.

"Wench, did you hear me?" Wolf queried, ignoring the challenging look she directed at him.

Dara set her chin at a mutinous angle. "I heard you."

"Then obey me."

"Non."

Wolf cocked a dark brow. There was something different about her today, but he was in no mood to find out exactly what. "You will obey me, Lady Dara."

Dara stubbornly shook her head and folded her arms across her breast. She looked away from Wolf. Let him hang her for spying, but she'd not grovel.

The simple, disobedient gesture slivered the thin thread that kept Wolf's temper in check. His hand shot out and closed about Dara's arm. He jerked her to her feet. Ebony eyes blazing with fury, he glared down at her and growled, "You, Lady Dara, are my prisoner, and you will obey me."

Her brilliant gaze locked with Wolf's, but she remained stubbornly mute. Be damned if she would obey him!

Wolf's grip tightened upon her arm. His fingers bit brutally into the creamy flesh beneath her tunic's long sleeve, but she made no sign that she felt any pain. His features flushed a deeper hue as he looked down into her rebellious sapphire eyes. His fingers relaxed upon Dara. The expression within her fathomless eyes reminded him of the young nun who had drawn him like a hummingbird to a rose.

Wolf's senses stirred. His anger cooled even as his blood heated and made him swell with desire. He clenched his teeth in frustration. Damn. He'd thought he had his wayward body under control during the past weeks. He'd shared his tent with Dara and managed not to think about bedding her after the first few days. Her withdrawal had helped stem his desire. He'd found nothing exciting about the mousy creature that she had become. However, his body was now making up for it in force. He was responding to the close proximity of her luscious body like a fresh-faced youth eager for a taste of his first female.

A bath in the stream beyond the trees would do more now than just cleanse his body. The cold water would hopefully help quell his sudden desire to ravage Dara. The thought taking firm root, he didn't ask her again to accompany him to the stream. He picked her up, tossed her over his shoulder, and walked from the tent. He'd be damned if he would allow the hot-tempered vixen to tell him what she would or would not do. Until fifty thousand crowns filled his coffers, she belonged to him, body and soul.

Hanging across Wolf's shoulder, his solid muscles pressing into her abdomen, her hair blinding her to everything except the tanned expanse of his back, Dara gasped for enough air to protest her abominable treatment. In such an awkward, humiliating position she could do little more.

Wolf strode on, ignoring Dara's discomfort. He followed the winding trail that led through the thick woods to the stream. The bubbling brook wound its way through the rolling countryside like an iridescent blue ribbon. Its rippling waters gurgled happily over the time-smoothed stones and eddied along a sandbar to form a pond, waist deep and perfect for bathing.

Wolf paused at the edge of the water only long enough to ascertain that they were alone. Seeing no one, he waded out into the stream and let go of his burden.

Dara slipped from his shoulder and immediately lost her footing on the slippery creek gravel. She sank below the water with a splash and came up spluttering with fury. Dragging the dark, clinging strands of hair from her eyes so she could see the object of her wrath, she drew back and pummeled Wolf's chest with her fists. "How dare you treat me in such a manner, you oaf!"

Effortlessly, Wolf captured her pounding fists within one hand, stilling her attempt to throttle him. His own dark eyes glowing with fire, he ordered, "Cease! I'll give you no more warning, Dara. The next time you think to hit me, it would be in your best interest to re-think your decision for I'll repay in kind."

"Your threats do not frighten me, you brute. Do what you will, but I'll worry no more. Life is worth nothing if I have to live in fear that each day will be my last."

Wolf arched a raven brow at Dara, wondering at her sanity. He didn't know what in the devil she was talking about. He'd placed her in no danger. He'd made sure that either one or both of the MacDonald brothers guarded her at all times to ensure her safety from their enemies as well as from any of his own men who might take it into their heads to accost her. "I know not of what you speak. Your life has never been in jeopardy."

"Umph!" Dara snorted. "If you think I believe you, then you are truly weak-minded. Play no more games with me. Do what you will and be done with it."

His earlier thoughts making him misconstrue Dara's statement, Wolf's eyes widened in surprise. Had the girl lost her senses? She was now telling him to take her innocence. Wolf tugged at his earlobe as if to correct his hearing. "Are you sure that is what you truly want, Lady Dara?"

Dara nodded, "Aye. It is far better than living with this hanging over my head. I can take no more. I want it done and over with."

The heart within Wolf's chest began to slam against his ribs with anticipation. He smiled down at Dara and drew her closer to his wet, hard body. "If that is your choice, I will willingly oblige your wishes. However, I think we both need to bathe first."

"What does it matter if I'm clean or dirty. It will end up the same, will it not?"

A thoughtful expression crossed Wolf's face and he nodded. "Aye, but it would give me more pleasure if you have a bath."

Dara's fury resurfaced. The man was truly a heartless beast. He must think her a simpleton if he thought she didn't know the reason he'd brought her to the stream. And it wasn't for a bath. Drowning was a far less messy way to be rid of her. He'd not have her blood soiling his hands after the execution. Fuming, she glared up at him and remarked sarcastically, "Of course. I must think of your pleasure at all times."

Wolf's lips curled up at the corners. "I would hope so. I will try to think of yours."

"You can be assured, I'll find no pleasure in it," Dara snapped, wondering at the man's sanity. How could he expect her to find pleasure in her own death? He had to be mad.

Wolf brought up his hand and cupped her cheek. He brushed her smooth skin with the pad of his thumb as he gazed down into her fiery eyes. "Oh, I think you will. Before I'm through, you will hear the angels sing."

Dara expected nothing else. She'd tried to live her life without committing too many sins. She was sure the Reverend Mother thought her destined for hell, but she felt she'd done nothing evil enough to suffer such a fate.

Dara cast one last glance about. She would die on a beautiful day. She looked up at Wolf, squared her shoulders and drew upon all the courage she possessed. Her whispered words were barely audible. "Then I'm ready." She closed her eyes and prepared herself to die.

Wolf circled her throat with his long fingers, caressing the slender ivory column, savoring the feel of her skin and the silken hair at the nape of her neck. He smiled smugly as he lowered his head to taste her lips for the first time. Like so many in the past, the girl had finally realized that she could no longer deny the attraction between them. Wolf felt like laughing aloud. They were all alike in the end.

Prepared for the worst, the touch of Wolf's mouth against hers momentarily stunned Dara into submission, until she realized how truly cruel the man was. He now chose her final moments to give her the kiss that she'd been craving. For weeks she'd been plagued by emotions that Wolf roused within her—emotions she couldn't explain. She had called them her demons because she felt bewitched by the man though he was her enemy. Tears sprang into her eyes, burning against her lids and creeping from beneath her thick lashes to trickle down her cheeks. She drew in a shuddering breath. She now knew how his mouth felt against her own, and it was devastating to realize she'd never know his kiss again. It would have been far easier to face what she knew was to come had she never experienced it. The touch of his lips made her want to forget her honor, her pride of family, and to live at any cost.

Wolf's mouth lingered upon Dara's, his tongue tasting and seeking entrance to the sweet cavern beyond her lips. Humiliated by her own perfidy, Dara began to push against his chest. She could stand no more torture. She wanted him to kill her and be done with it before she further betrayed what honor she had left. Dara jerked her mouth free and wiped her hand across her lips as she glared up at Wolf, her eyes full of accusation. "Have you no heart? Do you have to torture me before you end my life?"

Wolf looked down at her, bewildered. He had no earthly idea what she was babbling about. "End your life? I know in the past my kisses have made women swoon, but they have yet to be proven fatal."

"You mean you don't intend to drown me?"

"I meant only for us to bathe, but since you prefer other sport, I am more than willing to oblige your wishes."

"You mean you only brought me here to seduce me?" Dara said, momentarily dumbfounded.

"I didn't bring you here to seduce you, wench. You instigated it. Now come here and let us finish what you began," Wolf growled, tiring of her games. He reached for her again, dragging a reluctant Dara once more into his arms.

Dara, determined not to allow the beast any more liberties of her person, braced both hands against Wolf's chest and pushed with all her might in an effort to free herself.

Surprise etched Wolf's face when he felt his own footing give way beneath him. The gravel moved and he tumbled backward into the water. Flailing his arms to regain his balance and spitting fury and water at the same time, he rose out of the stream like a vengeful, gloriously handsome Apollyon. Again he reached for Dara.

The look on Wolf's face shattered all of her bravado. She leaped out of his path as he lunged forward, and with a squeal she turned to flee. Her wet skirts tangled about her legs and brought her to her knees. She, too, sank once more below the water's surface before she had time to regain her own footing. A hand dragged her upward by the neck of her soggy mantle. Raven hair webbing her in glistening wet silk, she hung in the air like a limp rag doll for several moments before Wolf set her on her feet and turned her to face him.

"Wench, I think it is time that you played my games instead of the other way around," Wolf growled, pulling her against him. " 'Tis time to show you that you can't tease me and not expect to pay the price. Though still young, you should have already learned that there are consequences for every action."

Wolf lowered his head, taking Dara's mouth with his own in a harsh kiss. He plunged his tongue inside her slightly parted lips and ravaged her mouth, plundering it as he had plundered her homeland. His arms came about her, crushing her against his passion-swollen body.

Dara tried to fight but found herself helpless to withstand his assault. The water swirled about them, as did the sudden tidal wave of emotion that came from the very depths of her being. Like the current of the water, his mouth and tongue stirred up sensations that had lain within her like undisturbed silt on the streambed floor. They surged up toward the surface like fine golden sand churned by the sudden rush of water after a spring rain. They muddied up all coherent thoughts and left her gasping for air as she clung to the strong, bronzed shoulders of the man who held her.

Wolf wound his fingers in the mass of her silken hair

and devoured her mouth until his own breath came in short, hard pants. Holding her prisoner with one hand, he unlaced her mantle with the other. The wet material clung stubbornly to her body, sticking to the sweet swell of her breasts and hips as he tried to ease the sodden garment downward. Disgusted by his inept attempt to free her of her clothing, he released her mouth long enough to scoop Dara up into his arms and walk out of the water.

Finding a mossy bed beneath a large tree, he set her down. Before Dara could calm her rioting emotions enough to muster a protest, Wolf took his dagger and cut away the tenacious mantle and undertunic. The soggy garments fell in a pool about Dara's feet, leaving only her wet chemise to protect her modesty. The dampness made the thin material diaphanous, revealing far more than it concealed. It clung enticingly to the coral peaks of her breasts, the curve of her waist, and the shadowy apex of her thighs.

Wolf stood mesmerized by the enchantress before him. He had known the girl was an extraordinary beauty, but he hadn't been prepared for the effect her exquisite body was having upon him. In all of his thirty-two years, no woman had stirred his senses as this one female was doing. All reason seemed to evaporate under the allure of her spell. She was like the mythical sirens whose songs men followed, even knowing that they were going to their deaths. Every sinew of his body was attuned to her. And he wanted nothing more than to throw her down upon the thick green moss and bury himself deep within her luscious young body. Like the beast for which he'd been named, he chose his mate.

Moving as if in a trance, his dark gaze never leaving her captivating eyes, Wolf reached out and cupped one proud breast. He flicked the nipple with the pad of his thumb and watched her lower lip tremble as she sucked in a sharp breath. Her nipple hardened revealingly in response to his touch, and Wolf felt a jolt of excitement so heady that he nearly shivered. The message her body sent him was plain. She also desired him.

Ebony and sapphire, sculpted ivory and bronze, stood separated by only a few feet, yet the current of electricity flowing between them melded them together as one even before Wolf drew Dara against his throbbing body. He gazed down into her glistening eyes and lightly stroked her lower lip with his thumb. His words were soft, yet firm with meaning, as he murmured, "You were meant to be mine, Dara of Rochambeau."

As she stood in the enchanted glade looking up at the man whose presence made everything within her quiver with newly discovered desires, Dara could find no words to refute his statement. Nor did she want to. Her attraction to Wolf was too strong to be denied. Desire overshadowed logic and loyalty. She was no longer the captive nor he the captor. They were two people who found themselves bound together by something far deeper than greed, God, or glory. It came from within their primeval souls to bring them together, to unite them as one and fulfill the destiny that God had divined when he'd first created man and woman.

Dara raised her mouth to meet Wolf's as he lowered his head to lay claim to her lips in a soul-searing kiss.

Chapter 6

"Ho, Wolf," a voice called, shattering the moment for the man and woman who stood poised upon the precipice of passion.

"Ho, Wolf," came the call again. Wolf ground his teeth together and released Dara's lips with a resigned sigh. He let his arms fall away from her and glanced in the direction of the stream. His body still burned for release, and he briefly considered ignoring his liege, but duty won out over physical desire. He ran his long fingers through his thick hair as he looked back at the woman standing so quietly before him. "Wait here. I'll see what the devil Bull wants, and then I'll return."

Dara shuddered and wrapped her arms about herself to ward off the chill that suddenly pervaded every inch of her body. Bull's call had the effect of a bucket of ice water dumped over her head. It shattered the spell Wolf's kisses wove and left her shaken by the knowledge of what she had nearly done. Dara drew in a ragged breath and fought against the bilious shame that made her stomach churn sickeningly.

She captured her lower lip between her teeth and bowed her head, chastened by her own wayward emotions. She squeezed her eyes tightly closed against the memory of her response to Wolf's hands and lips. Another shudder passed over her. She couldn't fathom the madness that had seized her. Nor did she know the cause for her sudden bout of insanity. Perhaps the pressure of being held captive had unhinged her mind, or the fact that she had been forced to the limit of her endurance from the weeks of watching her country laid to waste, or perhaps it was nothing more than Wolf's handsome face that had driven her insane. She only knew the affliction existed. She had no other excuse for her behavior because she couldn't blame her actions upon love.

Dara staunchly shook her head in denial. No. It was impossible for her to love Wolf. He was her enemy as well as France's. To feel anything for him beyond contempt would be to betray everything she held dear. Englishmen had done too much to her family for her to surrender herself to one of their lot.

Dragging in another ragged breath, she quickly retrieved the remnants of her clothing and pulled them on. After several frustrating tries she finally managed to tear the wet material enough to tie the severed seams back together. She turned toward the path Wolf had taken only moments before, and didn't look back. She didn't want to remember what had transpired upon the thick bed of moss, especially her eager response to Wolf's seduction.

"Ho, Wolf," Bull called when he saw Wolf step from the thicket of trees. "A messenger has brought news from Phelan."

A chill tingled down Wolf's spine. Bull's grim expression foretold the seriousness of the situation before the man volunteered further information. "What news does he bring? Is Ellice well?"

"I fear 'tis not good. The blasted Scottish laird, Angus Morgan, has laid claim to Phelan. He intends to take it by siege if necessary."

"I'll see the Scottish bastard dead and in hell first,"

Wolf growled, bristling instinctively, like his namesake set on protecting its territory.

"Then you leave immediately?"

Wolf nodded. "Aye. I won't leave Ellice unprotected. Since the majority of Edward's forces are here in France, he can't afford to send men north to protect my holdings."

"But he owes you that much. You are now a knight of the realm."

"A knight who bought his title with sweat and blood. I've worked too hard and too long to allow some Scottish laird to think he can sneak in England's back door and lay claim to what is mine because Edward has his eyes on France."

"Then we go with you," Bull said without hesitation.

Wolf arched a dark brow, and a slow smile curved his full lips. "You mean you'll leave a good fight out of friendship for me?"

Bull's own lips spread into a mischievous grin and devilment twinkled in his sky-blue eyes. "I would wager we'll not have long to do without a battle once we reach England." He laid a wide hand on Wolf's bare shoulder. "I know you too well, old friend. You'll not whimper and whine to the king about how badly you're being treated. You'll take matters into your own hands." Bull paused and his lips unfurled into a tight, grim line. "Remember, we also love Ellice."

Wolf nodded his understanding. "Then 'tis settled. We break camp and move the troops back to Bordeaux two months earlier than I had planned. Hopefully, the men will be satisfied with the plunder they have already amassed."

"Will you take your men back to Phelan?"

"Aye. I will welcome any who are willing to fight. I must have enough men if I am to protect Phelan. However, should any man want to remain in the prince's service, I will release him freely and with good cheer."

"You have no reason to fear. The pack stays with the Wolf," Bull said. Spying Dara over Wolf's shoulder, he arched an inquisitive brow at her passion-swollen lips and disheveled clothing. He flashed Wolf a shrewd look. " 'Tis fair to assume the lady goes with us?"

Wolf sensed Dara's presence but didn't glance at her as he said, "Aye. She knows far too much about the prince's plans with Navarre to allow her her freedom. I must take her back to England until the time comes when her knowledge can no longer do our forces harm. Then I'll be free to ransom her."

" 'Tis wise. I'll go and tell Ox and the others that we break camp at dawn."

Dara watched Bull stride out of sight before she said quietly, "I'll not go with you."

Wolf glanced over his shoulder at the young woman who had remained still and quiet as he and Bull discussed their plans. His dark gaze locked with hers. The lines about his mouth and eyes deepened. "You will do as I bid."

"Nay. I'll not allow you to take me to England. France is my home."

"Demoiselle, you seem to forget that you are my captive and have no say in the matter," Wolf said, once more the unrelenting captor. The lover of only a short while ago had vanished as he turned upon her and abruptly imprisoned her wrist within his long fingers. Without a word he started back in the direction of the camp, dragging an unwilling Dara along in his wake.

She struggled impotently against him, digging her heels into the damp earth, but nothing hampered Wolf's long strides. By the time they reached the camp, she was out of breath from grappling with the man made of sinewy iron. Wolf thrust her into his tent and ordered her to remain inside.

"Be damned if I will," Dara said, coming out of the tent nearly as fast as Wolf had put her inside. She faced her captor, breasts heaving from exertion and fury. Her eyes glittered her contempt as she glared up at the man who had managed to make her feel like a traitor to her family and country. He had taken advantage of her innocence, foully using her own emotions against her. "You beast, I'll not obey you again. Nor will I continue to remain as your hostage. Either you free me or kill me."

Wolf folded his arms over his wide, bare chest and looked down at the little termagant. Had he been in a better frame of mind, he might have seen the humor in the situation. She was like a gnat pestering a bull; not big enough to be anything but an aggravation. The muscles worked in his corded throat as he narrowed his thick-lashed eyes. "Lady, I would suggest that you heed my wishes or find yourself hog-tied until we reach England."

Adamantly, Dara shook her head. She mocked his gesture by folding her arms across her breasts. "Never. I will not meekly stand by and allow you to abuse me again."

One dark brow lifted in question. "How have I abused you, demoiselle? Until this moment I had thought you had been treated well. You have slept in my tent, eaten of my food, and have been protected from harm by my men."

"Humph!" Dara snorted. "I would not call what happened less than an hour ago being treated well. Nor will I stay here and allow you to degrade me again. I am no camp follower, nor am I a harlot to be used at your will."

Wolf's expression darkened. "As I recall, demoiselle,

I did not force my attention upon you. Your blood ran just as hot as mine."

Dara's cheeks crimsoned, and she quickly glanced about to make sure no one had overheard Wolf's ribald remark. To her chagrin, Ox and Bull stood only a few feet away, smiling broadly at the repartee between herself and their leader. Dara lowered her eyes to the ground in front of her, her face burning with humiliation. "You are wrong. I did not want your attentions."

"Ah, the little liar has returned. I had forgotten in the past weeks of your reticence, Sister, how well you do lie," Wolf said. "But no matter what untruths pass your lips, your body spoke honestly. You wanted me as much as I wanted you. And 'tis not yet finished between us, as you well know."

Dara jerked her eyes back to Wolf's. " 'Twas finished before it ever began. You are my enemy, and I'll never surrender to you."

Wolf smiled confidently. His ebony gaze swept over each of Dara's features before moving slowly downward. His eyes rested briefly on the swell of her breasts and the curve of her hips and then traveled the entire length of her. His lips curled smugly. "Ah, sweet little enemy, before we are through, you will come to me."

Dara jutted out her chin and spat, "Never."

"Never say never because never is a long, long time, little enemy."

" 'Twill be far longer than never before I come willingly to you. If you take me, it will be by force and no other way."

Wolf raised a hand and lightly ran his finger along the curve of Dara's flushed cheek. He smiled again when he felt the involuntary tremor that passed through her at his touch. "I have not as yet had to resort to rape, demoiselle. And I seriously doubt I'll have to force myself upon you. You are no different from any other woman I've known. In time the heat in your blood will make you come to me. However, I don't have the time to dally further today. There are far more important matters at hand at the moment than bedding you. Now return to my tent or find yourself gagged and bound." He arched a brow. " 'Tis your choice."

Flashing Wolf a mutinous look, Dara turned on her heel and marched back to the tent. She hadn't surrendered. She'd never allow Wolf to defeat her. Her acquiescence was merely a play for time. As long as Wolf believed he had her under control, she had the advantage, and in time would find a way to escape the monster. She would never allow Wolf to take her to England.

Wolf watched Dara until the tent flap concealed her from his view. The wench hadn't fooled him by her sudden submission. He could see her devious little mind already making plans to try to thwart him. But he was as equally determined to show the Lady Dara that he was not a man who could be led around by a ring in his nose. She was his captive. She belonged to him body and soul until the ransom was paid. And she would do as he bid, or she'd suffer the consequences.

"The lady intends to give you nothing but trouble," Ox said, his own gaze still on the tent flap.

"Aye. That's what she intends at the moment. But she'll come 'round like all the rest of her kind. She'll tire of the games and want what all the others have wanted. Be they lady or whore, friend or foe, women have needs just like we do."

Bull rubbed a wide palm across his beard-stubbled chin as he turned his curious gaze back upon Wolf. "I'm beginning to believe this wench is different from the rest."

Wolf's dark eyes came to rest upon his friend. He arched a raven brow. "How so?"

Bull smiled. "She must be different if she's slept in your tent all these weeks and you still haven't bedded her."

Wolf's skin flushed a deeper hue. " 'Twas by my choice."

" 'Tis strange that the Wolf hasn't been out to prowl since he captured the Lady Dara," Bull said, flashing his brother a sagacious look. He arched a speculative brow, and his grin deepened. "Could it be that the Wolf has found his one true mate?"

"Enough irrational speculation," Wolf growled. "The Wolf has been far too busy doing his duty for his king to worry about finding a lusty maid to ease his loins. Now 'tis time for you two to be about yours. We waste time in idle chatter. Have the messenger sent to me. I must send word to the Black Prince of my plans."

Dara turned on her side for what seemed like the thousandth time. Cradling her head on her arm, she stared through the muted shadows at the broad back facing her. It had been three weeks since Wolf had received the message from England. And it had been three weeks since her decision to make sure he didn't succeed in forcing her to go with him.

Dara bit down on her lower lip and glanced toward the tent opening. She knew she had to make her escape tonight or it would be too late. On the morrow, the English troops would turn westward for the final leg of their journey to Bordeaux. Once that happened, there would be too many miles between herself and her home for her, a woman alone, to successfully reach it again. Tonight was her last hope. She'd overheard the men talking and knew they were nearing the Dordogne River. Fortunately, her captor was unaware that Rochambeau lay only about three leagues from where they now camped.

Dara pushed herself upright and watched the shadow of the guard pass in front of the opening. Even as he slept, Wolf had made sure she didn't escape. Dara glanced once more at the man sleeping so peacefully upon his bed of furs. Quietly she slid her hand beneath her own pallet and retrieved the small eating dagger that she'd managed to conceal during their evening repast. She smiled triumphantly. Wolf thought himself so clever, but he'd failed to note the missing blade when the yeoman had come to collect the remains of their meal.

Dara held the knife up and ran her thumb down the sharp blade. It would do nicely to cut through the thick material of the tent wall. Wolf would be totally surprised when he awoke to find his tent had gained a new doorway and his hostage had vanished.

Holding her breath, she slipped from the furs and eased to the back of the tent. Slowly, she slid the blade through the fabric, and inch by inch widened the slit until it was big enough for her to easily slip through. Casting one last glance at the broad back of the man who had made her aware of herself as a woman, she tucked the dagger into her waistband and crawled through the opening to freedom.

Heart pounding, Dara crouched in the shadows to ascertain her avenue of escape. Seeing no guards nearby, she came to her feet and stealthily made her way toward the darkness ringing the English encampment.

Once in the safety of the shadows, Dara sagged against a thick-boled tree and looked back in the direction she'd just come. Her absence had gone unnoticed, or a hue and cry would have already gone out. Relieved, she glanced about the forest shrouded in darkness. She shivered. She found little comfort in the thought of having to travel through the pitch-black night. Nor could she stop her imagination from conjuring up hideous monsters of every description. She knew they awaited to pounce upon her from each bush and tree. Dara cast another look back toward the English encampment and stiffened her spine. She squared her shoulders determinedly. Her imaginary beasts were only minor terrors compared to the beast she'd have to face should she be recaptured. Wolf was far more frightening than anything her mind could create. The thought set her feet into motion. She turned toward the sound of the river.

The morning sun found Dara exhausted, yet still trudging barefoot down the narrow road that led toward Rochambeau. After stumbling through the forest, she'd had to leave her shoes on the riverbank when she'd crossed the Dordogne. It had been too deep to wade, and she'd had to swim to reach the opposite bank. After roaming around in circles for most of the night, near dawn she had managed to locate the rutted cart path that she now traveled. She hadn't been sure that she was even going in the right direction until she'd passed through a small village where a milkmaid had given her directions.

Dara forced one foot in front of the other, resolutely defying the cry of her tired, aching muscles. She was too close now to her home to stop. When she reached Rochambeau, she'd have all the time in the world to rest. Rochambeau's walls would protect her and her people from any danger once the thick gates were closed.

The thought kept her moving. Soon, she told herself, she would be safe. She'd not have to fear the English or any other enemy. Fatigued, Dara paused on the rise overlooking the vineyards that had sustained Rochambeau's wealth with fine wine. She couldn't believe what her eyes told her. Row upon row of trellises wound across the bare ground, supporting only withered vines.

She rubbed her eyes in an effort to dispel the horror of the image.

"No," she whispered, and began to run toward the tall granite walls of her home.

An eerie stillness hovered over the ancient castle like a thick gray cloud as she stumbled the last half mile to the iron-bound gates. Tears streaked Dara's ashen cheeks, and a sob of fear tore from her lips as she sped down the narrow shadowy passage, past the raised portcullis and across the bailey littered with debris. She didn't pause to take in the destruction. She ran up the steps and thrust open the oaken door to the great hall. The portal sagged at an odd angle, swaying from one hinge like a bird's broken wing.

Dara halted abruptly upon the threshold, blinded by the sudden change of light. She blinked into the cavernous hall where the morning shadows still inhabited the corners and vaulted ceiling. Only a few streaks of light filtered through the high, narrow, shuttered windows to relieve the darkness left by the night.

"Where is everyone?" she called. Her heart drumming a frantic tattoo against her breastbone, she listened intently for an answer that didn't come. Dara again called, " 'Tis Dara of Rochambeau. I've come home. Answer me when I call."

Silence as still as the family vault greeted her words.

Dara raised a trembling hand to her lips and bit down to stay the hysterical scream bubbling in her throat at finding her home deserted and in shambles.

Dragging in a long slow breath, she forced back the panic and told herself that she had to remain calm. This was her home, and it was her responsibility to find out what had happened. Her eyes once more swept over the hall. She had no doubt of what had happened to wreak such havoc. She had seen the English lay waste to far too many villages in the past months to think that an estate as rich as Rochambeau would escape their greedy sight.

Dara slowly moved to the center of the great hall. Misty tears momentarily distorted her vision as she viewed what the English had left of her once beautiful home. The Rochambeau standards had been torn down, the silk ripped into shreds. The whitewashed walls were blackened with soot from fires that had been made in the middle of the chamber. The tables, benches, and chairs lay broken in charred piles, used by the English looters as firewood.

Disgust thinned Dara's lips. Angrily, she swiped the tears from her eyes and damned every Englishman to the hell from which he'd been spawned. Slowly, she bent to retrieve a narrow strip of the standard that had once borne the image of the Rochambeau rams. Her eyes narrowed as she crumpled the silk in her hand and pressed it against her heart. She silently vowed to avenge herself upon those who were responsible for the devastation of the Rochambeau estates.

"Is it truly you, mademoiselle?"

Dara jerked about, her eyes searching the darkness for the body that went with the voice. "*Oui*. I have come home."

A moment later Dara was rocked nearly off her feet as a young girl burst out of the shadows and grasped her about the legs as she fell at Dara's feet. "Oh, mademoiselle. We feared the worst for you. When the King of Navarre took you away, we prayed that you would return to us. But when our prayers went unanswered, we thought you had surely died."

Relief coursed through her at finding her maid still alive. Dara raised the girl to her feet. "Renee, where is everyone? What has happened here?"

"They fled for their lives, mademoiselle. They were afraid to stay here after the King of Navarre opened the gates and welcomed the English soldiers." Renee shuddered visibly and bowed her head. Her voice shook from the memories. "They took everything, everything."

Dara's heart stilled. Renee didn't have to put into words what she had suffered. Her voice told Dara of her anguish, of the price she had paid. Dara momentarily savored her own good fortune before contrition set in. She realized that her fate would have been the same as Renee's had she not been captured by a man called Wolf. Any other soldier would have ravished her like the land of her birth. Guiltily, Dara placed a comforting arm about the young maid's shoulders. " 'Tis over now, Renee. I'll not allow anyone else to harm you."

Renee looked up at her with large grief-stricken eyes and slowly shook her head. "I fear even you cannot protect us now, mademoiselle." The maid raised a trembling hand and gestured at her surroundings. "The power of Rochambeau is destroyed."

"No, Renee. I will not allow you or anyone to believe such a thing. I will fight for my home and my people."

"But there is no one to fight for, mademoiselle. The few of us who are still here are either too old, too sick, or too young to stand with you. And you alone cannot stand against the enemy should they return. It is all in vain. All is gone, mademoiselle."

Dara unfurled her fingers to reveal the strip of silk. She shook her head as she looked down at all that was left of the Rochambeau standard. "*Non*. All is not gone. As long as I have breath in my body, a Rochambeau still holds what my ancestors fought and died to build. And I will do the same to preserve my brother's inheritance. Until he returns to rebuild what the English tried to destroy."

Renee flashed Dara a sympathetic look before quickly lowering her eyes to hide her skepticism. She knew what the English could do, had experienced first-hand their violence. Her mistress could never fight against the evil horde that had come to rape and plunder with Navarre's blessings.

Dara's stomach growled, reminding her that she'd not eaten since the previous night. "Do you have anything here to eat?"

"We have a bit of gruel. The soldiers took everything they could carry, leaving us with very little. They robbed even our gardens before they were ready to harvest."

Another flicker of guilt passed over Dara. She'd not had to suffer any deprivation. Fattened up for the kill, she thought cynically. Wolf had kept her well fed, so that he'd not have to bed a bag of bones when he chose to defile her innocence.

"Would you share your meal with me?" Dara asked.

"You have no need to ask. 'Tis rightfully yours, mademoiselle."

Dara's eyes misted. It was hard to understand the maid's loyalty after all she'd suffered. "Why did you stay, Renee? You could have left with the others."

Renee's glance once more took in the sooty walls and charred furnishings before they came back to Dara. " 'Tis my home, mademoiselle. I am only a servant and have no claim to this land through blood. But, like you, I was born here. I have no other place to go. Where I once claimed all who lived on Rochambeau as my family, you and those few who remain are all I have left."

"I am honored to be considered your family, Renee."

A timid smile touched the maid's lips. She didn't know how to respond. It was too bewildering to suddenly speak to her lady as an equal. Flustered, she said, "Come, mademoiselle. You must eat." Renee's eyes swept down Dara's tattered mantle. "The English left nothing untouched. They took all your clothing and jewels."

Dara smiled as she, too, glanced down at what had once been a very fashionable gown. Like her other garments, it had been ruined by the rain before she left the convent. She looked back to the young maid. "Do not worry, Renee. I have grown used to wearing rags. And there are far more important matters for us to attend to than worrying over my lack of clothing. We must first make sure that we all do not starve. Then we can begin to set Rochambeau back to rights."

Again a flicker of doubt passed over Renee's face, but she didn't argue. Unaccustomed to governing themselves, she, like the others, had hidden in the dungeon. Renee was glad to have someone once more taking charge of Rochambeau.

Chapter 7

Her hunger momentarily appeased by the thin gruel Renee and the aged gardener's wife had prepared on a brazier in one of the dungeon's many cells, Dara quickly took her leave of the dark, damp bowels of the castle. The confined quarters smothered the breath from her. A shudder of relief passed over her as she entered the great hall. Like the penance box at St. Marie, the dungeon had always produced an ungovernable fear in her.

Dara absently rubbed her arms as she crossed the hall and paused in the open doorway. Her lips thinned into a line of disgust as she looked at the destruction that had been wrought. It would take far more hands than Rochambeau now sheltered to rebuild what the English barbarians had destroyed. The dovecote, the barn, and the stables had been burned, as had the smithy and brew house. The hayricks were only ash, and the beehives had been crushed as if by some giant foot. An Englishman's foot, Dara mused resentfully, recalling her assessment of the Englishmen she'd encountered.

Dara ran a tired hand over her face and turned toward the family chapel. Her shoulders sagged under the weight of the burden now facing her. The responsibility of reclaiming her family heritage from the ashes of war lay firmly upon her. She had vowed to rebuild and keep Rochambeau for her brother, but if she were to accom-

plish what she had set for her herself, she would need
as much help as she could get from all quarters, including the Almighty. Though she'd been recalcitrant at St.
Marie, Dara suddenly felt the need to ask God's forgiveness and help.

Like the rest of Rochambeau, the chapel had been
ransacked. The gold-and-gem-encrusted cross that the
king had given her grandfather for his bravery in the
Eastern crusades had been stolen. Even the silk altar
cloth had been slashed to ribbons and left in a crumpled
heap upon the floor.

Taking in the devastation, Dara carefully picked her
way through the shards of broken glass that had once
filled the leaded window frame. The chapel windows
had been her father's gift to her mother upon the birth
of their son. The expensive stained glass had depicted a
scene of the Madonna and child.

Dara experienced a renewed sense of loss as she
looked at the empty window. Though she had never
truly known the woman who had given her birth, she
often came to the chapel to feel close to her. She had always found comfort in looking up at the stained-glass
window. Her father had honored his wife by having the
Madonna's features crafted into the likeness of Dara's
mother. The baby Jesus resembled her brother Paul.

Dara gulped in a ragged breath and sank to her knees
in front of the barren altar. She bowed her head and attempted to pray for the strength and courage she would
need to save Rochambeau. However, no prayer could
find its way past the one name that kept intruding into
her thoughts: Navarre, Navarre, Navarre. The muscles
worked in Dara's cheek as she clenched her jaw. No
matter how hard she tried, she couldn't conquer the
white-hot rage that burned within her. She was con-
sumed by hatred, leaving little room for prayer or anything else. The man had turned against his own flesh

and blood, his country, his people. He had willingly given Rochambeau to France's enemy in order to gain their favor.

Dara stared blindly down at the broken glass. She despised the English soldiers who had wrought havoc upon France. Yet she understood them. Unlike Navarre, they served their king. Her cousin possessed no such honor, no such loyalty. He was the devil's henchman in every sense of the word. He was a man who traded upon the blood of others to gain his own ends.

She raised her face to the shattered window, and her expression darkened. Her icy sapphire eyes reflected her hatred for Charles of Navarre. Solemnly, she picked up a piece of the stained glass and made a small slit on her wrist. The cut beaded bright red as she raised it into the sunlight spilling into the chapel. Her eyes narrowed as she looked at the blood running down her arm. She lifted her chin proudly toward the blue sky. "By my Rochambeau blood and God, I vow to make Charles pay for what he has done to my family. No matter what I have to do, I will see that he suffers the pains of hell for his treachery."

Prayer and piety forgotten under the surging need for vengeance, Dara came to her feet and walked from the chapel. She staunched the flow of her blood against the faded material of her skirt as she retraced her path back to the great hall and called for Renee. When the young maid came scurrying out of her dark hole, Dara ordered her to collect the others who had stayed at Rochambeau. It was time to set things to rights. She'd not live like a rat in the bowels of her own home. She was a Rochambeau, and by that evening she intended to eat by the warmth of the fire in her own solar, no matter if she had to sit on the floor.

By the time twilight began to wrap its mantle over Rochambeau, drawing the land and its creatures into its comforting embrace in preparation for the coming night, Dara had gained her wish. A fire gave off heat from the fireplace, and she sat in a chair in front of a table to eat her evening gruel. The gardener and the elderly smithy had managed to find the dilapidated furnishings in one of the storage rooms where old items had been stored for repair. They also managed to locate a straw mattress, which now lay against the wall where her four-poster bed had once stood.

Dara looked about her solar, satisfied with the progress they had made in such a short time. She knew that rebuilding the rest of Rochambeau would not be as easy as furnishing one chamber. However, it felt good to know that something had already been accomplished. No matter how small, it made her feel that she could succeed.

Hiding a yawn behind her hand, Dara came to her feet. Every muscle in her body ached with weariness. She'd been tired when she reached Rochambeau that morning, but managed to keep her exhaustion at bay throughout the day, until Renee and the other servants returned to their dungeon. Now she could no longer ignore her need for rest. She hadn't slept in nearly two days, and yearned for nothing more than to curl up on her stiff new bed and sleep for a week. Dara crossed to the straw-filled mattress and surrendered to her exhaustion. She curled like a babe, burrowing down into the lumpy center, and immediately slept.

" 'Tis unguarded. There be only a few servants left," Ox said as he slipped through the thick underbrush to give Wolf and Bull his assessment of the Castle Rochambeau's defenses.

"I expected as much. From the looks of the place, our troops have already been here and gone," Wolf said, his ebony eyes narrowing thoughtfully as his gaze swept over his wayward hostage's home. His anger at the Lady Dara had as yet to cool below a simmer. When he awoke that morning to find her missing, he thought his head would burst from the force of the fury that had run through him. Like a streak of searing lightning, it melted away all sound reasoning. He had ordered his men to scour the countryside until they found Dara.

Of all the hostages he'd ever taken in all his years of fighting other men's wars, Dara of Rochambeau was the most exasperating, infuriating, aggravating wench he'd ever encountered. He should have been glad that she disappeared; it freed him of having to deal with her. However, he'd felt no relief at her escape. The wench had thought to outwit him with her submissive act during the past weeks. And, damn it, she had succeeded. Wolf would admit that much. However, he was determined she'd not be the victor in this battle of wills and wits. He'd allow no one, especially a woman—a Frenchwoman, at that—to make a fool out of him. He would find her if it was the last thing he ever did. And when he found her, he'd make her sorry she'd ever crossed his path.

Wolf pushed back his coif and eyed the Rochambeau castle through the eyes of a warrior. He smiled grimly. "The fox has run to ground. 'Tis now time for the Wolf to dig her out of her lair."

Wolf swung himself back into the saddle and urged his destrier out of the forest and along the cart path that Dara had traveled earlier. Ox and Bull followed in his wake. Quietly, the still night giving no warning to those who slept inside the castle, Wolf and the MacDonald brothers entered Rochambeau's gates.

As was their habit in any dangerous situation, Ox and Bull flanked Wolf's back with swords drawn and ready. Though they'd seen no guards, experience made them wary. Men had died for letting down their guard against attack in enemy territory. The twins scanned the darkened hall as Wolf dismounted and entered. He stopped and listened for any sign of life. Only the distant sound of a crackling fire disturbed the stillness that hung over the hall like a black shroud.

"Stay here until I call," Wolf ordered as he turned toward the stairs. He paused on the first step and looked back to his men. "Let no one pass." He moved with the predatory grace of an animal out to hunt. Stealthily, he ascended the stairs to the floor above, his boots making no sound, his sword drawn and ready, its keen blade glinting a deadly silver in the pale beams of moonlight streaking through the high windows.

As if scenting his prey, Wolf paused to listen at the solar door before slowly easing open the portal. Scarlet firelight bathed the chamber, illuminating the girl sleeping upon her crude bed. Wolf smiled triumphantly. The vixen had been run to ground.

Wolf silently closed and bolted the door behind him before settling his tired body in the lone chair. He lay his sword across the small table and stretched his long legs out in front of him. Lacing his fingers across his hard, flat middle, he eyed the Lady of Rochambeau and wondered again at her ability to make him react in such an uncharacteristic manner.

A muscle in his cheek twitched from his bedeviling thoughts as his gaze took in the object of his day-long search. He noted the long, thick lashes that left feathery shadows upon her rosy cheeks, her childlike posture as she lay with her hands curled beneath her oval chin, her generous lips tinted an even deeper hue of red by the firelight.

Wolf recalled the taste of her mouth, and his body responded instantly to the memory. He swore under his breath, disgruntled with himself. He forced his eyes away from her luscious mouth to find them resting upon the sweet curve of her breasts. Wolf rolled his eyes toward the beamed ceiling and pursed his lips. He had to get hold of his wayward emotions, or he'd find himself forgetting that Dara's escape had cost him precious time.

He looked back to the girl sleeping peacefully unaware of his presence. His gaze then came to rest upon her battered feet. His lips thinned at the sight of the cuts and bruises. The wench had endured much to escape him. Wolf shifted in his seat. He didn't like the unusual sensation the thought aroused in the pit of his belly. He'd experienced a similar reaction earlier that afternoon when Ox had found Dara's shoes on the riverbank. His heart had nearly stopped at the sight of the small leather slippers. He had immediately jumped to the conclusion that the girl had preferred drowning to being his hostage. However, a short while later, when Bull and Ox discovered where she'd exited the river on the opposite bank, his renewed fury had wiped out the odd sensation as if it had never existed.

They followed the trail to the village, where they had to line up the mutinous inhabitants and threaten them with death before a milkmaid came forward to admit that she had seen Dara that morning.

Wolf's gaze narrowed, and he drew his lips back against his teeth. The wench had a reckoning in store for all the trouble she'd caused him. His search for her had cost him at least two days' travel time. That meant Laird Morgan had two more days to his advantage.

The lines about Wolf's mouth and eyes deepened at the thought of the danger to his daughter. He pushed himself out of his chair and came to his feet. He crossed to the fireplace, where the flames snapped cheerfully about the logs. His mood didn't match the atmosphere. Bracing a thick-muscled forearm against the mantle, he rested his brow against it and grimly stared down into the bright blaze.

Had he been wise, he would never have accepted this mission. He would have stayed at Phelan to protect Ellice from the vultures who hoped to take his land. Wolf's gaze drifted once more to the girl. Had he been wise, he would never have taken Lady Dara as his hostage. As Bull had predicted, she'd caused him nothing but trouble, and he feared she'd continue to do so until he could get her off his hands and out of his mind.

Wolf's expression darkened. Wisdom now had nothing to do with his future decisions about his captive. He had only two choices left to him in dealing with her. He could have her throat slit to keep her silent, or take her back to England with him. As he'd told Ox, she knew far too much of Navarre's involvement with the prince to be allowed her freedom.

Wolf refused to recognize the tiny voice that told him there were also other reasons for him wanting to take Dara back to England.

Dara unfolded like a flower. She arched her back and stretched her arms over her head. Her movements drew the material of her undertunic tight across her breasts as she yawned widely and opened her eyes to the new day. She smiled contentedly when she recognized her surroundings. She was home; safe from the Englishman who had held her captive. And for the moment safe from men like Navarre.

Dara gazed up at the ceiling overhead and rubbed the sleep from her eyes. Today would be the day she'd been awaiting since Navarre forced her to go to the convent. The first thing she planned to do was to send a message to the king, telling him of the traitor he harbored in his own household. Then she would send to the village for workers. Every hand that could be spared from the fields would be needed to repair and rebuild Rochambeau.

Her day mapped out, Dara sat up and made to rise from her bed. She froze at the sight of the giant with ebony eyes watching her. Closing her eyes, she silently prayed that when she looked again, Wolf's image would have disappeared. It didn't. She released a resigned breath and slowly came to her feet. She squared her shoulders, stiffened her spine, and lifted her chin in silent defiance as she prepared herself for the worst.

Wolf's stygian gaze moved over Dara's stiff little form with obvious contempt. His look dared her to challenge his authority by word or action. Lack of sleep hadn't improved his disposition from the previous day. He slowly uncoiled his lean body and came to his feet. He reached inside his tunic and withdrew a strip of thin leather. "Come here, wench."

Dara shook her head. "*Non*. I remain here."

The lines about Wolf's eyes and mouth seemed carved in granite. "I did not ask, I ordered. We leave within the hour."

Again Dara stubbornly shook her head. "I go nowhere. I am home and I will not leave Rochambeau again."

In less than a stride, Wolf closed the space between them. He swiftly subdued Dara's struggles, and his large hands captured her wrists. He jerked them behind her back and, in an instant, bound her hands together with a strip of leather. His work done, he stood back and smiled down at her. "You will learn to listen to me. I vowed you'd go to England bound if you didn't obey me."

Dara had no time to comment or protest his treatment of her person before Wolf's fingers encircled her waist and he tucked her under his arm like a sack of grain from market.

"Let me go, you beast," she squealed.

Paying no heed to her demand, he threw open the door and strode out into the passageway. He descended the stairs to find Ox and Bull surrounded by a scraggly bunch of peasants brandishing anything that could be used as a weapon against the intruders.

Ox and Bull held them at bay with drawn swords. A look of relief passed over their faces at Wolf's appearance on the stairs above them.

Wolf eyed the old men and women who thought to defend their mistress, and couldn't stop himself from admiring their spirit and loyalty. But he'd not allow their interference.

"Go about your business and you'll not be harmed," he ordered. When no one moved to obey, he glanced down at the still girl whose long dark locks hid her expression from view. He could feel her tension through the tautening of her muscles.

"Release our lady and be on your way, Englishman," Renee said, bravely stepping forward with a fire poker.

"Your lady is now my hostage, and if you want to keep your lives, you will step out of our paths," Wolf said.

A mutinous rumble passed through the group as they conferred among themselves and then looked back at the three English knights who threatened their lady. Haggard faces mirroring their suffering, they shook their heads. Again Renee acted as spokesman. She returned his threat. "Release our lady and you'll be allowed to live."

Wolf drew in a steady breath and set Dara on her feet. He encircled her arm with a large hand to stop her from tumbling headfirst from her perch on the edge of the narrow step. He brushed her hair away from her face and looked her directly in the eyes. His dark gaze conveyed his threat as he said, "Tell them you go with us, Lady, or see them give their simple lives to protect you."

Dara glanced toward the people who had no chance of winning a fight against three well-armed knights. She moistened her lips. Once before she'd given ground because she couldn't allow her people to uselessly spill their blood trying to protect her. Navarre had won that battle, and now the Wolf would win this one. Dara flashed Wolf a look of hatred before she said, "I am his hostage until King John or my brother pays my ransom. Raise no arms, for I need all of you here to act in my stead. You must keep Rochambeau for Paul. He is your lord."

"But my lady, they are only three," the old gardener protested, and raised his hoe threateningly over his head.

Dara nodded. Her eyes misted with tears as she looked at the crude weapons they had assembled. She swallowed back the lump of emotion that rose in her throat, and said, "*Oui*. They are only three, but how many of you, dear friends, will die in your attempt to save me?"

"It does not matter, Lady. We would protect you with our lives."

A crystal droplet spilled over her thick lashes and ran down her ashen cheek. "And I love you for your loyalty, but I can't ask that of you. Now let us pass."

Slowly, the group melted away, until only Renee was left holding the fire poker. "Lady, let me come with you."

Though she wanted nothing more than to have Renee's company on her trip to England, Dara again shook her head. "*Non*, Renee. You are the only one left here whom I can depend upon. You must oversee Rochambeau in my absence."

"Bid your mistress farewell, wench," Wolf said.

"Farewell, Lady Dara," Renee whispered, her lower lip quivering with emotion before she burst into sobbing tears.

"Good-bye, Renee," Dara whispered before she strode from her home with head held high.

Wolf led Dara to his mount and lifted her into the saddle before mounting behind her. He turned the destrier toward the gates. Soon the walls of Rochambeau Castle were only a memory.

Dara ignored Wolf and his companions as they made their way back to the encampment. Only her eyes spoke vividly of her feelings as Wolf lifted her from the saddle. Sparkling, ire-filled sapphire clashed with ebony, yet no words were exchanged between the two. The challenge had been issued, the battle lines drawn, and each combatant was determined to become the victor in this war of wits and wills.

Chapter 8

The small boat bumped ashore. Dara shivered. The day was cold, and apprehension had finally won its way to the surface. She'd managed to keep her trepidation under control as long as she had French soil beneath her feet. Now she did not have that consolation. Even the earth beneath her feet would belong to her enemy.

Everything seemed to be against her, even the very elements. The eerie gray fog swirling hypnotically in from the sea appeared to hold a threat as it moved about them. It seemed to possess a life of its own. Gauzy tendrils crept across the boat, winding elusively into each tiny crevice, searching out its prey.

Dara shivered again, finding little comfort in her thoughts or the bleak landscape before her. England, her captor's home, looked as unforgiving and forbidding as the man who sat stonily at her side. Dara glanced up at Wolf. Since leaving Rochambeau she'd had no opportunity to escape him again. Wolf had ensured her complete captivity by keeping her tethered like an animal and well guarded at all times.

Dara turned her gaze back to the stark granite bluff that time had sheared away with wind and rain. It could be no harder than the man who claimed this land as his own. Wolf of Phelan castle possessed no softness within his wide chest. The gentleness he'd displayed during her first weeks of captivity had vanished upon her return to his camp. He'd growled out orders and bit off the head of anyone in range when they were not carried out to his exact specifications. His temper spared no one. Seemingly driven by forces that he couldn't control, he nipped and snarled like his namesake and chewed up anyone who might hinder his return to England.

Wolf had no human feelings or frailties, and his men followed him as if he were a god. A frown creased Dara's brow, and she bit down on her lower lip, perplexed by the loyalty the man inspired. Their strange allegiance to Wolf bewildered her. Each would give up his life were it needed to protect their leader. Once they learned of Wolf's plans, not one soldier had chosen to remain in the service of England's famed Black Prince. They had been eager to get back to this godforsaken, desolate, windswept land that looked to Dara as if the sun had never warmed its cold, harsh face.

"Welcome to England," Ox said, after jumping into ankle-deep water and extending a hand to help Dara from the small boat.

Dara pulled the oversized cloak closer as she rose to her feet and accepted Ox's offer of assistance. As he lifted her from the boat and set her on firm, dry ground, she looked past the giant to the winding path that led to the cliff above. "I fear there is no true welcome here for me. I am no friend, but a captive. I do not come freely, nor was I invited here. This is to be my prison."

"A prison is often what you make of it, Lady. I've seen men who have been locked away in the darkest dungeon emerge with their spirits unscathed. They viewed their imprisonment as a mere hindrance, not a defeat. And then I've seen other men who are free to go at will imprison their own souls until their spirit dies of suffocation."

"Are you saying I am to blame for what I see before

me? That in truth this bleak landscape with its outcropping of granite and tufts of windblown grass exists only in my mind?"

"Nay, Lady. You cannot change what is. I say only that your time here can be what you make of it. You alone are responsible for your own happiness. I grant you, Phelan is no palace. It is far poorer than your Rochambeau even after its attack. Nor will you find your fine French courtiers under its slate roof. However, it is a good place to live. You will find food and a hearth to warm yourself by as well as good, decent folks who would see that no harm befalls you if you only give them a chance."

Dara glanced back to the man stepping from the boat. He turned his face toward the cliff, his black velvet eyes watching his men climb the steep trail to the horses that had been brought ashore earlier and now awaited to take them to Phelan. Standing in the gray ghostly mist, Wolf looked like the ruler of the underworld risen to claim those who trespassed against him.

A shiver tingled its way up Dara's spine, and she automatically drew her cloak closer about her shoulders. "This place will never be a good place for me to live. France is my home and always will be."

"Give over, brother. The lady is determined to remain miserable," Bull said, hoisting his armor from the bottom of the vessel. He tossed the oiled leather bag to a young vassal who awaited to help him carry it and his weapons to their mounts.

Dara bristled. The man talked as if she wanted to be unhappy, that he and his leader had nothing to do with her present situation. "I did not ask to be brought here."

Bull shrugged. "I'll not argue the point. If you don't realize that your time here can be much more pleasant if you'll just accept your situation, then I'll say no more."

"I don't want to accept the situation. I want to return to France."

Bull shrugged again. " 'Tis a shame that such a beautiful head holds so few brains." Leaving Dara stuttering with indignation at his insult, he turned and strode toward the narrow path that led up the cliff.

"You'd do well to heed my brother's advice, Lady," Ox said. "Life is far too brief to live one day unhappy if you can do otherwise."

"Oh, sage philosopher," Dara said, turning on Ox. "Tell me. Where did you learn your wisdom? Upon the battlefield?"

Ox's gesture was identical to his twin's. He lifted a shoulder and shrugged. "The battlefield teaches many lessons, Lady. One lesson you learn early is to appreciate the life you have every minute of the day." He turned and followed in Bull's wake.

Dara heard a deep chuckle and flashed Wolf a look filled with daggers. His smile faded and he swept her with his insolent glare. "Wench, you have much to learn, and I think it's about time to start your lessons." Again he raked his gaze over her. "I think I shall enjoy being your teacher."

"I need no lessons from you. I've already learned that all Englishmen are murdering cowards," Dara snapped, and turned away.

Wolf snaked out a hand and caught her by the arm, jerking her to an abrupt halt. His dark eyes glowed like smoldering coals as he looked down into her beautiful, startled face. "You have a great deal more to learn about Englishmen, wench."

"I want to learn nothing more of Englishmen if you're the prime example of the British male." Again Dara made to turn away, but found herself yanked against Wolf's hard chest.

His thick lashes narrowed and a muscle worked in his

cheek. His eyes moved slowly over her face before he lifted a hand and gently ran the tip of one callused finger across her full lower lip. His gaze locked with hers. "We will see how you feel about Englishmen after I've had you beneath me."

Unsure whether she was reacting out of fear or some other strange malady, Dara forced back the tremor that threatened. She stared up into his black eyes and felt her anger cool as her demons stirred, reawakening for the first time since Wolf had taken her to bathe. A warm, sultry current moved over her, making her skin flush. Nervously, she moistened her dry lips with the tip of her tongue and cleared her throat to tell Wolf he'd never have her beneath him. No words passed the lips that parted in unconscious invitation.

Unable to withstand the temptation, Wolf tipped up her chin and lowered his mouth to hers. One strong arm slipped about her waist and drew her against his battle-hardened body. He knew it was folly to dally when it was imperative that he set out immediately for Phelan. However, he didn't have the strength to resist what he had dreamed of, so many nights alone on his pallet, with Dara only a few feet away.

The misty tendrils of fog rolled in from the sea, webbing them in its gray cloak, shutting out the world around the man and woman who stood with lips melded, hearts pounding, and bodies pressed tightly together.

"Ho, Wolf," Bull called down from the top of the precipice. " 'Tis no time to dally. The horses are ready and word has arrived that Laird Morgan's troops are camped just beyond the border."

Wolf's arm momentarily tightened about Dara before falling away. He clenched his fist and looked toward the voice, but could see little of the man standing high above. He ground his teeth together. He was going to kill Bull with his bare hands. Twice now Bull had interrupted him when he'd stood on the brink of drawing a response from Dara. Twice he had felt her resistance waning with the awakening of her desire. And twice he had managed to make her feel far differently than her luscious lips proclaimed in the heat of anger.

"The third time will be the death of him," Wolf ground out, and looked down at the young woman still standing so close. Her sapphire eyes mirrored her confusion. Wolf smiled and lifted a hand to caress her cheek. "Lady, I have much to teach you about men in general. Before your lessons are done, you will know that none are alike, be they English or French. But the most important lesson I will teach you will not be about men. It will be about how to be a woman."

"I need no instructions on how to be a woman," Dara said, haughtily lifting her chin to hide her careening emotions. Her own irrational response to Wolf's kisses bewildered her, but she wasn't going to allow him to know the effect he had upon her. It was too humiliating.

The lines about Wolf's mouth deepened, as did his smile. "You need no instructions on how to be the female God made you, but you are greatly in need of tutoring on how to be a true woman instead of the haughty little girl. However, your lessons will once more have to wait until less trying times. I need to see to the defense of my home first."

Wolf turned toward the trail. "Come, 'tis time to ride to Phelan." He didn't wait for her. He strode agilely up the winding, narrow path.

Dara shivered, rubbed at her arms as she glanced about the now deserted beach, and then quickly followed in Wolf's wake. She felt it far safer to stay with an enemy known than to remain on the isolated beach to face the unknown.

* * *

The gates of Castle Phelan swung wide at their approach. The loud clatter of horses' hooves against the cobbles of the bailey alerted the castle residents that the master of Phelan had returned. They all rushed out to welcome him. The gesture was far different from the treatment he'd received when he'd first come to claim Phelan. The inhabitants' sudden change of attitude didn't surprise Wolf. Though Phelan lay only a short distance from Scotland's borders, and many of those who lived upon the estate could claim blood ties to their northern neighbors, Phelan's people were staunchly loyal to the English crown and would have welcomed the devil himself had he been intent upon protecting them from the barbaric Scots. It was common knowledge to even the peasants that the heathens across the border would slaughter them all in their beds if given the opportunity.

Even knowing he was considered the lesser of the two evils, Wolf met their warm welcome congenially. Until he proved himself to these hardworking people, he knew he'd not deserve their loyalty.

Wolf dismounted and tossed the bridle to a stable boy who rushed forward to offer his services. He didn't glance back at the woman who rode the small mare that had been intended to carry their baggage back to Phelan. He climbed the steps and walked into the castle, his attention centered upon seeing only one person.

"Papa," Ellice squealed, and launched herself at him from her perch on the stairs. He caught her in midair and swung her up over his head. In a glance Wolf assured himself that she was physically well, and laughed up at her as he slowly lowered her to eye level.

"Pet, you've grown since last I saw you."

Wrapping her arms contentedly about her father's neck, Ellice nodded smugly. "I'm nearly grown, Papa. Soon I'll be the true Lady of Castle Phelan."

Wolf lifted a dark brow. "I think you have just a few more years to add to your age before you can claim that title, pet."

"But you need someone to be your lady, Papa. Every castle has a lady."

Wolf again arched a raven brow. "Now how did you become such an expert on what a castle needs?"

"Nurse told me," Ellice said, proudly lifting her chin.

"What else has Nurse told you?" Wolf questioned as he crossed the hall to where a fresh keg of ale had been set out to quench the thirst of the new arrivals. He set Ellice on the edge of the table and turned his attention to filling a tankard with the dark, bitter brew.

Ellice held her plump little arms out in front of her and laced her fingers. She regarded them solemnly for a few moments before saying in her most grown-up voice, "Nurse said if you didn't marry, I would be Lady Phelan." Several dark curls tumbled over her shoulder as she cocked her small head sideways and looked up at her father. "Are you going to marry, Papa?"

Wolf nearly choked on his drink. The ale lodged awkwardly in his airway, and he coughed as he shook his head. "Nay, pet. I have no intentions of ever marrying, so you have no need to rush growing up. Only you will be the Lady of Phelan."

"You're a wonderful papa," Ellice said, throwing her arms about Wolf's hard waist. She looked up at him with eyes filled with adoration. "I'm so glad you're back. I missed you."

"And I missed you, pet," Wolf murmured softly. Emotion filled his throat as he tenderly brushed his fingers through her dark hair. How had he lived so many years without knowing the feelings that this one small child inspired within him? Her innocent, unconditional love humbled him. Unlike any other thing he'd ever encountered, it had the power to mellow the years of bitterness left within his scarred soul. Looking at her innocence, he could forget the hard-fought battles and the lives that had ended on the blade of his sword.

"What shall I do with Lady Dara?" Ox asked, drawing Wolf's attention away from his daughter.

A look of bewilderment flickered briefly over Wolf's face before he cleared his throat and said, "She is to reside in the chamber next to mine. Escort her there and summon a maid to serve her." His eyes traveled over Dara, taking in her windblown hair and soiled gown. "Also see to it that a tub and hot water are sent up for a bath. From the looks of her, she could well use one."

"Who is she?" Ellice questioned, eyeing the strange woman who opened her mouth and then abruptly snapped it shut like a fish out of water. Ellice's thick lashes narrowed thoughtfully. The woman acted oddly to her papa's suggestion. She seemed to object to his offer of kindness. Ellice's small mouth firmed into a tight line. There was something about the woman that didn't set well with Ellice. Nor did Ellice like the look that crossed the stranger's face when she glared at her papa. Though there was no malice in the woman's expression, somehow it seemed threatening. Ellice scooted closer to her father.

"She is Lady Dara of Rochambeau. She is to be our guest until she is ransomed," Wolf answered matter-of-factly.

A baffled frown drew Ellice's dark brows close over her tiny nose. "What is ransomed, Papa?"

Wolf smiled as he swung his daughter back up into his arms. "I'll explain it all to you a little later, pet. First I would have a meal and a bath myself." He strode toward the stairs. As he took the first step, Ellice peeped over his shoulder, her large, curious brown eyes once more assessing Dara from head to toe. The lady was beautiful, but there was something about the way her papa spoke of her that left Ellice feeling uneasy. Too naive to understand the burst of possessiveness that made her clutch her father tightly about the neck, Ellice wrinkled her nose at Dara as they passed from view.

Ox chuckled at the child's silent message. Though only five, Ellice sense a rival for her father's affection. Ox chuckled again at the thought of Wolf and his beautiful hostage. The atmosphere between them became as explosive as one of the ribaulds that Kind Edward had ordered manufactured. Ox had only seen the weapon fired once. It had created a great deal of flame, noise, and acrid smoke. So far all that was missing from Wolf's encounters with Lady Dara was the acrid smoke, and at times he could nearly swear he'd seen even that rising about Wolf when his temper ignited.

Ox glanced once more toward Dara and said, "Lady, if you will follow me, I'll show you to your chamber."

Stunned to learn that Wolf had a daughter, and bemused by the expression he had worn when they entered the hall, Dara had failed to give him a good setdown for his insulting remark about her needing a bath. She had opened her mouth, but no words passed her lips. Even after Wolf had ascended the stairs, she couldn't rid herself of the strange feeling his expression had created within her own heart. In all the months she'd spent near him, she'd never seen such happiness upon his face. When he gazed down at the child, the fierce beast within him altered visibly. His face became so tranquil and tender, he looked nothing like the devil she thought him. Seeing another side of the man she'd thought to possess no heart or soul, she realized that the Wolf of Castle Phelan could love like any other mortal.

The revelation exploded in Dara's mind, leaving her momentarily staggered. During the past weeks, she'd allowed herself to forget that Wolf had never actually mistreated her. She had heaped every sin and all the blame upon his head in order to ignore the demons his very presence stirred into life within her treacherous body. For her own peace of mind she'd found it far better to believe he was the devil incarnate than to recognize her own weakness toward him.

"Lady Dara," Ox repeated. "Wolf has instructed me to escort you to your chamber. And I would do so in the near future if you would allow me. I have need of a few hours rest for myself before we set out to find the Scots."

Drawing her thoughts away from the enigmatic master of Castle Phelan and the questions brewed by the sudden discovery that he had sired a child, Dara looked at the tall man awaiting her answer. Recalling his earlier reprimand, she smiled sweetly and dropped into a graceful mock curtsy. "I would not want to be responsible for making you lose your rest, Sir Knight. Especially since I have no other choice than to accept your escort."

Ox's laughter filled the hall and drew looks from several of the new arrivals, who were now seated at the long tables enjoying freshly baked bread and a sharp yellow cheese along with their ale. "Lady, you'll survive. I have no doubt."

The smile faded from Dara's lips. "*Oui.* I must survive, for I will see those responsible for my misfortune punished."

Ox's smile also evaporated. His thoughts, too, turned to far more serious matters. He gave a sad shake of his close-cropped head. " 'Twould be best if you let go of your thoughts of revenge, Lady Dara. The man you seek to destroy has far more power than a mere lord possesses. He is married to the King of France's daughter and has the ear of England's monarch. I fear you have set yourself a task you cannot achieve without endangering your own life. Navarre will never allow you to live should he believe you can do him harm."

Dara stilled. Until Ox had put her fears into words, she had fought to keep herself believing that someday she would be returned to France to avenge her family. The color slowly ebbed from her cheeks. She looked up at Ox and spoke with as much conviction as she could muster. Her words sounded weak even to her own ears. "Paul will ransom me as soon as he returns to Rochambeau."

"Do you truly believe your brother will return?"

Dara's lower lip quivered as she drew in a shaky breath and said, "I have to believe. It is all that keeps me sane in a world that has gone completely mad."

A look of understanding flickered across Ox's rugged countenance. He'd seen hardened soldiers who believed the impossible just to keep one foot trudging in front of the other on long marches, to make it from one day to the next without breaking. "Then believe what you will, Lady Dara. I'll say no more."

Ox turned toward the stairs, and Dara, shaken by the sudden realization that Navarre could even control her destiny in England, followed quietly in his wake.

Moonlight streamed in through the narrow cross-slit windows, bathing the room and the girl soaking in the huge brass-bound tub in silver. She lifted a slender, shapely leg out of the soapy water and squeezed out the cloth. The frothy bubbles of the soap slid back into the steaming water, leaving her skin slick and silky.

Dara luxuriated in the hot bath. It had been so long since she'd enjoyed such a simple pleasure. Not since the night Navarre had forced her to leave Rochambeau had she bathed with hot water. At the convent such luxuries were forbidden by the Reverend Mother. She considered them implements of the devil, made only to encourage the sins of the flesh. The Reverend Mother thought a good scrubbing with lye soap and cold water made one dutiful and hearty.

Dara washed her foot, stroking the sole with the lathered cloth. No matter what the Reverend Mother believed, Dara could find nothing sinful about the soft tallow soap and warm water. Everything else in her life was so bleak, she'd not deny herself this small comfort. And though she'd been insulted by Wolf's remark, she was now truly grateful for his foresight. He'd known how exhausted she'd been when they arrived at Phelan, even when she refused to recognize it herself.

Dara lay back, thoughtfully considering her captor and her new prison as she finished her bath. She'd already washed her long hair free of the salt spray that had collected in the dark strands during their voyage across the Channel. It now floated about her like skeins of newly dyed silk. Absently, she drew the thick lather over the tops of her breasts like a white frothy shield as she inspected her new living quarters with a chatelaine's critical eye.

Ox had not lied when he said that Phelan was no palace. In truth it was little more than a deteriorating fortress. In years past the castle might have seen better times, but now its granite walls were cracked. No one had seen fit to chink the seams in the stone where rain and the freezing cold of winter further widened the damage. Dampness also marked the beams overhead to indicate a leaky roof.

Dara pursed her lips in disgust. She couldn't tolerate such lack of concern for property. It was an unnecessary waste. Since her earliest memories, she'd been taught to preserve, not destroy. The land was only yours temporarily. It was the duty of each generation to hold it in trust for the future. What you took from the land, you returned with care, and in turn it would always be there to provide for you and your children and your children's children. Phelan's dilapidated condition only mirrored its master's attitude. He was a destroyer, not a builder. The villages and towns he'd ordered laid to waste in France gave proof of that fact.

Dara seized upon the memory of watching the towns and villages burn to revive her anger against Wolf. She couldn't allow herself to recall how he'd looked earlier in the hall with his daughter or it would awaken her demons again. She'd managed to get them back under control and locked away in their tiny compartment, and she most certainly didn't want them loosed again. Wolf was her enemy, and she could view him in no other way if she wanted to survive as a whole person to return to France.

Laying her head back against the rim of the tub, Dara closed her burning eyes. She drew in a deep breath and fought against the nearly uncontrollable urge to burst into tears. How she longed to see Rochambeau. However, now she feared she might never see it again. Ox had made her face the fact that she had sought to ignore. Navarre was ruthless in his schemes for power. He'd find no hardship in having her killed if he believed that she could harm him. And he'd do everything in his power to ensure that she was never ransomed.

Her chilling thoughts seemed to cool the warm water, making Dara shiver. She quickly came to her feet and reached for the linen towel the maid had left for her. Hair streaming down her back, she wrapped the thick linen around her body and stepped from the tub just as the door swung open. Startled, Dara spun about to face the intruder. When her eyes met his ebony stare, she stiffened and raised her chin defensively.

"What do you want?" she asked, clutching the towel tightly to her breasts.

Wolf's gaze slid over her, and his lips quivered as if

he found her remark humorous. He closed the door behind him before he looked once more at Dara and asked in return, "What are you willing to give, Lady?"

Dara took a nervous step backward as Wolf crossed the chamber. He paused within an arm's length and waited for her answer. She swallowed uneasily but held her ground. Lifting her chin in the air, she refused to let him coerce her into retreating another inch. "I have nothing to give to you or any Englishman."

Wolf's ebony gaze raked over her once more, taking in the wet hair clinging so enticingly to her bare shoulders, the tops of her full breasts revealed above the towel, the curve of her hip and her long, shapely legs bared beneath the edge of linen. He smiled as his gaze once more claimed hers. "I fear you mislead yourself. You have much to give, Dara of Rochambeau."

Dara's skin heated under Wolf's intimate perusal. Every inch of her seemed to awaken and tingle with expectation. The demons stirred and clamored against their enforced incarceration. They chewed at the bars of their prison and prized at the lock that withheld their freedom. They seemed to gain strength as she caught the scent of Wolf's clean, masculine odor.

Dara shook her head firmly, denying her demons their freedom. "*Non.* You are wrong. Perhaps your wife has something to give you, but not I."

"Ah, lovely Dara. I have no wife," Wolf mused softly, raising a hand to her cheek.

Dara's demons jumped with joy at the news that he had no wife. Again they prized at the bars to their cells.

Wolf lightly brushed his knuckles against her flawless skin. "And I am never wrong when it comes to women."

The demons screamed in protest as Wolf's words set Dara's temper afire. Her anger cut off the passion that fed them and firmly slammed the door upon their escape. Dara snapped, "Your arrogance does not surprise me. But be assured, you are wrong about *this* woman. Now get out and leave me to my dilapidated prison."

A muscle twitched in Wolf's cheek. He took in the chamber in a glance. It was true Phelan was in a state of disrepair, but he intended to make improvements just as soon as he settled things with the Scots. Wolf's brows lowered in an ominous frown. No matter how true her assessment of his home, the haughty, high-handed wench had no right to abuse his hospitality by rudely pointing out the fact to him. She was here at his beneficence. She breathed now only because he'd brought her to his castle. "Phelan is my home, and you will respect it as such, Lady."

Dara gave the chamber a scathing glance. " 'Tis little more than a hovel. You would do better to use some of the coin you gained from laying waste to my homeland to restore this heap of stones before it collapses about your head." She waved her hand toward the beam above them. "It already rots." She pointed to a crack running from ceiling to floor. "And crumbles."

Wolf's gaze didn't follow the direction she indicated. Helpless to stop himself, he found his attention drawn to a far more interesting display created by her movements. The globes of her breasts inched higher with each wave of her hand, until the edges of her coral nipples peeped temptingly just above the edge of the linen towel. His irritation over Dara's appraisal of his home completely overshadowed by the tide of passion swallowing him, Wolf struggled to maintain control. He failed. Like the ocean reacting to the pull of the moon, he couldn't stop himself from reaching out and drawing Dara into his arms.

Dara gasped in surprise at Wolf's unexpected assault. She looked up into his black, smoldering eyes and her own widened. She swallowed uneasily as her demons shouted gleefully at their sudden liberation and burst free of their prison. She shook her head as his mouth lowered over hers to silence further criticism of his home as well as any protest.

Wolf slid his fingers through her damp hair and captured the back of her head to stay her movements. He deepened the kiss, thrusting his tongue between her lips and into the sweet cavern beyond. He spread his other hand across her round bottom and pressed her closer to his hard, throbbing body. He'd be denied no longer. Since the moment he'd set eyes upon Dara of Rochambeau, his need for her had fermented in his blood like new grapes prepared to make fine wine. Though he had sought to deny his desire, it had grown more poignant with each passing day. And he had finally reached his limit of self-denial. Tomorrow he would go in search of his enemy, and like all soldiers, he had prepared himself for the event that he might never see another sun rise or hold another woman within his arms. And he would not go into eternity without first knowing this woman who had nearly driven him insane with her presence in his tent each night.

Wolf teased Dara's lips and tongue until she accepted his erotic challenge. Her tongue dueled with his while her senses swam and her belly quivered with a strange, breathless yearning. Instinctively, she molded her body even tighter to Wolf's and raised her arms about his neck. Her towel fell free, floating gently downward to lay at her feet.

Wolf's hands roved hungrily over Dara's bare back, stroking the graceful curve of her spine to the tiny dimples at the base before spreading over her rounded buttocks. Every muscle in his body screamed from the tension coursing through him, yet he tempered his caresses, fully aware that the girl in his arms had never known a man. He'd finally managed to break through her defenses, and he'd not rush her now.

Restraining his own urge to throw her down upon the bed and sink himself into her soft warmth, Wolf drew back and gazed into Dara's passionate little face. He smiled at the expression he saw burning in her eyes. The husky timbre of his voice reflected the tenuous grip he held upon his own emotions. "You are far more beautiful than the dawn, and more alluring than the night."

His breath froze in his throat as his eyes moved over Dara's nakedness. He bent and touched his tongue to the quivering pulse that mirrored the beat of her heart. A thrill of excitement shot through him as he felt her heart leap in response to his touch. He breathed in her fresh scent and flicked the throbbing cadence again. "Ah, sweeting, your skin is honey to my lips. I want to devour you like the great wolf I am."

His gaze locked once more with Dara's as he lifted her into his arms and crossed to the bed that lay piled with furs. He lay her down and quickly shrugged out of his own clothing. Naked, his only adornment the medallion, his bronzed body hard and swollen with passion, Wolf stood proudly before Dara, giving her time to understand his need, allowing her to comprehend that once he came to her on the bed, there would be no turning back.

Dara's breath caught in her throat, and her heart seemed to stop at the sight of his male beauty. Her gaze slid over him, burning its way downward to the turgid flesh that rose unashamedly like a warrior's lance from amid a dark velvet forest. Dara's eyes widened momentarily at the power of his desire before they shot back to his handsome face. Her cheeks flamed a lovely rose, and her lower lip trembled slightly as she moistened it with the tip of her tongue. Slowly, she reached out to touch Wolf's steely thigh. She glided her hand upward over the furred bronzed skin until her fingers lay close to his tumescence. Though slick and hard, his skin felt like velvet. Quietly she said, "I know not what to do. Will you teach me, Wolf?"

Wolf released the breath that had been locked in his lungs since the moment Dara's small hand began to ascend his thigh. He prayed she'd stop before she touched his arousal, but had also prayed she wouldn't. Unable to withstand further torment, he came to her. Pressing her back into the furs, he claimed her lips in a soul-searing kiss, sating himself upon her mouth until the need to taste all of her overcame everything else. He left a trail of fiery kisses along her cheek, down the slender column of her neck and shoulder to the bounties of her breasts. He buried his face against the soft, swelling mounds, inhaling her heady female fragrance. His breath burned against her skin as he murmured, "You smell of life and spring."

Dara's arms came about his heavily muscled shoulders as Wolf took a nipple possessively between his lips and flicked it teasingly until it budded hard. She arched against his caress, giving him full access to her burning flesh.

Wolf slid his hand down her side, lifting up her hips, cupping her sweetly rounded derriere in his palms as he pulled her against his chest. The medallion pressed into her belly, branding its symbols into Dara's skin as his lips branded her breasts. He trailed tiny kisses over the round globe and down into the valley before ascending to the next coral-tipped peak. He suckled her, drawing from her the deep, dark sensations that heated their bodies and quickly warmed the metal of the talisman that hung between them.

Dara's head fell back, her damp raven hair spreading across the bed, down past the strong hands that held her so intimately locked against hard male flesh. Her body quivered with the strange, new, exciting sensations his mouth and hands aroused. As she panted for breath through slightly parted lips and clung to Wolf's shoulders for support, her demons began a metamorphosis, transforming into something she could not name.

The taste of her breasts only whetting his appetite to know more of the secrets of Dara's luscious body, Wolf slowly made his way downward, leaving her skin on fire with kisses that tingled across her sleek belly to the glade of curling raven silk. He nuzzled her, breathing in her scent before raising himself at her side and looking at her. Silently he beseeched her for entrance to the paradise of the honeyed glen that he longed to explore.

His erotic assault making her tremble, Dara instinctively spread her legs for Wolf and watched mesmerized as his strong hands slowly stroked her inner thighs, ever moving upward. Her breath froze in her throat, and she pressed her eyes closed as his fingers fluttered closer to her womanhood. Anticipation, fear of the unknown as well as her need to feel his touch, made her heart seem to still. She gasped from the jolt of pleasure that careened through her when Wolf lightly brushed the tips of his fingers against the soft, moist folds of her sex. Her eyes flew wide and locked with his as a new wave of desire shot through her.

"You are so hot and wet," Wolf murmured, his voice strained from his own need. He delved a long finger into her satiny sheath and touched the maidenhead that proclaimed Dara's innocence. A visible shudder shook Wolf and a low moan of need escaped his full lips as he buried his face against her. He drew in the rich, feminine scent of her and felt his own turgid sex throb in response to the musky fragrance that confirmed Dara's arousal.

Unable to deny himself further, Wolf spread his

hands beneath her buttocks and lifted her to his mouth. He sought out the tiny passion-swollen bud and teased it until Dara moved her hips against him. She rolled her head from side to side and whimpered his name, pleading for release from the exquisite agony he was inflicting upon her with his mouth and tongue. The core of her burned like molted lava. Her nails raked at Wolf's shoulders. Intuitively, she knew that only his swollen shaft could put an end to her sweet misery.

At the sound of her primal cry, Wolf could no longer suppress his own desires. He covered her like the sun eclipsing the moon. His bronzed body shadowing her ivory flesh as he took her lips with his, he drove himself into the slick, wet passage that eagerly awaited his arrival.

Wolf thrust himself deep into her virginal body, ripping away her maidenhead and absorbing her cry with his own mouth. He tasted his own blood as Dara sank her small teeth into his lower lip and recoiled against the stinging pain. He stilled; buried deep within her soft body, he lay motionless to allow Dara's body to grow accustomed to the intrusion of his swollen flesh. He rained small kisses over her face, brushing his lips against her brow, eyes, and tiny, perfect nose. Each kiss carried an apology for the pain he had inflicted as well as the promise of the pleasure to come.

When at last he reclaimed her lips, Dara's desire had again flamed. The pain of moments before was forgotten as her body began to pulse about his hard male shaft. Guided by natural impulse, she moved against Wolf and clung to him as his tumescence filled her time and time again with lightning.

Dara reveled in the wild current of sensation that began in her belly and rippled continuously outward until it encompassed every sinew of her entire being. She arched against Wolf, drawing him deeply within her, and his name escaped her lips in an awed cry.

What Dara had called her demons, now were her angels. They blessed her with an ecstasy so beautiful that she couldn't describe the sensations that possessed her. She gloried in the euphoric tranquility that flowed through her quivering body, sating all her needs, allaying all her doubts and worries about her future or her past. She had found her haven.

With a feral groan that seemed torn from the very depths of his being, Wolf also sought his release. His blue-black hair touched his shoulders as he arched his corded neck and thrust deeply into Dara's wet warmth to end his quest for paradise. He spilled his seed within her receptive body, and then collapsed over her, his hot, sweaty body melding to hers.

Content, Dara tenderly brushed back a raven curl that had fallen over Wolf's brow before wrapping her arms about his neck. She smiled with satisfaction as she gazed up at the beamed ceiling. Never in her wildest fantasies had she dreamed that making love would leave her so awestruck. When supervising the preparations for the winter larder or any chore that brought her into contact for longer than five minutes with the servants, she had often heard them discuss their encounters with the opposite sex. But until today Dara hadn't truly given credence to all the wild stories. She'd believed the maids had exaggerated their tales of rapture just to see the effect it would have upon their lady. She'd been sure they had created many of the incidents of which they spoke just to see her blush with embarrassment.

In all truth, she'd never been sexually attracted to any man until the English knight had unexpectedly entered her life. It wasn't that she didn't like men. In fact she'd always enjoyed male companionship more than she did the females of her acquaintance. They were far more interesting in general. They had seen and done things that no woman could ever hope to achieve. However, she'd viewed the men she knew like her own brother, until they began to look at her as something other than a friend. When that happened, she had quickly put an end to their relationship. She saw no reason to make herself uncomfortable or to create hope where there was none.

Dara hadn't lied when she'd told Navarre that she had no intention of marrying any man she didn't love. Her father had often stressed the fact that the greatest gift that God had bestowed upon him was the love of the woman who had mothered his children. He had never aligned himself with other powerful families by using his children as pawns or pieces of barter. Her father had wanted both of his children to find the kind of happiness he'd known, by allowing them to choose their own mates when the right time came.

Dara's smile deepened. Her father would be proud to know she had followed his wishes. Dreamily, she stroked her fingers through Wolf's thick, curling hair and savored the feel of his skin pressed against her own flesh. Lying beneath Wolf, she felt whole. He made her feel secure and safe. He was a wonderful lover, a strong and courageous warrior as well as a man who possessed a tenderness that few of his ilk could claim. And he had conquered her heart as surely as he had conquered France. Dara's blissful expression faded as reality intruded and inexorably drove out the wonder left by Wolf's lovemaking. Her lips thinned into a flat line. She shivered as she stared up into the shadows unrelieved by the firelight. The darkness seemed to pervade her very soul.

Dara swallowed back the sickening wave of bilious remorse that rose in her throat. She drew in a shuddering breath and delved deep within her well of Rochambeau courage to keep herself from succumbing to the wild urge to gnash her teeth and wail her grief. She blinked back a blinding rush of hot tears and firmly reined in her emotions. It was far too late for hysterics. She had allowed herself to capitulate to Wolf's seduction and her own wayward emotions, betraying herself and her heritage.

Wolf felt Dara tense beneath him and raised himself on his elbows. He looked down into her bright eyes and knew from the expression within their luminous depths that their interlude had come to an end. No matter how intimately their bodies remained joined, the distance between them had become nearly insurmountable.

A dagger seemed to lodge between his ribs. He swore under his breath and rolled away from her. He sat up on the side of the bed and reached for his clothes. Without a word he jerked them on before looking back to the woman who hurriedly covered her own nakedness with the furs. Wolf sucked in a deep breath and sought to deny that her rejection affected him. What had he truly expected from Dara of Rochambeau, a noblewoman of France? Like the noble bitch who birthed him, it was time to extricate herself from the situation by laying all the blame at his feet. She couldn't concede that she had been an equal participant in their lovemaking, or she'd have to admit she'd soiled herself with a lowly commoner. With a swipe of his hand, Wolf brushed the hair back from his brow and squared his shoulders defensively, awaiting her attack. When it did not come, he immediately countered in his own behalf. "Lady, 'tis best to remember that I was not here alone, before you judge me too harshly. You also took part in what just transpired between us."

Unable to deny his words, Dara looked away from his penetrating eyes, mortified that he was right. She had no reason to reproach him for what she had allowed, had even wanted to happen. She had followed the urgings of her own wayward body, too caught up in the new, heady sensations Wolf aroused to realize the extent of her own transgression. Provoked by her own demons, she had wanted him to make love to her as she'd wanted nothing else in her life. Dara's cheeks crimsoned from the knowledge and her stomach churned. How she loathed her own weak, treacherous flesh.

Puzzled by her silence, Wolf stood and extended his hand to her. "Come, Lady. Your evening meal awaits in the hall below."

Dara ignored his proffered hand and glared up at Wolf with glassy eyes. "How can you speak of food after what just happened?"

Wolf shrugged stoically and rubbed a hand over his middle. "Easily. The angry roar of my stomach reminds me of the reason I came to your chamber in the first place." A mocking grin curled up one corner of his full-lipped mouth. "But the sport 'twas well worth a few hunger pains."

"Is that how you look upon what happened between us? As sport?" Dara asked, her voice constrained with the emotions she sought to control.

"How would you have me view it?"

"I would have . . ." Dara's words faded, and she cleared her throat and began again. "I would have you . . ." Again words failed her. Unable to tell Wolf how she felt, Dara looked down at the hands she held clasped in her lap.

"Lady, 'tis your choice. Do you want things between us to return as before? Or would you be willing to share my bed each night?" Wolf held his breath, awaiting her answer.

Dara stiffened. She would give her soul were it possible to return things to what they had been only an hour earlier. That could never be. You could not stop the hands of time and reach back to adjust events to your satisfaction. She could only recognize the fact of her own stupidity and vow never to let herself be so foolish as to fall prey to her own demons again.

A hollow ache centered in Dara's chest as she looked up at the man towering over her. His handsome features were held in a stern mask and offered no warmth for her.

A sudden sense of loneliness swept over Dara, and she swallowed back a new rush of hot tears. "Sadly, nothing can ever be as before. What we did should never have happened. It was wrong. You are my enemy and I am yours. When I allowed you to take my innocence, I betrayed everything I hold dear."

"I take it from your answer that you reject my offer to become my mistress?" Wolf said, eyeing Dara through thick, narrowed lashes. Her rejection again left him feeling as if he'd been slapped. A muscle twitched in his cheek. He curled and flexed his fingers at his side in an effort to suppress the urge to reach out and circle Dara's slender throat to choke off any more hurtful words.

Dara stiffened. "How can you be so nonchalant?"

"Because I have no need to play the game of a vilified innocent. I am honest about my feelings and do not seek to place the blame for my own actions upon others. 'Tis true our kings are at war, and that you see us as enemies. But you wanted me as much as I wanted you, Dara of Rochambeau. And I see nothing wrong in that. We gave each other pleasure for a few minutes in time; nothing more. And should you be honest, you would admit to yourself that you'd enjoy being my mistress were I a fine lord instead of a poor knight. Your body was made to be loved."

Hearing none of the pain laced in Wolf's words, Dara came to her knees as if struck by a bolt of lightning.

Her hand cracked against Wolf's cheek like the thunder following in its wake. Her blood simmering, she swore, "You bastard. I am no harlot."

Wolf captured Dara's wrist in a bruising grip before she could snatch it back. His fingers bit into her flesh with brutal pressure as he glowered down at her. He bent close and growled, his breath hot on her face, " 'Tis true I'm a bastard, but it has yet to be proven that you are not a harlot. Your hot little body might belie your protests, wench." His gaze raked scathingly down Dara's nude body. "You are fortunate that our coupling has left me sated and in no mood to raise a hand to you. However, I would refresh your memory to one thing. There are far more pleasurable ways for me to punish you than to lay my hand across your soft backside."

Wolf brushed his lips roughly across Dara's to emphasize his ominous threat. He smiled as he straightened, and then thrust her from him, resolving to never allow himself to feel anything for her beyond anger. Dara fell back against the furs. "Now, clothe yourself before I change my mind. 'Tis time we joined the others for our evening meal."

Dara rubbed at her wrist and replied mutinously, "I'm not hungry."

"I did not ask if you were hungry. I said we would join the other members of my household for the evening meal. And you will eat what is put before you. I'll not allow you to starve yourself to death to spite me. I seriously doubt even your stupid king would ransom a dead woman." Wolf crossed the chamber to where Dara's mildewed trunk sat. He threw open the lid and drew out a tattered gown. A look of disgust flickered over his face before he turned and tossed it on the foot of the bed. "Will you clothe yourself, or shall I do it for you?"

Dara hurriedly reached for the lavender gown and

pulled it over her head. She struggled to be free of the clinging material as she struggled to be free of the heartache that Wolf's callousness created. The gown slipped down over her, the discolored material falling gently about her feet while the back gaped open. She clutched the bodice to keep her breasts from spilling free and tried to reach the lacings. To her dismay, she found it impossible. No matter how hard she might try, she could not dress herself without assistance. Casting an exasperated look toward the door that led to the small antechamber where the maid awaited to assist her, Dara immediately discarded the idea of calling for help. It would be far too embarrassing to allow anyone to see her in her present state. Her situation would be obvious to anyone who saw her undressed with Wolf in her chamber.

Resigning herself to ask for Wolf's assistance, she turned to the man who had caused all her troubles. At last she managed to say, "Would you help me dress?"

Understanding her dilemma, Wolf closed the space between them and, without a word, took her by the shoulders and turned her around. He laced the gown expertly, and then maneuvered Dara back to face him. He looked down at her and spoke sternly, as if he were her father. "Lady Dara, you are here within my home, and I expect you to act with courtesy to those who live under my roof. I understand your feelings about me, but you will treat others with respect, according to their position, as you would in your own home. They have done nothing to harm you, and I'll not have you inflicting your anger at me upon their heads. I'll have peace within my home."

"Send me back to France, and you'll have the peace you seek," Dara said, undeterred by Wolf's exacting orders.

"I'll have peace with you here," Wolf said, his voice stern with his own resolution.

Dara bravely shook her head and looked Wolf directly in the eye. "Nay. I'll give you no rest until you free me."

Wolf's ebony gaze didn't retreat. "Oddly, I find I would have no rest should I free you, so I prefer to keep you close. And should tonight be an example of what lies in our future, then I eagerly accept your challenge, even welcome it, Dara. We can be lovers or enemies as long as you remember you are mine until you are ransomed. I hold your life within my hand, and you will obey me when I tell you to set aside your barbed words and your deception while dealing with members of my household. Do you understand me?"

"I understand all too well," Dara ground out. "I am your slave to use and abuse until you tire of me."

Wolf reached out and wrapped his hands in Dara's hair, drawing her near. He peered down into her eyes, his expression stony. "So far you know nothing of abuse, my noble little enemy. Now cease this prattle. 'Tis time to dine."

Dara's gaze moved over his features, noting for the first time the lines of weariness that webbed his eyes. The retort that sprang to her lips died an easy death as she unconsciously reached up to smooth the lines away. She caught the mistake before she made it. Nonplussed by how easily she could forget that she stood within mere inches of her enemy, she pressed her wayward hand firmly against the folds of her skirt and lowered her eyes to the floor. She didn't want Wolf to see the sudden rush of confusion that swept over her. Drawing in a fortifying breath to steady her voice, she said, "I am aware of my place here. As your prisoner, I realize that I live on your beneficence."

Wolf nodded his satisfaction. "I'm glad you are beginning to understand. It will go much easier between us."

Dara's head snapped up. Bitterness filled her voice as she said, "Nothing can be easier between us after tonight. We have crossed the boundaries that kept each of us in our own world."

Wolf eyed Dara darkly, pricked by the words that reminded him of so many of her noble peers. She considered herself above a mere mercenary who had gained his knighthood upon the battlefield. "Is that so bad? Perhaps we can come to an understanding that will suit us both."

Dara shook her head. "Nay. There can never be an understanding between us. I would rather die than betray my family and country again in your arms."

Truly sensing for the first time the depth of Dara's inner torment, Wolf found himself oddly relieved by her answer. He drew her against his chest as if she were Ellice and lay his chin against her dark hair. He felt the shudder that passed through her and knew Dara also fought against the same desires that afflicted him each time they were in the same room. She could not have responded to his lovemaking in such a manner otherwise.

Wolf closed his eyes, wondering at the strange new creature he'd just discovered and the emotions she'd aroused within him. Unlike the other women he'd known, Dara felt guilt over her response to him as an enemy, not as a person of lesser rank. Though she experienced the height of fulfillment within his embrace, she was torn between her loyalty to her family and country. Wolf drew in a deep breath. He hadn't comprehended the war that she waged within her, or the sense of her own treachery to those she loved.

Her sense of honor was like a man's. Wolf frowned at the revelation. The thought was entirely new to him. He had never considered a woman actually possessing such feelings. Until this moment, he'd believed only men to have the integrity of such high principles, while women were oriented to more mundane matters of life.

Something tugged at Wolf's heart. This woman—so small, so beautiful, and so sexy—had shown far more courage and loyalty than some men he could name. There was nothing common about her. She had bravely confronted him at the convent to protect the sisters of St. Marie, and she had come close to outwitting him as well. She had again shown her courage and loyalty when he'd come after her at Rochambeau. Instead of seeing her people die to protect her, she had surrendered to his demands, sacrificing her freedom to save a few peasants' lives. From his own experience with noble ladies and their feelings toward those of lesser rank, Wolf knew that few in her position would have been so generous.

Unconsciously, Wolf tightened his arms about Dara. He had bedded many women, yet none had given as freely of herself as his beautiful French captive. Dara of Rochambeau considered him her enemy, yet when he'd stirred her passion to life, she had held back nothing. Unlike other fine ladies who wanted to experience his prowess in bed but who also reminded him of the honor they were bestowing upon him for being allowed to bed someone of higher rank, Dara had surrendered her innocence without regard to his base heritage.

How he loved this woman! Wolf's eyes flew wide as the startling thought crossed his mind. He quickly rejected it. He could not love Dara of Rochambeau. She was his hostage, nothing more. She was beautiful and desirable, but he couldn't allow himself to become emotionally involved with her. And were he even fool enough to consider such a fantasy, her rank separated them more thoroughly than even the Channel that separated their two countries. He could not allow himself to love Dara. She was of noble birth, while he was a bastard knight, a mercenary, a man who lived by his sword and would, most probably, die by the sword.

Brusquely, Wolf set Dara away from him. His stony expression revealed none of his tortuous thoughts as he said, "Lady, it grows late and our repast grows cold."

Suddenly deprived of Wolf's comforting embrace, Dara looked up at the man who had held her tenderly only moments before. His expression was unreadable, his stygian gaze as unfathomable as the midnight sea. Sensing the distance Wolf was putting between them, Dara shivered and absently rubbed at the gooseflesh that prickled her arms. She didn't know what she had expected to see in his face, but she hadn't anticipated the sense of bereavement that accompanied his sudden withdrawal. Too confused by her own veering emotions, and unable to say or do more, Dara nodded and followed Wolf from the bedchamber. She kept her gaze away from the man at her side as he led her down the passageway to the stairs. They descended the steps to the main hall, where everyone had gathered to partake of their evening meal.

Chapter 9

Glowering, Dara sat mutely at Wolf's right hand and tried to force down a few bites of the tough roast beef the brazen serving wench had haphazardly shoveled onto her trencher of stale bread. The girl has been too busy eyeing Wolf as if he were part of the meal to consider the way she served the unappetizing fare. Annoyed by the girl's despicable behavior, as well as the man who sat like a king at the head of the table, enjoying the woman's boldness with a wry smile curling his shapely lips, Dara chomped down on the stringy meat and wished she could throttle Wolf. God! How she wanted to strangle the cur. He had no consideration or respect for anyone. His own daughter ate at the same table where he philandered with the serving maid.

Silently fuming, Dara chewed faster and faster, venting her fury upon the piece of roast that seemed to grow in size with each bite. She sought to swallow the beef, but gagged as it lodged against the bilious lump that filled her throat when she considered Wolf's lack of propriety. He didn't attempt to stop the wench when she deliberately brushed against him or bent provocatively close to allow him full view of her heavy breasts.

Blaming her queasy stomach upon the unsavory meal, Dara refused to admit that jealousy might be at the root of her nausea. Eyeing her trencher, she suspected Phelan's cook of confiscating one of the saddles from the stable and preparing it for Wolf, who probably couldn't distinguish a good piece of meat from a bad one. Either that or the cook was too lazy to slaughter a young beef and indeed had used a cow that died of old age.

Disgust, nausea, and anger combined to make Dara feel she would burst at any moment if she didn't leave the hall. She'd had all she could take of the unpalatable meal as well as Wolf's lecherous behavior. She tossed her knife onto the table and shot Wolf a reproving look. The poor fare of his table didn't surprise her. It only served to reaffirm the wretched state of a household he seemed to take such pride in calling his own.

"What's wrong, Lady? Does my board not suit your taste?" Wolf asked, cocking a dark brow at Dara even as he speared another tough piece of beef.

Grimacing, Dara watched Wolf raise the meat to his lips and then take a hefty bite with his even white teeth. He chewed, seemingly unaware of the poor quality of the beef and the slightly rancid smell that rose from it.

Noting Dara's expression, Wolf washed down the tough beef with a large swig of ale before he said, "Lady, I asked you a question. Why do you not eat? Do you find something wrong with the food?"

" 'Tis exactly as I would expect to be provided here," Dara said. "And I fear I am not up to the war that must be waged to eat at your table, my lord knight. I value my teeth as well as my stomach far too much."

Wolf arched a dark brow and speared another piece of beef. He eyed the meat curiously for a long reflective moment before his gaze once more claimed Dara's. "You find something amiss with the meat?"

"I find it unsuitable for human consumption," Dara answered honestly.

Her candor stung, but Wolf refused to show that he'd been affected by her words. He smiled at Dara.

"Wench, you abuse my hospitality at every turn. You criticize my home, my food, and myself. Will nothing please you?"

Get rid of the witch that eats you with her eyes, Dara thought, but said, "There is only one thing that would truly please me, as you well know. However, I know you will not release me."

"You are right, Dara. I will not release you until your ransom has been paid. But I would bargain with you."

"I make no bargain with the devil," Dara said.

A wry smile curved Wolf's mouth. "Ah, little enemy, one would think you a pious little nun." His grin deepened. "But you and I both know otherwise, don't we?"

"I know only that you have no conscience. You seduce me, and then within the hour your roving eyes have landed upon the wench who would serve herself upon your platter should you ask."

Wolf arched a dark brow. "Jealous, little enemy?"

"Jealous over a lout like you? Never! I care nothing about who you bed. But even a vile-mannered beast like you should be aware that young eyes watch every move you make."

Wolf glanced toward the small girl sitting between Ox and Bull. She smiled up at him as she chewed a piece of the meat, her large brown eyes worshipful. Wolf shifted in his seat. In his attempt to make Dara realize that her rejection hadn't bothered him, he'd allowed the serving wench's impudent behavior. Wolf's face flushed with guilt. His vanity had made him completely forget about his daughter.

Wolf looked back to Dara and feigned disinterest. Though he might need it, he'd not allow her to censure him in front of his men. He was the master of his own domain. "My daughter is my concern, Lady."

"*Oui*, that is true, but like everything else you possess, she had great need of attention." Dara glanced about the hall. "Your home, your food, and your daughter all show your lack of care as well as your neglect."

"Be quiet, wench," Wolf ordered, his vexation surfacing. He didn't need Dara to remind him that as a mercenary he was ill prepared to bring up a daughter as a lady of quality. He had done his best to give Ellice the type of life that she deserved. He had fought and shed blood to gain it for her.

"Silence will not change anything," Dara said, pushing back her chair and coming to her feet. "Now if you will excuse me, I will retire. I have had enough of ill manners and bad food for one night."

"You are not excused, Lady. You will sit back down and finish your meal," Wolf growled, glowering at Dara.

Dara shook her head. "Nay. I will not." She turned and marched toward the stairs without a backward glance at the hall, which had suddenly grown silent. Nor did she see Wolf come out of his chair as she ascended the winding stairs. Face flushed with anger, every muscle in his hard, lean body taut for battle, he followed in her wake.

Dara breathed a sigh of relief as she closed the chamber door behind her and relaxed. With every step she took she'd expected at any moment to find a furious Wolf blocking her way. Her heart hammered against her ribs from her own bravado. She'd defied Wolf in front of his entire household and managed to make it to her chamber without suffering his retribution.

An icy hand seemed to settle against the nape of her neck, raising the fine down as a chill tingled along Dara's spine. She had been foolhardy to test Wolf's temper after their earlier encounter. But she couldn't have stopped herself from harrying him after the episode with the serving wench, any more than she could have stopped the sun from setting.

What on earth has come over me to do such a thing? Dara wondered, crossing to the fireplace where the coals smoldered like the passion Wolf's presence aroused within her. She was at the man's mercy, but it seemed some devil within her was determined to get herself throttled at his hand.

Dara jumped with a start as the door slammed back against the granite wall. The entire castle seemed to tremble from the impact. She swallowed uneasily as her gaze came to rest upon Wolf's furious countenance. Black eyes burning like the devil's own, he stood scowling at her. Instinctively, Dara retreated to the far side of the chamber for self-preservation.

Wolf smiled grimly. "Lady, you can't hide from my wrath."

Her back against the damp, cracked granite, Dara stiffened her spine and feigned a courage she was far from possessing. "I'm not hiding." She forced her feet to carry her a step forward. "Nor do I fear your wrath."

"Perhaps you should," Wolf growled, slowly eyeing Dara from head to toe. His gaze lingered on the soft mounds covered by the lavender material of her gown.

Though fully clothed, Dara felt suddenly naked beneath his insulting leer. She had the urge to cross her arms over her breasts but suppressed it. Regally, she raised her head and glared back at Wolf. "I have nothing left to fear from you, Sir Knight. You have taken everything from me except my life. Do you come now to extinguish it as well?"

"You may wish that I had killed you by the time I'm through," Wolf said, his voice low and softly menacing. Slowly, he closed the space between them. "And I promise, Dara of Rochambeau, you will regret your defiance."

Before Dara could move out of his reach, Wolf's hands encircled her upper arms and pulled her roughly against his hard, unyielding body. His dark gaze locked with hers. "Lady, during the past months I have been patient with you, but I will not have your defiance in my home."

"Are you going to spank her, Papa?" Ellice questioned from the doorway where Wolf had failed to close the portal behind him when he entered the chamber.

Wolf clenched his jaw and squeezed his eyes tightly together for a long, unsettling moment. A muscle worked in his cheek as he struggled to regain control over his temper. Finally he looked once more at Dara, his dark gaze holding hers, silently ordering her to remain quiet as he dealt with his daughter. He let his hands fall to his sides and turned to the small girl. "No, pet. I'm not going to spank Lady Dara."

"Then how are you going to punish her for disobeying your order?" Ellice asked, bewildered. Nurse always paddled her bottom when she didn't abide by the rules.

Wolf shrugged, unable to tell his daughter how he'd like to punish his beautiful hostage; how his body ached to feel her beneath him again; how he wanted to hear her cries of ecstasy as he spilled his seed deep within her luscious body. Wolf cleared his throat and sought to dispel the images his imagination conjured up. "How would you suggest I punish her?"

Ellice lifted one small shoulder in a shrug that mirrored her father's. Her dark velvet gaze came to rest upon her rival for Wolf's affections. She frowned. She wanted the woman to go back to where she'd come from. Or to be put where no one would see her. Ellice smiled up at her father, her small face alight. "You could put her in the dungeon."

Wolf glanced back to Dara. "Aye. Perhaps that is what I should do. She'd give me no trouble locked away down there."

Dara's sharp intake of breath could be heard across the room. She paled visibly and caught her lower lip between her teeth. Her wide eyes held a look of stark terror.

The muscles across Wolf's hard flat belly constricted at the expression on her beautiful face. Unwittingly he'd found the chink in the brave armor Dara wore in front of the world. He had found her weakness. She was terrified at the thought of being put in the dungeon. Wolf's heart twisted within his chest. He opened his mouth to comfort her, but she gave him no time to speak. Her plea tumbled out in a breathless whisper, "Please, Wolf. I'll do anything you ask. I beg of you. Don't put me in the dungeon."

Shaken by her appeal, Wolf looked back to his daughter. "Go to your chamber, Ellice. 'Tis time for you to be in bed."

"But Papa," Ellice whined, "I want to see you punish her for being bad."

"Ellice, this is none of your affair. Now do as I say or you'll find yourself earning a paddling for your own disobedience."

Unwilling to tempt such a fate, Ellice flashed a mutinous glance at the stricken, white-faced woman, gave her father a pouty look, and then turned and ran from the room, a sob tightening her small chest. She didn't know what had happened to her father but was certain it was all the Lady Dara's fault.

Ellice clambered up onto her bed and buried her face in the pillow before she allowed her tears to fall. She balled her small fists and beat at the down mattress as she cried out her vexation. She would like to lock Lady Dara in the dungeon and throw away the key, so she'd never interfere with her and her papa again. Ellice cried herself to sleep.

Wolf watched his daughter until she passed from

view down the passageway. Assured she had obeyed him, he closed the door and latched it. He needed no other interruptions. Turning, he looked once more at Dara. She hadn't moved. Pale and taut, she stood warily regarding him, as if he'd suddenly turned into a stranger. "Dara, I'm not going to send you to the dungeon. It was only a feeble jest."

Dara raised a trembling hand to her ashen lips and sucked in a shuddering breath. Her words came so softly, Wolf had to strain to hear them. "I would die."

Heart pressed between the steel vise of his conscience, Wolf crossed the chamber to Dara in less than three strides. He took her into his arms and damned the voice that told him he shouldn't coddle her, that he should show her who commanded Castle Phelan. She needed his comfort and to hell with everything else. "Hush, love. You will not die. I will not allow it."

Dara wrapped her arms about Wolf's lean waist and huddled within his embrace as if it were her sanctuary. A shudder passed over her as she pressed her cheek against the hard planes of his chest and squeezed her eyes closed. Logic told her she was making a fool of herself by surrendering to her irrational fear of being locked away, but she couldn't stop herself. Nor could she stop herself from accepting the strength and comfort Wolf offered. He was her enemy, but he was also her haven. Like her fear, her other feelings were illogical, but that didn't stop them.

Tenderly, Wolf lay his cheek against Dara's dark hair and breathed in her sweet fragrance. His blood stirred at her heady scent but he managed to quell the heat before it settled in his loins. He'd not use Dara's terror to bring her to his bed. He wanted her, true. But he wanted her to desire him as well. He had tasted the fire of her passion, and he'd not be satisfied with her merely accepting his lovemaking out of a sense of obligation or fear.

Wolf lifted Dara into his arms and lay her on the bed. He removed her slippers and tucked her beneath the covers before he lay down beside her and drew her comfortingly against him. He lightly brushed his lips against her brow as she rested her head on his shoulder. " 'Tis been a trying day for all of us. Sleep now, my lady. I vow no harm will come to you."

Dara looked up at the man who had so unwittingly wrought her terror. Her heart swelled with emotion. Wolf spoke no word of apology but his every action showed his regret for his offhand threat. Dara snuggled against his side and closed her eyes, suddenly at peace. Tonight had been cataclysmic, yet somewhere out of the upheaval of raging emotions, she'd had to confront her own feelings for the man who held her. And she realized she had fallen in love with her enemy.

Dara awoke alone. Curled amid the furs to ward off the chill of the early morning hours, she stared at the vacant space at her side. The only sign that Wolf had remained with her all night was the scent of him upon the pillow. She inhaled the clean, masculine fragrance that clung to the linen. She couldn't stop the sudden burst of emotion that swept over her. She reached out and touched the fabric where Wolf's head had lain. She knew she should hate Wolf. As a Rochambeau and a daughter of France, he was her sworn enemy.

Dara rolled onto her back and pensively stared up at the thick beams overhead, torn between her loyalty to her family and her emotions for the man who held her captive. It was her duty as a Rochambeau to do everything within her power to fight Wolf. But she now found she lacked enthusiasm for such battle. So much had changed within her during the past months that it was hard to place duty before her own heart.

Dara's brow knit with a perplexed frown. How could

she fight her own emotions? How could she win a war waged between her mind and her heart? In such a contest there could be no victor.

Feeling suddenly as ravaged as France under Edward's assault, she threw back the furs and sat up. She must come to terms with herself, to negotiate a truce or find herself destroyed.

Dara slid her feet to the floor and crossed to the narrow window overlooking the bailey. She immediately spotted Wolf. Suited from head to toe in silver mail, he wore a belted black surcoat over the fine metal. The medallion that he always wore gleamed dully against the ebony background when the sunlight caught the tarnished brass. As usual, Wolf stood flanked by the twins while he addressed his men. Mounted, they listened intently to their liege lord.

From so far above the bailey, Dara couldn't hear Wolf's words, but knew by his men's expressions that the matters of which he spoke were serious. They were going to fight, not take a morning ride for their health. A few moments later Wolf mounted his destrier and led his men through the gates.

Her heart suddenly lodging in her throat to shut off her breath, Dara watched the squad disappear over the rise. Wolf rode out in search of his enemy; an enemy that didn't love him, an enemy that would gladly see him dead to usurp his place within Castle Phelan.

A chill rippled down her spine. The thought of his death pierced her like a dull dagger. It ripped painfully through her chest and sliced a jagged path into her heart. Dara trembled from the assault of the sudden battle taking place within her.

She drew in a shuddering breath and accepted her mind's defeat. Her love for the man who made her blood turn into liquid flame had conquered all logic and reason. Her heart had proved far more powerful than her loyalty to Rochambeau and the ancestors who filled the family crypt.

Dara glanced toward the clear blue sky and thought of the man who had died at Crécy. She knew her father would understand if he were alive. He had often said that the love shared between a man and woman should be treasured above all else. He would not deny her Wolf's love because of men long dead. She had served her family well and loyally during the past years, working to preserve her brother's inheritance, always putting Paul's future before her own while he chased his dreams of glory. The responsibility of Rochambeau had lain heavily upon her shoulders, and she had willingly carried the burden, without resenting the restrictions it placed upon her own life.

Now her own destiny awaited. The time had come to make a choice between her past and her future. Her troubled gaze traveled from the inner courtyard to the high walls surrounding the outer bailey, where the villagers had gathered the previous night to welcome the master of Castle Phelan. The furrow across her brow deepened. The choice might not be hers to make. Wolf had never given an indication that he cared for her any more than he cared for the serving wench last night. Though he'd given her comfort, he'd not professed undying love. Even when he'd made his offer to her to become his mistress, he hadn't desired anything more from her than the use of her body to appease his lust.

Dara turned away from the window. When the time came, Wolf intended to ransom her back to King John. She stared morosely at the gloomy chamber. It mirrored her expectations of a life with the man who had unwittingly claimed her heart. And as long as Wolf looked upon her as only his hostage, no matter what else transpired between them, she could never allow him to know of her feelings.

Dara crossed the chamber to the polished metal mirror that hung over the large carved chest that now held her tattered clothing. She peered at her image and was amazed to find a haggard, worried face staring back at her. It little resembled the confident Lady of Rochambeau that she had once been. As though blind, she raised her hand and traced each of her features with the tips of her fingers to assure herself that the face still belonged to her.

Dara's expression darkened. She narrowed her eyes and clenched her jaw. She didn't like what she saw in the mirror. It seemed only a shadowy replica of herself. She had been a woman who prided herself on her independence, a woman who had always taken matters into her own hands; the woman who had acted in her brother's stead, the woman who had managed her family estate as well as a man, the woman ready to fight the English for her country.

"Where have you gone?" she asked, reaching out to touch the image of the anxious face reflected on the mirror's cool metal surface.

The decaying beams overhead, the cracked granite walls, the rough-hewn flooring, even the heavy oak bed where she'd slept in Wolf's arms, seemed to shout the answer: You've given up.

Dara shook her head in denial. "No. I haven't given up."

Then fight for what you want, the voices enjoined.

"How can I fight when Wolf feels nothing?" Dara whispered.

Make him feel. Make him need you.

Dara paused, her face lighting at the idea. Once more her gaze swept over the chamber. She could help Wolf, make herself so valuable to him that he'd never want to ransom her. Her face fell. "But that won't necessarily make him love me."

No. But it's a start. Let things come as God wills.

Dara nodded decisively and squared her shoulders. She had never been one to meekly surrender anything without a fight. When she cared about something, she'd do whatever it took to assure the outcome she desired. And gaining Wolf's love meant far more than anything else she'd ever encountered. It would be a challenge, but she'd willingly, even eagerly, accept it.

Something akin to relief swept over Dara. She no longer felt adrift. She smiled at her reflection, feeling much like her old self. No longer would she be a woman pining for a small token of affection from the man she loved. From this minute forward, she intended to take the advice Ox had given her upon their arrival. The responsibility for her happiness was her own and no one else's. Only she could make herself happy, and she planned to start doing that very thing, this very morning.

Today would be a new beginning for her. For now, she would turn her energies and skills to making Wolf's household into a place where civilized people could live. Once that was done, she intended to turn her attention to Wolf's daughter. The child needed to be taught how to be a young lady, not a spoiled little animal.

Dara's stomach rumbled from hunger. She rubbed at the hollow ache below her ribs. She prayed Wolf's men had left at least a small piece of bread to appease her appetite until she could see a palatable meal prepared. Eager to begin setting Wolf's household to rights, she quickly brushed the tangles from her hair and braided it. She retrieved her slippers from beneath the bed and, smiling, went downstairs.

It took little time for Dara to bring some semblance of order to Wolf's disorganized household. Her air of authority staunched any doubts in the servants' minds about who was in charge. Sensing from her confident manner that they would find themselves without a position should they disobey, they assumed she had Wolf's support and carried out her directives without complaint.

Experienced in supervising a household twice as large as Castle Phelan, she divided up the work, setting each group of servants to certain tasks. Within the first couple of hours she had the hall cleared of the old rushes and replaced with freshly cut ones that were sprinkled with herbs. She had set servants to clearing the corners of cobwebs, readying the soot-blackened walls for whitewash, cleaning ash out of the fireplaces, changing and washing the linens, weeding the neglected herb garden she'd found near the beehives, gathering the ripening fruit from the fruit trees, and setting the storeroom to rights.

Then she finally set her sights on the most offensive place: the kitchen. The cook had already heard of the whirlwind cleaning dervish that had taken over Castle Phelan in its master's absence. He did not challenge her authority when she inspected the larders and granary. Nor did he consider objecting when she frowned in disgust at the food he'd prepared for the midday meal. Chastened like a small boy caught in his slothful ways, he quickly followed her order to set a freshly killed stag to roast along with a dozen fresh birds from the dovecote. Next she turned her attention to the baker, inspecting the hard, blackened loaves that he prepared once a week. She ordered fresh bread made, and threatened the baker with a good beating should anything come to the table again in such a sad condition that it could only be used as a trencher. There would be no more wastefulness within the Phelan kitchens. The flour and food would be prepared so that it could be eaten instead of thrown to the hounds to bury like a hard bone. By midafternoon Dara wearily sank into the large chair that Wolf had occupied the previous night. She gazed about her, awed by the changes that had been wrought in such a short time. The air smelled of fragrant herbs, and a warm fire burned in the clean hearth. She smiled, satisfied with the results of her campaign. It would take a great deal of work, but Castle Phelan could be made livable.

"You have no right," came a small, angry voice from behind Dara.

She looked over her shoulder to see Ellice, her dark brown eyes sparkling with ire. Dara drew in a deep breath and reined in her own temper. At the present moment she was too tired to deal with a recalcitrant child. However, there seemed no way around the confrontation with Wolf's daughter. The child stood with her small hands braced against her waist, glaring up at Dara, ready to defend her territory. Dara smiled, seeing herself in the small, belligerent face. She knew exactly how Ellice felt. Had anyone come into Rochambeau and usurped her place in her father's household, she would have been furious and hurt.

"You have no right. You are not the Lady of Phelan. I am."

Dara nodded. "You are right. And I beg your forgiveness."

Ellice's small brow puckered with a puzzled frown. She hadn't expected the interloper to agree with her. But she wouldn't be deterred by the woman's agreement. "I want you to go away. You're not wanted here."

Again Dara nodded. "I understand your feelings, Lady Ellice. But I fear I can't go away. I am your father's hostage until King John of France pays my ransom."

Unable to suppress her pleasure at being addressed as Lady, Ellice couldn't contain the tiny smile that dimpled her cheeks for a fraction of a moment before she raised her small chin proudly in the air and eyed Dara with antagonism. "You have no right to order Papa's servants about."

"Yes, you're right. I just wanted to help. I know how busy your papa is, and thought I could be of service while I'm here," Dara said calmly. She was fully aware that this conversation with Ellice could be the catalyst for their future relationship. She had to bridge the child's hostility, or she'd never be able to help her become the young lady she deserved to be, instead of the wild little animal she'd acted the previous night.

"Papa and I don't need your help. Everything was just fine until you came."

"Lady Ellice, I'm sorry you feel that way. I had hoped we could become friends, since I had to leave behind all my friends in France."

Ellice eyed Dara thoughtfully, considering her offer. It was tempting. Even at the age of five, Ellice recognized and envied the authority and confidence that Dara possessed. Nurse had told her about true ladies when they had discussed her becoming the Lady of Castle Phelan. And Ellice knew Lady Dara was a lady. She wasn't like Nurse or the other serving wenches. They were kind to her in their own way, but could not teach her the things she needed to learn to be the chatelaine in her papa's household.

Ellice caught her lower lip between her small teeth and worried it indecisively for a long moment. Her papa would be so proud of her if she learned to be a real lady like the Lady Dara. A sudden need to please her father overpowered her jealousy. She cocked her small head to one side and asked, "Would you teach me how to be a lady?"

Dara smiled her pleasure at the question. Though still young in years, the child sensed, more than recognized, the things lacking in her life. Dara nodded. "*Oui.* I would teach you all I know of being a lady."

Ellice moved a hesitant step closer to Dara's chair. "I would know how to order servants about as you do."

"There is much more to being a lady than just ordering servants about. First we must begin with your manners."

Ellice frowned. "What's wrong with my manners?"

Hiding her smile, Dara answered, "A lady does not eat her food like one of her father's yeomen gobbling down his ale and bread before a battle. She must eat daintily, taking small, delicate bites so as not to soil herself. Nor does a lady stalk about as if carrying the weight of heavy armor upon her shoulders. She should move gracefully with head held high."

"What has eating and walking to do with giving orders to the servants?" Ellice asked, mutinously having second thoughts about Dara's offer of friendship. It now sounded much more like the lady wanted to chastise her.

"Everything, Lady Ellice. You must be a lady to receive the honor due a lady. You can't gain the respect of your servants or your peers otherwise. If you act like a man-at-arms, you will be treated accordingly."

Though not totally comprehending Dara's words, Ellice agreed hesitantly. "If that is what is required to make me into a lady that will please Papa, then I will do it." She paused and eyed Dara skeptically. "But I don't really see the need for all the foolishness. It seems a great waste of time to learn how to eat when I already know how. You simply have to pick up your food and put it into your mouth."

"True. But a true lady knows the proper way to put it into her mouth," Dara answered, warming to the small girl's innate charm. She would truly be captivating when she learned to be a lady.

Chapter 10

The hair on Harlow Norton's neck rose in warning. He glanced over his shoulder to see a squad of Englishmen bearing down upon him. Harlow leaned forward, lying close against his mount as he kicked the small shaggy pony in the side, urging him across the open field, fleeing as fast as the animal's short legs would carry him. Harlow ground his teeth together at the thundering sound of the destriers quickly closing the distance between them. He'd known when he'd accepted this mission from Laird Morgan that it could be dangerous. Wolf of Phelan's reputation for being a relentless enemy was well known even in the hinterlands of Scotland.

A nervous sweat broke out across Harlow's upper lip. He wasn't a coward, but he didn't relish the thought of falling into the Wolf's hands. The merciless bastard would have him tortured just for sport before putting him to death for spying for Laird Morgan.

His thoughts giving him impetus, Harlow drove his heels once more into the pony's heaving sides. He'd never allow the Wolf to take him prisoner. It would be far better to die on the field with the sun on his face than to rot in Phelan's dungeon.

Harlow glanced toward the north, where his home lay. He'd never see it again. He clenched his jaw, damning his own carelessness as well as the man in pursuit. The bastard had returned to England unexpectedly. Like his namesake, he'd sneaked back into his den to garner his forces against the impending attack.

The lines about Harlow's eyes deepened. His only regret was not accomplishing his mission. When the Wolf and his men returned, he'd been nearing Phelan, disguised as a beggar seeking a few morsels of food and a night's rest. No one had paid any heed to him in his tattered rags when he entered the gates. They were too caught up in welcoming Wolf home. The guards had failed to note his quick, stealthful disappearance into the stables. He'd waited until all had taken to their pallets before he'd sneaked out of his hiding place to assess the castle's defenses.

Harlow glanced once more over his shoulder. Unfortunately, his information would never reach Laird Morgan.

The earth seemed to shake under the thunderous onslaught of English knights. Their destriers' long legs ate up the distance as iron-shod hooves chewed the turf into clods that flew in the air from the force of their passage. Again Harlow kicked his small shaggy pony in the side, and he felt the animal give a shuddering surrender beneath him. The shaggy beast stumbled to a wheezing, trembling halt.

Harlow looked down at the lowered head and mentally made the sign of the cross. His reconnaissance would not now lead to the siege Laird Morgan had planned. He slid from the pony's back and gave the animal's lathered neck an understanding pat. Though bred for a stout-hearted nature, his Scottish pony was no match for the destrier bred for war.

Harlow turned to face the Englishmen who quickly surrounded him with lances drawn and pointed in his direction. Accepting his capture and failure, he prayed he'd have the courage to force the Wolf to end his life quickly.

Immediately recognizing the knight dressed in silver and black, he addressed the Lord of Phelan. "Sir Wolf, 'tis not oft' that a poor fellow like myself is greeted by such enthusiasm on his way to market."

The medallion about Wolf's neck swung free as he leaned forward and folded his arms over the saddle pommel. It swayed hypnotically back and forth as he scrutinized the red-haired Scotsman for a long, tension-ridden moment. "You speak as if you believe we are simpleminded fools, Scot."

Understanding his ploy had failed to convince the Wolf that he'd mistakenly captured a poor peasant, Harlow quickly shook his head and grinned up at Wolf. "Nay, Sir Knight. I don't think it. I know it."

Wolf's lips twitched at the man's audacity. He couldn't stop himself from admiring the Scot's boldness. The man understood his precarious position, yet he still had the impudence to insult his captors. However, Wolf's admiration for the man's courage didn't alter the situation. This was his enemy and would be treated as such.

"Then you are the fool, Scot," Wolf said, smiling coolly down at his captive. He glanced toward Bull. "What say you? Should we hang the spy here, or take him back to Phelan for a little entertainment this eve?"

Bull glanced past Wolf to his brother and grinned. "We've lacked for entertainment since roasting our last Frenchman in Bordeaux. Perhaps even a dumb Scot could provide a few minutes of amusement for our men. They do thirst to shed some heathen blood."

"You English curs," Harlow swore, withdrawing his sword. "Fight me now. I'll not be sport for English dogs."

Wolf's laughter spilled across the field, ridiculing the man who stood ready to fight and die at the hand of his enemy. "Surely you jest, Scot. The odds are against you."

Temper as hot as the color of the hair on his head, Harlow snarled, "I don't think so. Twelve sniveling Englishmen against one good Scot. The odds seem in my favor."

At the Scot's taunt, an angry murmur rippled through the circle of men. Wolf flashed them a quelling look and they were quickly silenced. He turned his black-ice gaze back to Harlow, all good humor gone. "As I said before, you are a fool, Scot."

"Perhaps a fool, but no coward," Harlow taunted, hoping to spur the Englishmen's anger to such an extent they'd have no choice but to end his life in the middle of the open field.

With the easy grace of a man used to the weight of steel armor, Wolf dismounted and withdrew his broadsword. His expression boded no good for the Scotsman. His face as hard as the granite wall of Castle Phelan, he turned to Harlow. "We shall see if one Scot can take the day against one good Englishman. Ready yourself to fight."

Harlow cast a scathing glance toward the mounted men surrounding them. "Do you fight alone, Sir Wolf?"

"Always," Wolf growled, raising his blade. The polished steel caught the sunlight, reflecting against the brass medallion in the center of Wolf's chest.

Harlow's eyes widened at the sight of the medallion, and the arm holding his sword went limp at his side. He could no more raise his arm against a man wearing the Morgan family crest than he could slit his own throat.

"Damn you, Scot. Do you cower before the first blow has even been struck? Are you so craven that you would die without trying to defend yourself?"

Harlow's eyes locked upon Wolf's furious face. "I can't."

Wolf's thickly lashed black eyes narrowed. "Recreant, raise your weapon."

Harlow shook his head and dropped his sword upon the ground at Wolf's feet. "Nay, my lord. I can't fight those who carry the Morgan blood."

"Has your cowardice driven you insane, wretch?" Wolf growled. "I am English, not Scot, and certainly not of Morgan blood."

Again Harlow shook his head. He raised a hand and pointed to the medallion hanging in the center of Wolf's chest. " 'Tis the Morgan crest ye wear, Sir Wolf. 'Tis no Englishman's blood ye have in yer veins."

"You're mad, Scot," Wolf said, resheathing his sword. "And I'll not put an end to a madman's life. Go back to your lord, and tell him that I have returned to Phelan. And I will keep what is mine. If he wishes to uselessly waste his life and those of his men, he is welcome to come and try to take Phelan from me. However, give him this warning. I will not go as easy on the next fool he sends. The next will be hanged and quartered as a spy deserves. Now get you gone before I change my mind and make the world a better place by ridding it of one more fool."

Harlow bowed to Wolf. "I will give Laird Morgan your message, my lord. And I will tell him of what I've learned here today."

"Fool, you've learned nothing beyond your own cowardice. Now be gone," Wolf said, and turned his back on Harlow.

Without looking back at the Scot, he mounted his destrier. He cast a fleeting glance northward before urging the animal in the opposite direction. A bitter white line etched his grimly set lips as he kicked his mount to a faster pace and tried to outdistance his thoughts, his past.

The implication of the Scot's words disturbed him far

more than he wanted to admit. It brought back the pain the small child within him still carried, the pain he'd thought long salved by his own accomplishments. He didn't want to think of his beginnings, or why his parents had abandoned him, or whose blood he carried in his veins. He was his own man. He had made his own way in the world and had achieved far more than many who could claim noble bloodlines. He needed no past. He had earned his knighthood with his sweat and blood, and needed to claim no English or Scot lord as his father to feel proud.

Wolf pushed back the silver mail coif and ran his long fingers through his sweat-dampened hair as he drew his destrier to a walk. The animal entered the forest, picking his way through the trees that bordered the open field where Wolf had captured the Scot. The thick leaves overhead dappled the sunlight across the dark loam of the forest floor, muting it into cool shadows that seemed to hover tauntingly in Wolf's mind. No matter what he told himself, deep in his heart he knew that he wanted to know of his past.

"Damn," Wolf swore beneath his breath, and slammed his fist against the saddle pommel. Could he never be free? Would Ada's revelation haunt him until his dying day? He clenched his jaw and let another curse escape into the cool forest air. He had to come to terms with himself once and for all, or end up driving himself mad.

"Heed the Wolf's words, fool. The next time we set eyes upon you, 'twill mean your death. Now be gone," Bull ordered before turning and following in Wolf's wake. Ox flashed one last troubled look at the Scotsman before ordering the men about.

Dumbfounded by the turn of events, Harlow watched the English knights ride out of sight. He laced his fingers in his thick red hair and scratched his scalp, bewildered by what he'd just learned. By all that was holy, he'd never have believed the Wolf could hold claim to the Morgan bloodline. But there was no mistaking the medallion the Wolf wore about his neck. It was identical to the one Laird Morgan wore, and if legend was to be believed, there had only been two medallions struck. Over two hundred years ago the first Laird Morgan had had them wrought for himself and his lady. And since that time, they had been passed down through each generation from each lord to his lady as a symbol of their bond and love.

Again Harlow ran his fingers through his tousled hair. He didn't know what to think, but he was sure one man would have the answer. Taking the pony's reins, Harlow turned north toward home. He didn't have time to allow the pony to rest. He had to reach Morgan Keep as soon as possible.

"What are ye a-blabbering about, man? Did confronting a few Englishmen send your wits into Hades?" Laird Morgan growled. He leaned forward in the massive chair that had been the seat of the laird of the Morgan family since Morgan Keep's construction over a hundred years earlier. A symbol of his birthright and rule, the Morgan medallion swung about his neck. His ebony gaze froze Harlow in place. "I sent ye to assess Phelan's defenses, not to come back here with tales of visions ye've concocted in that simpleton mind of yers."

"I've concocted no tale, Laird Morgan. I speak the truth, though I know 'tis hard to believe."

"Hard to believe? 'Tis impossible. The medallion of which you speak was lost over thirty years ago."

"But Laird, could ye not be mistaken? I know what I saw. 'Tis the same as the one ye wear about yer neck."

Laird Morgan glanced down at the bright talisman,

and his frown deepened. He shook his head. "Nay. 'Tis impossible."

"But could not the other have been found by the Wolf?"

Again Laird Morgan shook his raven head. "Nay. The medallion is lost forever." He looked back at Harlow, his frown unrelieved. "And fool that ye are, ye failed to put an end to the Wolf when ye had the chance."

"I could not raise my hand against the Morgan crest, no matter who wore it."

"Enough," Laird Morgan growled, coming to his feet. Harlow's report had dredged up memories that he'd thought long buried, painful memories that still made his heart ache. "I've heard enough of this foolishness." He turned and stalked out of the hall, leaving his retainers staring at the man who still stood before the Morgan chair, as bewildered by his laird's actions as he'd been at finding the Wolf wearing the Morgan medallion.

Laird Angus Morgan strode up the narrow, winding steps to the top of the tower. His dark expression reflected his mood as he crossed to the wall and stared past the castle's crenellations toward the rolling hills to the south. Angus released a long breath and felt his heart twist. How he still yearned for his sweet Allyson. It had been nearly thirty-three years since the day he'd given her the Morgan medallion and vowed his undying love.

Angus pressed his lips into a tight line as the memories rose up to assault him as if it had been only yesterday that he'd stood beside Allyson and had been secretly married by the priest in the tiny hamlet of Etal. Both had known from the moment of their first meeting that their relationship would never be condoned by Allyson's parents. Yet that hadn't stopped them from falling in love. Allyson, the daughter of the Lord of Phelan, had been the embodiment of everything he'd ever wanted in a woman. She had beauty, grace, and a heart so kind, so loving, and so good, that it had warmed him to his very soul. Even now, after all these years, the thought of her could make him feel the warmth of her love.

Angus bowed his head and ran a weary hand over his face. Had he only known what lay in their future, he would have taken Allyson and ridden into the highlands where no one could have ever found them. However, hindsight did little good. Allyson and his child had both been lost to him because of her conniving father. Lord Phelan had learned of their relationship and imprisoned his daughter to prevent her from escaping him before he could arrange a marriage that he felt far more suitable, one which would help him recoup the wealth of his family and revitalize his crumbling castle. When he finally realized that Allyson carried Angus's child, he had not changed his mind. He became determined to keep her secret by locking her in the tower until the child was born.

Angus felt the welling of the old grief and the sting of tears as he turned his ebony gaze toward England once more. His love, his life, the only woman to ever claim his heart, had given birth to his heir, only to die a few days later of childbed fever. Word had reached him a week later that he was a father, a widower, and that his son had soon followed his mother into death on the same day. Devastated, Angus had grieved for Allyson until his father insisted that he marry to provide an heir for succession. After five years he'd finally relented and taken the beautiful Hedda to wife. But he'd found little happiness in the match. The woman's name had been accurately chosen. Warfare was all he'd had from their union. She had died giving birth to his daughter, Kirsten.

A tiny smile eased Laird Morgan's pensive frown.

Kirsten had been nothing like her mother. She reminded him more of Allyson than of Hedda. She'd been born with a loving spirit, always caring for the sick or taking in injured animals. It was never a surprise to find some wild thing scurrying about in the castle towers. Kirsten was the bright spot in a life that had seen little light since Allyson's death.

"Papa," Kirsten said softly from the doorway. "May I join you?"

Laird Angus's smile deepened as he turned to look at the child of his loins. He held out his arms to her, and she immediately ran into them, snuggling against him as if she were still a child instead of a young woman nearing her eighteenth birthday. Angus ran his hand through the smooth, dark hair that lay down her back to her waist. It felt like fine silk beneath his fingers. The pain in his heart eased. God had taken his wife and son from him, but he had also seen fit to bless him with this loving child. Angus would not complain further. He would be satisfied. "How has your day gone, imp? What will I find in my bed tonight—a fox or a weasel?"

Kirsten chuckled and looked up at her father. "Neither. I released the vixen this morning to return to her den. Her leg has healed." She eyed her father critically. "Now if I can but keep people from hunting her, she'll be safe."

Lord Angus chuckled. "You have nothing to fear from me, chit. I hunt a Wolf, not a fox."

Kirsten's smile faded. "I heard what Harlow said. Could it be true, Papa?"

Angus shook his head. "Nay, child. There is only one medallion left. And 'tis mine."

"But Papa, Harlow is one of your most trusted men. He'd not conjure up such a tale. Nor is he a coward."

"Aye, I well know that. However, I can't take what he says as fact. He does not lie, but I fear his vision is failing him. There can be no other medallion like mine."

Kirsten scanned her father's handsome face with eyes as black as his own. "You know what happened to the other Morgan medallion, don't you, Papa?"

Laird Angus once more glanced southward and nodded. "Aye, child. I know what happened to the medallion, for I am the one who gave it away."

Kirsten's inquisitive eyes widened, and she asked softly, "Will you tell me?"

Drawing in a deep breath, Lord Angus looked down at his daughter. He nodded. It was time to tell her of his past, of the woman he'd loved and the son he'd lost before he'd known of his existence. " 'Tis a long story, Kirsten."

Sensing from the use of her Christian name the seriousness of his mood, Kirsten placed a comforting hand on her father's arm and smiled her understanding. "Papa, I have all the time in the world. I would know, so I can help ease your pain."

"Then you shall know all, Kirsten. And I beg of you to understand that nothing I say will change the love I hold for you." Lord Angus drew his daughter to a well seat cut into the tower wall and sat down. He took her hand within his own and began the story at the point of his first meeting with his beloved Allyson.

At the end of the tale, Lord Morgan glanced once more to the south. "Now you know why I challenge anyone who lays claim to Phelan. 'Tis mine by right of marriage, since Lord Phelan left no heirs."

"I'm so sorry, Papa," Kirsten said, tears of sympathy glistening in her eyes.

Seeming to shake the past from him, Angus looked back to his daughter and smiled tenderly down at her. He lightly brushed his knuckle against her flawless cheek. "You have no reason to be sorry, little one. Had things been otherwise, then I would not have had the pleasure of your company here in my old age."

Kirsten's lower lip trembled, and she brushed at her eyes with the back of her hand. "But you would have had a son and the woman you truly loved. You would have had years of the happiness that fate has denied you."

Angus took his daughter into his arms and held her against his heart. "I would change nothing. You have brought more happiness into my life than a man like me deserves."

"I love you, Papa," Kirsten whispered against the thick velvet covering his chest.

"And I love you, Kirsten. Never believe otherwise."

For a long moment they sat together, treasuring the love that bound them as father and daughter. At last Kirsten broke the silence. Without looking up at her father, she asked, "Papa?"

"What?" Angus answered absently, his thoughts once more upon Harlow's tale.

"What if what Harlow says is true?"

"As I've already said, it can't be."

"But what if it is? Could not Lord Phelan have lied when he said the child died?"

"Nay, Kirsten. I also suspected Lord Phelan of manipulating things to his own benefit. But the man I sent to Phelan came back with the same news. The daughter of Lord Phelan had died, and there was no babe within the castle."

Kirsten leaned back and looked up at her father. "But does that mean the child died?"

Lord Morgan shook his head. "I know not. All I know for certain is that I gave the Morgan medallion to Allyson and have thought all these years that it was buried with her."

"Should you not at least question the man who possesses the medallion that Harlow believes is the twin to this?" Kirsten asked, lifting a finger to the shining talisman against her father's chest.

Angus's cheeks twitched from the smile he tried to suppress. "Minx, 'tis said curiosity killed the cat, or 'twas perhaps a lass. Are ye trying to persuade me to confront the rascal who now lays claim to land that rightfully belongs to me?"

A twinkle in her eye, Kirsten smiled sweetly up at her father. "I have no doubt that you will do the right thing, Papa. Nor do I believe I have the power to persuade you to do anything that you don't want to do in your heart. I'm only suggesting that there might be an alternative."

Lord Morgan couldn't suppress his smile any longer. "Minx, I know exactly what you're trying to do. And I will think upon it."

Kirsten's smile widened. " 'Tis all I ask." She bent and placed a kiss upon Angus's cheek. "Now I must see to Janet's cough. She managed to get herself soaked in the last rain, and the cold has taken hold in her chest."

"Then see to your remedies, child. And I'll see to the handling of the Morgan affairs," Angus said, coming to his feet. He offered his daughter his arm. When Kirsten stood, he lightly brushed his lips against her brow before releasing her to go about her duties.

Kirsten paused at the doorway and looked back at her father. "I love you, Papa. And I know you'll do what is right, no matter what you decide."

"I will always try, Kirsten. But at times, 'tis often a hard task."

Chapter 11

Wolf could be heard barking out orders before the heavy iron-bound doors of the keep swung open and he entered. His mood as sour as newly pressed green grapes, he paused upon the threshold to take in the hall before him. His ebony eyes narrowed with annoyance as his icy gaze swept over the chamber, acknowledging the changes wrought in his absence. Wolf slapped a heavy gauntlet against his thick-corded thigh, and his lips firmed into a churlish line. The sight of the fresh rushes at his feet set a new wave of fury roaring through his blood, though he sought to maintain control over his temper.

Wolf drew in a cooling breath, only to find himself inhaling the sweet fragrance of the herbs Dara had ordered scattered over the floor. He flashed a searing look over the assembly of servants and retainers, searching out the culprit responsible for the sudden transformation within his home.

He clenched his jaw. Only one person would have the audacity to overstep her bounds in such a manner. And only one person felt his home not quite good enough for her. Wolf's gaze settled upon the woman standing quietly near the stairs. As regal as a queen, Dara of Rochambeau stood watching him with head held high. Wolf ground his teeth together. He'd be damned if he'd allow the little interloper to take over his home. He had bedded her, but that gave her no rights over his household. He desired her body, but he'd not stand meekly by and allow her to usurp his authority. The haughty wench would learn her place.

Flashing Dara a look that would have wilted a battle-hardened soldier, Wolf turned and strode across the hall. In his present state of mind he didn't trust himself not to turn Dara over his knee right then and there as he'd often threatened. Ignoring the serving maid who hurried forward to serve him, Wolf poured himself a tankard of dark ale. A foreboding look from his black eyes sent the young girl scurrying toward the safety of the kitchen.

Sparing no thought to the child he'd overlooked on the stairs behind Dara, he drained down the entire contents of the tankard before refilling it.

Noting Wolf's black mood, Dara gave Ellice a small reassuring smile and crossed the chamber to where the master of Phelan stood so unapproachably aloof from the rest of his household. Moistening her lips, she broke the silence that hung over the hall like a sodden cloak. She hoped to bring some semblance of normalcy back to the chamber for the sake of the small, anxious girl who had waited all afternoon to see her father. "Sir, 'tis good that you have returned home. We had begun to worry."

"Why in hell would you worry if I never returned? Or do you fear that without me you'd be sent back to Navarre, and he'd have your pretty throat slit from ear to ear?" Wolf growled, unconsciously venting a few of the emotions that had been building within him since his encounter with the Scot. It didn't truly matter that his victim was the woman whom he'd taken to his bed the previous night, or that at any other time he would have appreciated her efforts to bring some semblance of order to his household. In his present state of mind, he needed to lash out and free the pent-up emotions the

Scot had managed to dredge up from his past, emotions that should have been long dead, emotions he thought he'd annihilated after Ada's death.

Wolf's knuckles whitened from the pressure of his grip about the tankard's wooden handle. He glared down at the woman who had forced her way into his life and was now trying to lay claim to more than his bed. "Is there anything else that I might do for you, wench?"

Dara glanced uncertainly back at the child who had retreated into the shadows of the stairwell. Her temper spewed over. The bastard! How dare he act like such a beast when his daughter had worked so hard to make herself look like a lady in order to please him. Eyes glittering like blue diamonds, Dara looked back at the man who unwittingly possessed her heart. She squared her jaw determinedly and braced her hands on her hips. Her words came soft and quiet, seethed through clenched teeth for his ears alone. "You can do nothing for me, you ill-tempered wretch. But you could think of your child instead of acting like the great ass that you are."

Fuming, Dara turned and stalked to the stairs. She took Ellice's small hand into her own and gave it a reassuring pat. "Come, Lady Ellice. Your father has had a long day in the saddle." She flashed Wolf a withering look. "We must give him time to rest. He'll be more agreeable at the evening meal." Dara started to lead Ellice up the stairs.

"Lady Dara," Wolf said, his voice booming thunderously across the hall. The granite walls seemed to vibrate from the very force of it.

The men loitering near the ale table stilled apprehensively, recognizing from experience the tone he used when he went into battle. The servants preparing the long tables for the evening meal eased quietly into the shadows, wanting to place as much distance between themselves and their angry lord as possible. They didn't envy their master's beautiful hostage.

"I have not given you permission to leave."

Dara paused and drew in a fortifying breath. She glanced down at the child who stood regarding her through eyes so much like her father's. "I believe your father has decided he isn't tired after all."

Ellice glanced to where her father stood with arms folded over his wide chest, watching them through narrowed lashes. Confused, she moistened her lips and looked up at the woman at her side. "Why is Papa so angry? Did we do something wrong?"

Dara tried to give Ellice a reassuring smile. The futile attempt ended in a lopsided, wavering grin. "Nay, child. You've done nothing wrong. He is angry with me. I have a tendency to forget that I am only a captive here."

"Papa will help remind you," Ellice said, striving to help Dara's feelings about her poor memory.

"I know," Dara said, turning resignedly to retrace her steps down the stairs. Her feet lagged as she crossed the hall once more.

"Good evening, Papa," Ellice said happily, drawing her father's black gaze away from the woman who still held her hand. "Do you like the way I look?"

Wolf's brow furrowed as his puzzled gaze swept over his daughter for the first time. Ellice wore a clean gown and her long silky hair had been braided and wrapped in a coronet about her small head. A tiny gold net kept it in place. She looked the image of a miniature lady. Wolf's frown deepened, chiseling lines across his forehead and at the sides of his mouth. He looked back to Dara. "Is this farce your idea as well?"

"Don't you like the way I look, Papa?" Ellice asked, hurt and puzzled by her father's reaction.

"Lady, you will go to your chamber and await me

there," Wolf growled to Dara, and watched her ascend the stairs before turning his attention back to his daughter. "You look very lovely, pet, but I think 'tis a bit much for one so young."

"But I'm now truly the Lady of Phelan, Papa."

"Yes, sweeting, you are my lady and someday you will be recognized as the Lady of Phelan. But I would not rush things before 'tis time. I am a selfish man and would keep you small for a while longer. Now go upstairs and have Nurse loose your hair. I want the daughter I left this morn seated at the table with me this eve."

"But Papa, I want to become a lady like Lady Dara."

"As I said, pet, in time you will. Now obey me or find yourself without supper."

Ellice blinked back the rush of stinging tears that filled her eyes, and ran up the stairs as fast as her small feet would carry her. Her father had broken her five-year-old heart. She'd tried so hard to look like a lady for him. She'd done everything Lady Dara had instructed. And she'd been so sure he'd be pleased with the way Lady Dara had arranged her hair. She looked so grown-up, so much like a real lady with the gold netting covering her braids. But her papa had hated the way she looked. All her efforts had been for naught.

A sob escaping her, she turned the corner and collided into a soft female form that nearly sent her toppling backward. Wiping at her glistening eyes, Ellice looked through a blur of tears to see Dara. Her lower lip began an unconquerable tremble, and she whispered, "Papa doesn't like the way I look."

Dara's heart went out to the small child. Kneeling, she took Ellice into her arms and cradled her comfortingly against her breasts. "Hush, Lady Ellice. Your father is exactly like all fathers, mine included. They don't like to see that their daughters are growing up. They want to keep them little girls for as long as possible. It is something we women have to understand and forgive."

Ellice leaned back and looked at Dara. Her questioning, hopeful, ebony gaze locked with sympathetic sapphire. "Truly?"

"Yes, Lady Ellice. Like all fathers, Sir Wolf fears he'll lose you if he allows you to grow up."

"But I must grow up to be the Lady of Phelan. Even Papa has said so."

"Your father just doesn't want to rush the passage of time, 'tis all. He loves you well, Lady Ellice. And he wants to keep you for himself for as long as possible. He knows in the near future your beauty will have knights and lords from far and wide beating down Phelan's doors to ask for your hand. And then he'll lose you."

"Nay. Papa will never lose me. I never intend to ever leave Phelan," Ellice said, throwing her arms about Dara's neck. Her need for comfort had momentarily vanquished any rivalry she felt toward Dara. After giving Dara a fierce hug, she leaned back and looked at her once more. A tiny, smug smile made her cheeks dimple fetchingly. "Truly, Papa has nothing to fear about me being wed, because I don't even like boys."

Dara couldn't stop her own smile. She well remembered a time in her own life when she didn't like the opposite sex. And it hadn't been that long ago since she wondered if she'd ever find a man who physically attracted her. Then Wolf had entered her life, turning her world upside down even as he unknowingly claimed her heart.

However, it would do little good to tell Ellice how things can suddenly change in life. Her five-year-old mind couldn't comprehend the ungovernable force created by loving a man. It vanquished everything in its path. Love was torment; love was rapture. No one could explain love to those who had not experienced it themselves.

"I'm sure your father will be pleased to learn how you feel. Now 'tis time for you to do as your father bid you. I would not have him angry with you because of me." Dara dropped a light kiss upon Ellice's brow and came to her feet. She stepped back to allow the child to pass. Dara watched her until she entered the chamber at the end of the corridor.

Satisfied that she had eased Ellice's mind, yet dreading her own confrontation with the child's father, Dara released a long breath and turned to her own chamber door. She came to an abrupt halt at the sight of the man standing in the shadows with his strong, muscular arms folded over his wide chest and one shoulder braced against the granite wall that looked no softer than his expression. Dara stiffened as Wolf's gaze raked over her from head to toe and then settled back on her face. She sensed the anger seething through him. He seemed to exude it through every pore of his hard body. Dara raised her chin defensively in the air and prepared herself to face his wrath.

"What game do you now play, little enemy? Since you have no power to challenge me otherwise, do you seek to worm yourself into my household in order to find a way to destroy me? Do you think to hurt me through my child? Or do you think to bring me down by turning my people against me?"

"Don't judge everyone upon your own deeds," Dara retorted, giving in to anger in order to vanquish the pain his words inflicted upon her heart. How could the man be so dim-witted as not to see that everything she'd done had been to help him, not harm him? The thought added fuel to the fire of Dara's temper. She gave Wolf no time to respond. She flashed him a scathing glance and stalked into her chamber.

Fury clouding his face like a brewing thunderstorm, Wolf clamped a long-fingered hand about the edge of the door Dara tried to slam in his face. He firmly closed the portal and dropped the latch into place. The clang of the rusty metal seemed to reverberate through the still chamber as he slowly turned his angry glare upon the woman who stood bravely defiant in the middle of the chamber. His breath froze in his throat, and his heart seemed to slam against his ribs at the sight.

The last rays of the evening sun spilled in through the narrow cross-slit windows, framing Dara's breathtaking beauty in a radiance of golden light. Momentarily spellbound by the vision, Wolf felt heat surge in his loins. He ground his teeth together in frustration as his sex swelled against his tight-fitting braies.

His fury draining away like muddy water after a torrential rain, Wolf swore under his breath, cursing himself for his inability to maintain control over his emotions when he was near Dara. He didn't want to lose his anger. He had come to put her in her place, to let her know exactly where she stood in his life. Another low curse emerged from Wolf. Could he never be near this woman for any reason without wanting to bed her?

A resounding "No" echoed through Wolf's mind. How could he remain furious with her when his own body undermined his anger? She had the power to arouse every male instinct he possessed, no matter how infuriated he became. In her presence he forgot all logic and allowed his sex to guide his mind. Even now as he tried to understand the hold she had upon him, he wanted nothing more than to throw her down upon the bed and sink himself deep into her warmth.

Wolf fought the urge, clamping a firm hand down on his wayward emotions. He couldn't give way to his desires. He had to make Dara realize her place in his home for Ellice's sake, if for no other reason. He couldn't allow Dara to inch her way into his daughter's life and then, when King John paid her ransom, leave Ellice. The child needed a mother, but not a surrogate who would one day vanish from her life. And that would happen eventually. Lady Dara of Rochambeau would leave Phelan one day. That much was assured. She was a lady, and like all of her kind, she'd never lower herself to find him worthy to husband, no matter how he and his daughter felt. His lack of heritage prevented any relationship between Dara and himself beyond what they now shared.

Wolf curled his hands at his sides in impotent fury. The long afternoon had done nothing to eradicate the feelings the Scot's words had stirred to life. He looked at Dara and in that moment hated her and himself for what could never be between them. The shadowy figures of the man and woman who had sired him and then abandoned him still reigned over his life.

The pained look in Wolf's ebony eyes extinguished the anger Dara had sought to keep kindled against him. She had seen the same look in his eyes before, but hadn't recognized it because she hadn't recognized her own feelings. Now that she had opened her heart to this man who seemed to need no one, she realized that he hurt like any other person. She didn't understand Wolf, nor did she know the reason behind his pain. All she knew was that she loved this man and wanted to ease his pain if he'd allow her.

Guided by instinct alone, Dara crossed the few feet separating her from Wolf. She lay her hand against his chest and felt the strong, steady beat of his heart beneath her palm. She looked up into the dark, penetrating eyes that watched her as if she'd suddenly gone mad and gave him a timid smile. "Will you not let me help you?"

Wolf's strong fingers closed over Dara's. He did not return her smile as his intense eyes locked meaningfully with hers. "There is only one way you can help me, Dara of Rochambeau. My body craves to ease itself upon yours."

Dara's heart surged against her ribs, and her demons did a little jubilant dance as she looked up at Wolf. She moistened her suddenly dry lips. She knew the proper answer to his question. She should act offended; rant and rave, kick and scream her outrage, curse and condemn him for such a suggestion. However, the look in his eyes and her own body's response to the mere touch of his hand routed such a retort. Her demons had escaped and would not be denied. Dara smiled, loving the little monsters more by the minute.

Governed by a heart that dared defy the world to love this man, Dara reached up and wrapped her arms about Wolf's strong, corded neck. She laced her fingers in the raven hair softly layering his neck and tentatively raised her lips to his mouth. She felt the shudder that passed through Wolf as he wrapped his arms about her and pressed her tightly to his hardened body.

Surrendering to his need of comfort, he claimed Dara's lips with his own, tasting, savoring, drowning in the sweetness of her mouth. When she opened her lips to allow his tongue to delve into the moist cavern beyond, he gave an audible moan. His hands moved over her, rapidly divesting her of her clothing. The gown fell about her feet as he swept her up into his arms and carried her to the bed. Hampered by the restrictions of his own clothing, Wolf reluctantly released Dara's mouth and smiled down at her. "A moment, demoiselle. I need to rid myself of these garments."

Her demons in full control, a bewitching, provocative smile curling her lips, Dara came to her knees beside Wolf. Her breasts brushed against the soft velvet of his gipon as she teased the shell of his ear with the tip of her tongue. Her smile deepened when she heard him suck in a sharp breath. Giving a breathy chuckle low in her throat, she whispered seductively, "Nay, Sir Wolf. I will act your squire on this eve."

Intrigued by Dara's sudden transformation from termagant to beguiling witch, Wolf cocked a dark brow at her, but did not move or object as she began to unlace his gipon. She knelt naked on the bed and tugged the garment over his head.

Wolf drew in a sharp breath as the material slipped off and he found himself looking directly at the soft mounds of her coral-tipped breasts. He swallowed hard but couldn't suppress the urge to reach out and touch the satiny flesh. He cupped the round globe, gently stroking the budding peak with his callused thumb. He felt Dara still, and then lean closer to his touch.

A thrill of excitement shot through Wolf, extinguishing all thoughts beyond the woman who clung to his shoulders. He buried his face in the valley between her breasts and inhaled her heady fragrance as he wrapped his arms about her trim waist. Another shudder passed over him when he felt her fingers running gently through his hair. Wolf squeezed his eyes tightly closed. Never in his wildest imagination had he ever envisioned the sensations her touch stirred to life within him. He throbbed with need, his sex hard and hot from the blood that had turned to molten lava in his veins.

Drawing in a ragged breath, he circled her waist with his hands and set her away from him. He looked up into her passion-softened eyes and said huskily, "Demoiselle, much more and I fear I'll be of little use to you after you finish removing my clothing. Now be done with it before I am."

A puzzled look passed over Dara's face, yet her demons were too busy urging her on to ask what Wolf meant. She quickly unlaced Wolf's undertunic and pulled it over his head. The breath caught in her throat at the sight of his wide bronze shoulders and chest. She couldn't stop herself from reaching out and running her hands over the smooth skin that covered muscles made of iron. Her fingers momentarily traced the markings on the medallion about Wolf's neck before they began to follow the ridge down his hard flat middle to the laces that secured his braies. Guided by her demons, Dara looked up at Wolf as she slowly released his throbbing manhood. He shifted his hips to accommodate her, and she slid the last garment down his hips and sinewy thighs.

The linen fell to the floor unheeded as Dara lowered her gaze to the tumescence she'd revealed. Gently she touched the satiny rod that proclaimed his desire and felt it surge beneath her hand. Her eyes jerked back to Wolf's face to find his burning gaze locked hungrily upon her breasts. Surrendering to the hot current that made her moist with need, she lay her hands upon his shoulders and straddled his lap, sinking down upon his turgid sex, burying him deep within her. She gasped her pleasure before eagerly claiming his mouth in a hot, wet kiss.

The muscles in Wolf's shoulders bunched as he captured her round bottom in the palms of his strong hands, bringing her hips into rhythm with his. He thrust upward and felt the quivering response deep within her as he touched her very core. Her lithe young body caressed his pulsating manhood, creating thunder and lightning in his blood. Her breasts pressed like hot coals into his chest, and her fingers bit into the flesh of his shoulders and back as she clung to him, riding him, urging him on.

She was the huntress Diana, and he her Pegasus. They soared into the realms of the gods, traversing the sultry velvet heavens, touching the sun together as his hard shaft penetrated her softness to the very depths of her femininity time and time again.

Dara felt the beginnings of ecstasy. The breath stilled in her throat at the wonder of it. The muscles in her thighs began to quiver, and her heart pounded like tribal drums in her ears. Instinctively she arched her back and met Wolf as he thrust upward to shatter the crystal prism that held all the colors of the universe. They exploded before her eyes like a thousand enchanting stars, showering her in sensations. Hot rapturous reds blended with glittering gold, bright exquisite silver merged with dark sensuous blue, and then brilliant yellow sunshine spilled through her, making her feel like a glorious rainbow of bliss.

Eyes wide with wonder, and trembling from the power of her own release, Dara watched the transformation on Wolf's face as she felt his hot essence fill her. She clung to him, savoring the knowledge that within her she had captured his seed and it would bear fruit.

Staggered by the thought, Dara slid her hand down Wolf's heaving, sweaty chest to the junction where their bodies joined. Slowly she raised her fingers and lay them against her taut belly. She looked in awe at the slightly convex plain that would soon bulge with life, and wondered how she could know that she had conceived Wolf's child. She had no answer. But in her heart she knew that her womb now harbored the beginning of life.

Wolf stilled as he watched Dara. Her soft expression revealed far more of her thoughts than she realized. Still bemused by their lovemaking, she was seeing into the future, a future with him, with his children. She was envisioning a fantasy that could never become a reality.

A chill passed over Wolf, raising gooseflesh on his sweaty skin. He lifted Dara away from him and set her on the bed. He drew the covers up and gently tucked them about her before he left her side. Unable to look at the woman who watched him with puzzled eyes, Wolf crossed to the window and stared out into the twilight of evening. He would give anything to tell Dara her dreams would come true. But he couldn't. Nor could he allow her to delude herself into believing that they could have a future. Once she knew of his heritage, or his lack of it, her feelings for him would change completely.

A heavy weight settled in Wolf's chest as he resigned himself to the inevitable. He glanced down at the medallion before he looked back to the woman sitting so still and quiet on the bed. Her expression bewildered, her luxurious hair tumbling about her shoulders in wild disarray, her lips swollen from his kisses, his brand blue upon her throat, she held the sheet up to her breasts. Though it had been only minutes since she'd pressed her nakedness eagerly against him, she now sought to shield her nudity from his view.

Wolf ground his teeth together in frustration and gripped the cold stone window facing until his knuckles whitened from the pressure. He struggled with a new burst of desire. Only minutes had passed since he'd held her in his arms and experienced the height of ecstasy, but he was fully ready to bed her again.

Wolf ran a hand through his tousled hair and cleared his throat. It was time. He couldn't go on like this. He had to tell Dara the truth of his past before she thought herself in love with him, before it was too late for her to keep her dignity. Before he humiliated himself by surrendering to the urge to take her into his arms and tell her he loved her.

Chapter 12

Though the night was warm, Dara shivered. The look on Wolf's face did little to soothe the disquiet his sudden departure from the bed had created. The glow left by their lovemaking had completely dissipated, leaving her feeling vulnerable and filled with mounting doubt. Wolf had left her so abruptly, it seemed he couldn't bear to touch her any longer. She didn't know what she'd done to cause him to react in such a manner. She'd only meant to please him. Another chill traveled up Dara's spine at the memory of her earlier faux pas. She'd also only meant to please him today when she'd acted as his chatelaine.

Dara lowered her eyes to the bed and nervously fidgeted with the furs that lay at her side. She'd allowed her demons free reign, and had in Wolf's eyes disgraced herself by acting the wanton.

Abashed at her own abandon, Dara's cheeks crimsoned. She'd acted out of love, wanting to give as much pleasure as she received. She glanced at Wolf through the curtain of her long lashes. His expression did little to comfort her. The unapproachable look on his face seemed to widen the chasm she'd created between them with her aggressive lovemaking.

Dara's insides cringed. She could nearly hear the Reverend Mother's stricture against giving way to the sins of the flesh. She'd said the devil preyed upon those too weak to resist his urgings. When they surrendered to the demands of their flesh, they became Satan's handmaidens. Lucifer used their bodies as instruments to spread evil in the guise of pleasure.

Capturing her lower lip between her teeth, Dara worried it uneasily. She could not believe that what she'd shared with Wolf was evil. It had been too beautiful. However, she didn't know how Wolf viewed her behavior. The Church taught men that women were weak creatures easily swayed to sin, preaching that men should beware of succumbing to the temptation of female wiles, for they risked losing their souls.

Dara's heart twisted as she looked up at the man she loved and saw the hurt look had returned to his eyes. Her words came softly, apologetically, from her heart, "I only wanted to please you."

Wolf didn't respond for a long moment. At last he nodded solemnly. "You pleased me well, Dara."

Unable to read his odd mood, Dara questioned, "Then you are not angry with me for the way I—I acted?"

An enigmatic smile touched Wolf's lips as he answered quietly, "Nay, little enemy. A man treasures a woman who is eager for his lovemaking."

A pensive frown marred Dara's brow as she studied the complex man who had claimed her heart and soul. "I don't understand. I feel I have done something terribly wrong, yet you will not tell me what it is."

Wolf's hand closed about the medallion. The feel of the symbols upon its surface did little to give him the peace of mind he sought. Nor did it reassure him that he was doing the right thing. Yet he knew there was no reason to prolong the inevitable. He had to put an end to this before either of them could be hurt further. Wolf's confusion made his voice cold and harsh. "I won't marry you."

Dara blinked at Wolf, bewildered by his sudden fierce avowal. "I haven't asked you to marry me, nor do I expect it."

Wolf gave a brisk nod. "Good. Then you understand that what we share is only temporary, that you and I have no future together. When your ransom is paid, you'll be returned to France."

Dara again clamped her teeth down on her lower lip to stay its sudden trembling. She'd known from the beginning she had no future with her English knight. The knowledge, however, did not stop the pain created when she heard it put into words.

Dara's eyes glistened with pent-up emotion as she asked the question she'd feared to have answered after learning Wolf had a daughter. Though she had refused to even voice it to herself, the words now slipped past her pale lips. "Is it Ellice's mother? Do you still love her?"

A muscle worked in Wolf's smooth-shaven cheek. "Had she lived, I would have made Jeanine my wife. But she has nothing to do with us."

Dara cringed visibly. Wolf still loved the woman who had given birth to his child.

The hurt look on Dara's beautiful face tied Wolf's insides into insidious knots. He muttered a profanity learned upon the battlefield and strode across the room. He had to keep his distance or find himself succumbing to the need to comfort her. He absently kicked at a dead coal that had fallen onto the hearth. The gray ash left by the heat and flame of the fire reminded him of how bleak his own life looked at the thought of losing Dara.

"Damn," he muttered, and looked back to where Dara still sat. "I am a mercenary who earns his living by fighting other men's wars." Wolf paused and drew in a bracing breath. "And I'm also the bastard that you so aptly called me. I have no family or name. I am Wolf of Phelan only by the strength of my arm in battle."

Puzzled by his outburst, Dara looked at the man who still stood gloriously naked. Her gaze moved over his perfect features, down the corded neck to the heavily muscled shoulders and to the plains of his wide chest where the medallion lay against his smooth, bronzed skin. The gleaming emblem held her gaze for a long moment, then she looked once more at Wolf's face. "I need not know of your lineage, Wolf. I gave myself to you, not to your sires or your ancestors. I care only for the man who held me so tenderly in his arms and made me into a woman."

Her words were worse than a dull, rusty dagger to his heart. He flinched visibly. God! How they hurt. She was saying all the right things, yet he knew he could never accept them. He had to make her realize that in time she would come to despise him for being base born. "I thought you understood. You are the one who said we came from different worlds, that we are enemies and can never be anything else."

"That was before," Dara said softly, her eyes reflecting all the love that filled her heart.

Wolf's dark brows knit. "Before what, demoiselle?"

Dara swallowed uneasily, and then answered honestly, "Before I knew I had fallen in love with you."

Wolf jerked as if he'd received a heavy fist to his middle. Nostrils flaring, he sucked in a sharp breath as the muscles across his belly contracted visibly. He now knew how prisoners felt when they were put to the rack. It took every bit of willpower he possessed to keep his features expressionless. " 'Tis only a maid's fantasy. Young women often suffer such delusions about the man they give their virginity. Guilt over their response to lovemaking makes them believe lust is love."

"Are you saying my love for you is only in my imagination?" Dara asked, suddenly seeing red. She'd opened her heart to this man, and now he ridiculed her by telling her that what she felt was merely lust in disguise.

Wolf nodded, hating every word he uttered. "Aye. 'Tis most common. In time, when you return to your home, you'll look back on our time together as it truly is, a few moments of stolen pleasure. And your husband need never know of our tryst. There are ways to fake your loss of virginity. They say a prick on the thumb with a needle works well to leave evidence of your purity."

"Get out," Dara ground out, her voice trembling with rage. She pointed to the door. "Get out before I show you how to fake your death. However, I fear I'll have to use a dagger to draw blood and it might in truth prove fatal."

Wolf crossed the chamber to where Dara had dropped his clothing. He picked them up and dressed himself with a self-assured air that didn't reflect the tension coiling in his belly. At last he stood clothed beside Dara's bed. He looked down into her furious little face and suppressed the urge to kiss her until she lay moaning her pleasure beneath him. Gruffly he said, "Lady, leave off your fantasies and your meddling in my life. While you are here, we can give each other pleasure, but remember, you will leave Phelan. This is not your home, nor is Ellice your daughter. I will not have my child suffer because you have deluded yourself into believing you are in love with me."

"You beast. I would never hurt Ellice, nor have I deluded myself on anything about you, my bastard knight. You are truly a bastard in every sense of the word. Now get out before I go completely mad," Dara seethed. She buried her face against her raised knees and pressed her clenched fists to her sides in an effort to control the urge to pound them against Wolf's chest until he denied his own cruel words.

"Lady, you are welcome to busy yourself about my kitchen and hall. You may meddle with the servants all you like, but I'll not have you interfere with my daughter."

Dara jerked her head up to stare incredulously at Wolf. "Interfere? You dim-witted brute! Ellice came to me. Though you may not be aware of how uncivilized you and your men live here in this great crumbling fortress, your daughter is. She is only five, but she realizes that she must learn manners to be a lady. You are living proof that manners are not born."

Dara's words made Wolf take pause. His forehead furrowed, drawing his dark brows close over the bridge of his narrow nose. "Is what you say true?"

"Aye. I have no need to lie. Ellice is a young girl, she needs and wants a woman's guidance."

Wolf felt his world close in about him. He knew Dara was right. His daughter needed the guidance of a lady to become a lady. He was torn in two different directions. By allowing Dara to continue to instruct his child, he could help and hurt Ellice at the same time. Suddenly weary to the bone, Wolf rubbed a hand over the back of his neck and nodded. "I will think upon it."

Wolf closed the door to Dara's chamber. He strode down to the hall and went directly to the ale table. He wanted to drink himself into oblivion. Perhaps then he'd be able to forget his past, and the future without the woman who had managed to bypass all the barriers to claim his heart.

For once at peace with one another and the world around them, Ox and Bull sat on the long bench in front of the fireplace, enjoying their own tankards of ale. The two brothers watched Wolf curiously as he downed two brimming tankards of the dark, potent brew before refilling the vessel and settling himself in the leather monk's chair reserved for his use. He didn't acknowledge his friends' presence but sat sipping his ale and staring moodily into the flickering flames of the fire.

Arching a dark brow, Ox flashed his brother a questioning look. Bull shrugged a silent reply before turning his attention back to his drink. Ox glanced once more at Wolf. He knew Wolf's mood had something to do with the Scot they'd captured that morning. His friend had been in high dudgeon when they'd finally caught up with him in the forest. Ox glanced toward the stairs and wondered what had transpired between Wolf and his captive. He could feel sympathy for the girl if Wolf had taken out his ill humor upon her.

Wolf's actions also puzzled Bull. He glanced about the hall and wondered what had displeased his friend so greatly. The Lady Dara had wrought changes within the castle that Bull had begun to believe impossible. For all the months they'd resided at Phelan before going to France, the laggard servants had acted incapable of cleaning the castle or preparing a decent meal for its master. The rushes had been rotten underfoot and filled with vermin, the food too tough to eat without several tankards of ale to wash it down. But after only one day under the Lady Dara's supervision, a sudden metamorphosis had taken place among the slothful minions. Following her directives, they had proved themselves capable of serving their master well.

Bull's stomach rumbled with anticipation at the smell wafting from the kitchen. The scent of herbs, roasting meat, and freshly baked bread set his mouth to watering. Rubbing the hard flat plain beneath his ribs, he looked at Wolf and grinned his pleasure at the prospect of a well-cooked meal. "Methinks the Lady Dara has done us a favor and seen to it that we will dine well tonight."

Ignoring Bull's remark, Wolf drained his tankard and held it up to be refilled. A serving maid quickly appeared from behind the wooden screen that shielded the kitchen doors from view and obeyed his silent command. She returned a full tankard to Wolf and dropped a quick curtsy before hurrying behind the screen to await further orders. Moodily, Wolf turned his attention to his drink.

Unable to draw Wolf out of his doldrums, Bull took a long sip of his own drink. After a thoughtful moment, he cocked his head to one side and ventured another direction for conversation. His handsome face alight with curiosity, he said, " 'Tis strange the way the Scot acted today after seeing your medallion."

Ox's head jerked up and he looked at his brother. He gave a slight shake of his curly head in an attempt to warn his brother away from the subject of the Scot and the medallion. However, it was too late. He watched Wolf stiffen and slowly turn his cold, black glare upon Bull. Ox felt like groaning aloud at his brother's ill-timed remark.

"What is it you find so strange, Seamus? That he was mad or that a bastard like me could be sired by a Scottish laird?"

Wolf's use of his Christian name sent a chill down Bull's back. He'd again unwittingly broached a sore subject. Cursing himself for every kind of a fool, Bull shook his head and tried to extricate himself from the mire his heedless words had created. "I meant no offense, Wolf. I only thought it strange that Laird Morgan would send such a coward on a reconnaissance mission." Bull feigned a chuckle and ventured to make amends. "And I'd not find it strange to learn your sire was of noble birth. You would make him proud be he English or Scot."

"Aye, so proud that the bastard never acknowledged

my existence. So proud that he and the noble bitch who gave birth to me felt such contempt for their offspring that they abandoned him, not caring whether he lived or died." Wolf's words were razor-edged with contempt.

Understanding far more about human emotions than his hapless brother, Ox intervened before Bull could further bury himself in a pit with his blundering tongue. "Do you think Laird Morgan still intends to lay claim to Phelan, knowing you've returned?"

Wolf's face was as glacial as the cliffs overlooking the sea on an icy winter's morn. He came out of his chair and looked down at the twins. His words were laced with venom. " 'Tis my fondest wish, for I will send him to the hell that he deserves." Wolf turned and stalked out of the hall.

Ox turned on his brother. "Damn me, but you are a great fool. How does the sole of your boot taste?"

Bull's features clouded. His dark brows knit across the narrow nose identical to his brother's except for the small scar Ox had left upon it during one of their frequent brawls. "Fool? I did nothing wrong. I meant only to lighten Wolf's mood, but all the angels in paradise couldn't alter his ill humor."

"Lighten his mood?" Ox rolled his eyes heavenward before shaking his head in disbelief. "Brother, I would suggest that you leave off trying to be an emissary of congeniality if what just transpired is any example of your diplomacy. Your wayward tongue has the power to sever friendships and start wars."

Bull seemed to swell with indignation. He glared mutinously at his brother. "Damn you, Ox. Leave off this harangue. I've had enough of your tongue to last me a lifetime."

"You'd do well to listen to my advice, brother. Had I not interrupted you earlier, I fear you'd now be in the dungeon or worse."

Bull's head seemed to sink into his shoulders. "I said leave off your tongue-lashing."

Ox eyed his brother belligerently. He'd not retreat when he was in the right. "You deserve far more than a tongue-lashing for your stupidity. Do you not realize what bedevils Wolf?"

Bull's control snapped and he came to his feet, his fists clenched at his sides. Fury blurred any thought to what was bedeviling his friend. All he wanted was to thrash the daylights out of his smart-mouthed brother. He growled, "I suggest you step outside, brother, or are you too big of a coward to call me stupid when I can do something about it?"

Ox came to his feet and marched to the door. He'd give his brother the whipping he sorely deserved. It was time Bull learned some manners and used his head for more than a place to set his helm. Ox swung the door open and walked down the steps to the bailey. Bull followed close upon his heel. As Ox turned to prepare himself for Bull's assault, his brother launched himself upon him from the steps. Ox tumbled backward from the force of his brother's weight. His breath left him in a great whoosh as he rolled with Bull, pummeling his brother with his fists. The twins' peace with each other had once more come to an end, and they turned their attention to their second love, battle.

Chilled by the misty dawn air that filtered into her chamber through the narrow window, Dara absently rubbed at her arms and drew the blanket closer about her shoulders. Circles of weariness shadowed the dewy skin beneath her luminescent eyes, yet she could find no rest. After Wolf's departure the previous evening, she'd paced the chamber for most of the night, cursing and raging against the fates that had thrown her headlong into Wolf's life. She had foolishly allowed herself to fall in love with him, fully knowing there could never be a future for them. As he'd reminded her last eve, they were enemies.

Dry-eyed and unable to sleep, Dara sat huddled in the chair, watching the horizon slowly lighten from stygian blue to a deep slate-gray before paling into mauve and rose. A streak of gold shattered the last hold the night had upon the land, drenching the tops of the tall pines in brilliant sunlight. Dara drew her gaze away from the morn blooming across the landscape and looked back at the heavily timbered four-poster where she'd given herself so wantonly to Wolf. She couldn't force herself to lie on it again. Memories made the soft mattress into stone.

Dara hugged the blanket closer and cast a weary glance about the chamber, as if guarding herself against another assault of memories that had tortured her during the long, dark hours of the night. It hurt too much to think, to keep remembering Wolf's rejection and the confirmation of his love for Ellice's mother.

Dara had thought she'd come to terms with herself. However, in the light of morning, the pain still pierced her as fresh and new as the moment Wolf uttered the words that rent her heart asunder.

Drawing in a shaky breath, she pushed herself to her feet. She knew after last night, she could not remain at Phelan. She had to find a way to escape before she found herself groveling at Wolf's feet, begging for his affection like a lap dog. She had exposed her deepest emotions last night, and he'd made them seem like a childish fantasy. She could endure no more. She'd turned her back on everything she held dear to follow her heart, only to have it destroyed.

Dara's lower lip began to quiver, and her eyes burned with the need to weep. The blanket fell about her bare feet as she pressed the balls of her hands against her eyes. She refused to cry again. She'd shed the last of her tears in the wee hours of the morning. The time for crying had passed, as all things did, and now she had to decide her own course of action. She had to leave Phelan, but she had no earthly idea where she could go in this foreign land. She had no idea where she might seek refuge.

Brushing her tangled hair back from her face, she picked up her gown and slipped it over her head. She stepped into her slippers and drew in a resolved breath. She could take only what she wore upon her back. The things she left behind were like the heart she carried within her, merely ragged pieces, good for nothing more.

Quietly, Dara crossed the chamber and opened the door. She peered out into the shadowy passageway, and then moved stealthily toward the stairs. Her feet made no sound upon the stones as she descended. Afraid she'd be apprehended by the guards on night duty, she paused in the shadows of the stairwell to ascertain their whereabouts. Her gaze swept over the great hall where Wolf's most trusted men and household servants lay on pallets, sleeping soundly.

Whistling, fluttering, whining, and muttering snores filled the air, creating a continuous drone that easily covered the sound of Dara's passage as she crept between the pallets toward the tall iron-bound doors. She flashed a cautious look about, and then, without waiting to wonder why there were no guards stationed at the entrance, she eased open the portal and slipped out into the cool dawn.

The bailey was still, no one stirred, even the roosters had as yet to rouse from their night's rest to awaken the other livestock. Dara stayed close to the walls until she reached the gates. For protection against an attack at night, the portcullis had been lowered. Yet the small door cut into the gate opened easily from within. Her heart drumming frantically against her ribs, Dara raised the bar and quickly slipped outside. She was free of Castle Phelan. Taking no time to savor her escape, she dashed across the uncultivated field to the nearest trees. Hiding herself from view and breathing heavily from exertion, she sank down upon a bed of dew-dampened moss to collect her wits enough to decide what she should do next.

Dara glanced at the tall granite walls of Castle Phelan. She couldn't believe the ease with which she'd escaped.

She pressed her lips into a resolute line, determined not to dwell upon the shattered heart that she also left within Castle Phelan. Wolf had made his feelings clear. Now her only hope was to find a sanctuary that would keep him from reclaiming her as his captive. Dara rose to her feet and squared her shoulders. She turned north, unaware that she would soon cross the border into Scotland.

By late afternoon she began to feel the consequences of her stubbornness the previous night. She'd refused to go down to the hall to sup with the man who had rejected her love. Nor had she tasted the food he'd had sent up to her on a tray. Now her stomach growled with hunger. She hadn't eaten since the midmorning meal the previous day. And the trembling that beset her knees proved that she should have filled her stomach before setting out on this journey into the hinterlands of this barbaric country.

However, Dara hadn't planned that far ahead. She'd acted upon impulse. She hadn't stopped to consider anything beyond wanting to get as far away from Wolf as possible before he realized she'd fled. Hopefully, he'd take her absence at the midmorning meal as a show of stubbornness, and not know of her flight until late in the evening when it was time to sup again.

Hungry and thirsty, Dara pushed her way through a thicket of alder bushes. The sharp-toothed leaves prickled her skin and snagged at her gown, yet she was heedless of the discomfort, as the sound of gurgling water drew her like a magnet.

Thinking only of appeasing her burning thirst, Dara sank down on her knees and cupped the water in her hands, greedily slurping from her makeshift vessel. The crystal liquid trickled down her chin and fell onto the taut material across her breasts, creating an ever-widening circle of moisture. At last, her thirst satisfied, she wiped her mouth on the back of her hand and got to her feet. She froze instantly at the sight of the tall, dark-haired man mounted upon a black stallion across the stream.

Ebony eyes raked over her, lingering appreciatively upon the swell of her breasts and the soft curve of her hips before locking once more with her frightened, sapphire gaze. A small smile curled up the corners of his shapely lips. " 'Tis legend that these forests are full of wood sprites, but you're the first I've ever seen in my long life."

Dara's heart slammed against her breastbone in relief. For a moment she'd thought the man Wolf. The stranger's resemblance to her captor was uncanny. He possessed the same black eyes and similar features. As the shock began to fade, Dara realized the man was also much older than Wolf. His smile hewed age lines about his eyes and mouth. And where Wolf's hair was as blue-black as a raven's wing, the years had altered this man's raven locks to a salt-and-pepper gray. The stranger was a large man, but Wolf's youth gave him a more powerful build.

Nervously, Dara looked up and swallowed uneasily.

A stranger in a strange land, she knew little of the people who inhabited these isles. Dara instinctively took a step back. This man, though smiling at her, could well be a bandit set to rob and murder. She took another step away.

"Do wood sprites not speak?" he asked, arching a dark brow quizzically.

"They speak when they have something to say," Dara answered, flashing another uneasy glance about for a means of escape. The thick alders prevented her from bolting in the opposite direction, and to each side of her was only the open field that the stream meandered through like a blue-silver snake.

The man folded his arms over the pommel of his saddle, relaxing as he leaned forward. " 'Tis wise. People ofttimes allow their tongues to run away with them and say things that they do not mean."

The sound of another horse approaching cut short further conversation. The man looked up, and his face lit with pleasure at the sight of a young woman riding toward them like the wind. Her windblown hair fell about her shoulders like a mantle of silk as she drew her mount to a skittering halt. Her sweet laughter filled the afternoon air at the stern look her father sought to bestow upon her. Her face rosy with excitement, her dark eyes dancing with mirth, she held up a gloved hand to stay her father's censure. "Papa, don't fuss. Violet wanted to run. And you know I didn't have the heart to deny her."

"Kirsten, your animals are going to be the death of you or me. Which one of us, I'm not quite sure as of yet. But I suspect it'll be me. My poor old heart will give out from all the worry of your wild rides."

Chuckling softly at her father's exaggeration, Kirsten looked at the young woman across the stream. Her smile faded as her gaze swept over the girl's tattered gown. Yet what touched Kirsten's heart was the look in the woman's sapphire eyes. She reminded Kirsten of a hurt, frightened animal caught in a trap. Kirsten glanced back to her father and saw that the girl's wild, desperate look had touched him as well. "Papa, have you played the great bear and frightened this poor girl nearly to death? She acts speechless."

Laird Morgan turned twinkling eyes back to Dara. "Nay child. She is a wood sprite. They do not speak unless they have something to say."

Kirsten's sweet laughter spilled into the late afternoon air. She looked once more at Dara. "Do wood sprites have names?"

"They do. I am called Dara."

Kirsten nodded. The girl's accented English indicated that she had come from foreign shores; however, Kirsten accepted her reticence about revealing too much of herself. " 'Tis a nice name for a wood sprite." She glanced toward her father. "Now that we know wood sprites have names, I wonder if they also get hungry, Papa?" Kirsten looked back to Dara. "Could I perhaps persuade you to come back to Morgan Keep to partake of our evening meal with me and my father, Laird Angus Morgan?"

Recognizing the Morgan name, but too weary to recall where she'd heard it before, and too relieved by the girl's generous invitation to refuse her hospitality, Dara returned the smile. She suddenly felt safe. "This wood sprite would be most grateful for your hospitality, my lady."

"Then Dara Woodsprite, you are welcome. Come, you may ride back with me on Violet. And you can tell me all about how it feels to be a wood sprite and exactly what a wood sprite does. I've heard all the old people talk about them, but until today I didn't really believe they existed." Kirsten smiled mischievously at Dara and winked.

"I will gladly tell you all the wood sprite secrets that I know, my lady," Dara said, picking her way across the brook on a path of several large stones peeking above the water's surface.

"How exciting. And after you tell me your secrets, I'll show you some of the creatures who share your forest with you."

"Does that mean we have another furry guest within the donjon?" Laird Morgan asked, dismounting to assist Dara up onto his daughter's horse.

Kirsten flashed her father a loving look and nodded. "You'll love him, Papa. And I promise, he'll not bite your toes too hard when you pass on your way to bed."

"Then 'twill be better than the vixen," Laird Morgan grumbled, grinning good-naturedly. He rubbed at the calf of his leg. "She didn't appreciate my stepping on her tail and decided to repay in kind by taking a nip out of my leg."

Dara couldn't stop her own smile at the banter between father and daughter. She felt she'd fallen into another world, a world where there were no enemies, a world that knew only love.

Harlow Norton's eyes widened and he quickly stepped into the shadows of the stable as Laird Morgan and Lady Kirsten rode through the gates with their guest. He blinked several times to clear his vision, yet when he looked again at the scene, nothing had changed. The girl riding behind Lady Kirsten was the Wolf's woman. He'd watched her ride through the gate of Castle Phelan within its master's entourage. And she'd entered the castle with Wolf's most trusted henchmen, the two giant twins who had been with him on the field yesterday.

Harlow thoughtfully rubbed his chin, wondering at what game the Wolf now played. Had he sent the girl to spy on those within Morgan Keep, or to reconnoiter its defenses as he himself had done at Phelan?

Harlow couldn't answer his own questions. But he did know a bad fish when he smelled one. The girl riding with Lady Kirsten, no matter how much she looked like a tattered angel, was up to no good. Wolf had sent her here to do his dirty work.

At the thought, Harlow's freckled face flushed a deep red with ire. He'd not allow the vixen to bring harm down upon Laird Morgan or anyone within the Morgan household. He'd see that the wench's true reason for coming to Morgan Keep was exposed if he had to watch her night and day. His family had served the Morgans faithfully for generations, and he'd not be the first Norton to fail in his duty.

Harlow watched Laird Morgan, Lady Kirsten, and the newcomer enter the castle. He'd have to await the right moment to tell Laird Morgan of what he knew. It'd not do to let the wench know he suspected her of spying for the Wolf.

The Wolf, Harlow mused, again running a hand over his chin. The man had created a quandary in Harlow's life. He didn't know what to believe. He knew what his eyes had told him. The Wolf wore the Morgan medallion. But he also knew what Laird Morgan had said. Harlow shook his head and turned his gaze southward. It seemed the Wolf had not accepted the thought of having Morgan blood any more than Laird Morgan had accepted the fact that Harlow had seen the second medallion about his enemy's neck.

Lord! Such a quandary, Harlow mused, shaking his head. He might never get the puzzle solved. Harlow quirked his head and looked once more at the donjon of Morgan Keep. His eyes narrowed. The arrival of the dark-haired wench might prove beneficial after all. She might come in handy in helping him find the answers he sought. She might also be the bait that Laird Morgan needed to draw the Wolf into a trap.

Harlow smiled smugly, tucked his hands into his belt and rolled back on the heels of his feet, happily planning his first meeting with the defanged Wolf. It would be far different than the encounter yesterday.

Chapter 13

"I think you are a very lucky beastie," Kirsten said, lifting the young wolf onto the table. She'd laid out the medicines she needed to help heal the wound he'd received from a villager who had found the pup trying out his hunting skills upon a flock of sheep. "Aye, Lucky is a fitting name after all you've survived." Kirsten noted the slight wag of the animal's tail and rubbed his dark head affectionately. "I'm glad you like your new name. And in the future you'd do well to avoid the village flocks. I might not be around to save you the next time."

Turning her attention to the task at hand, Kirsten glanced at the seeping wound. Pleased to see that there was no drainage of yellow pus, she nodded her satisfaction. Dipping her fingers into the wooden bowl that held the healing herbs, she applied another poultice of goose grease, boiled crushed turnips, comfrey, and wood sage to the pup's hindquarter, and then wrapped it with a linen bandage.

Awed, Dara observed Kirsten from her vantage point near the window. The wolf would allow only Kirsten near him. His white-fanged snarl and angry growl kept the residents of Morgan Keep at a safe distance.

Watching Kirsten care for her wild patient was like watching one of the magicians that frequented the village fairs. She was amazing. She could take a snapping, snarling beast and make it as gentle as a lamb with only a few softly spoken words.

Dara saw the young wolf look up at Kirsten through iridescent green eyes. And she could have sworn that he smiled as he rolled his long pink tongue out of his mouth and swiped it affectionately across Kirsten's face.

Kirsten's easy laughter filled the air as she wiped the moisture from the tip of her nose and cheeks. She patted the dark head comfortingly. "You'll soon be well, Lucky. The wound is healing nicely, and within a few days you'll be ready to go back to your family in the woods."

"How do you do it, Kirsten? I've never seen anyone who could tame wild animals as you do," Dara said, keeping her own distance from the animal.

Kirsten looked at the girl she now claimed as a friend. She smiled as she stroked the pup's head. "I don't tame them. Nor do I do anything different than I did for you, Dara. They sense that I just want to help them. They also know they have nothing to fear from me. Instinct tells them they can trust me as a friend."

Dara understood. She knew exactly how the young wolf felt. Kirsten had a way of making one feel safe. She gave of her friendship without questions or conditions. She also had the most loving nature of anyone Dara had ever encountered. Kirsten's heart seemed large enough to encompass the world. In the short time Dara had known her, she had never spoken an unkind word about anyone or anything. In Dara's view, Kirsten was as close to being a saint as even the Reverend Mother could wish of a mortal soul. Kirsten saw no evil in others, only the good.

Guilt pricked at Dara's conscience. She turned and looked out the window overlooking the courtyard. Eyes turned inward, she didn't see the men sweating and grunting under the afternoon sun as they practiced with their lances and swords in mock battle. She voiced the question that had been niggling at her since Laird Morgan and Kirsten had taken her into their home three days before. "Why have you not asked me about myself?"

Kirsten lifted her patient and placed him on the floor, and he immediately found a cool dark corner to curl up in. She dusted her hands together, and then busied herself putting her medicines away in a leather-bound box. "I want to know only what you would have me know, Dara. And when you are ready, you will tell me."

"Did you ever think that I might be an enemy to you and your family? Or that I might be a thief or murderer set to slit your throat while you sleep?"

Kirsten shook her dark head and laughter twinkled in her ebony eyes. "Nay, Dara Woodsprite. Wood sprites do no harm to those who find them. And you have an honest face, though I also suspect it comes with a stubborn streak behind it."

Dara cocked a delicately arched brow at her friend. "Why do you think I'm stubborn?"

Kirsten lifted a shoulder in a slight shrug. "I suspect it's because you've never asked us to take you back to your home or to notify your relatives of your whereabouts. And you hold tenaciously to your secrets. Wouldn't you call that stubborn?"

"Were I in your place, I'd called it suspicious."

Kirsten snapped the brass latch closed and looked up. "How so?" she asked.

"Because anyone without something to hide would have been honest and told you why they were wandering around, lost in the forest," Dara said, shifting uneasily.

"Perhaps you're right, but I prefer to believe that she was too frightened at the time and needed to learn to trust us. I also believe that someone or something has hurt her very badly, because I often see the pain in her eyes."

"You're far too astute," Dara said quietly. She turned her gaze out the window once more. It was hard not to think of Wolf. He was in her every waking hour as well as her dreams. "And 'tis not easy to speak about."

Kirsten crossed to Dara and took her hand. "Come, friend. It will be far easier to speak freely in the garden where we can't be overheard. 'Tis also pleasing to the senses, with the sweet smell of roses filling the air."

Dara quietly walked with Kirsten down the long, cool corridor and out into the midday sun. Kirsten led her to a bench carved from stone that stood in the shade of a large oak tree. They sat down and for a long, indolent moment just savored the sweet fragrance of rose and lilac drifting upon the current of the gentle breeze. At last Kirsten looked at her friend and smiled reassuringly. "Do you think you can tell me about it now?"

Dara's eyes misted. She raised a hand to cover her quivering lips and swallowed back the pain that tightened her throat. Drawing in a deep breath, she looked directly at Kirsten. "There are reasons I've been unable to tell you who I am and how I came to be here."

Kirsten smiled sagely. "Papa and I suspected as much, but I'd not allow him to bombard you with questions."

"And I thank you for your understanding. But it's time that you knew the truth."

Sitting with hands gracefully folded in her lap, Kirsten remained silent, patiently awaiting Dara's explanation.

"I am Dara of Rochambeau of France. I was brought to England as the captive of Wolf of Phelan."

Kirsten's eyes widened in surprise. She flashed a quick glance about the garden to ensure that no one had overheard Dara's revelation before she leaned forward and whispered, " 'Tis our secret, Dara. No one else at Morgan Keep should learn of your true identity. It would serve you ill, for the Wolf of Phelan lays claim to land that rightly belongs to Papa."

A brick of lead seemed to drop sickeningly into the pit of Dara's stomach as the memory that had been hiding in the shadows of her mind since first hearing the Morgan name now exploded into full light. The night of her arrival at Phelan, Wolf and his men had discussed Laird Morgan during the evening meal. Dara managed to suppress her groan of frustration before it escaped her throat. She had been befriended by Wolf's enemies. The irony of the situation was that she should be glad. However, she felt no joy in the fact that she had found shelter with the very man who hoped to destroy Wolf.

Kirsten's next words jerked Dara back to the present. "You must promise me that you'll not tell Papa who you are."

Puzzled by Kirsten's insistence, Dara asked, "Would your father harm me because I am Wolf's hostage?"

Kirsten shook her head. "Nay. Papa would not harm you, but he might decide to use you to bring the Wolf to him."

Dara's bitter laughter floated over the garden. Her eyes misted as she looked at Kirsten and shook her head. " 'Twould serve no purpose. Wolf would not come. He is glad to be rid of me."

Hearing the pain in Dara's voice, Kirsten finally understood the look she'd seen in her friend's eyes in the past days. She reached out and took Dara's hand, giving it a comforting squeeze. "You love him, don't you?"

Dara lowered her eyes and captured her lower lip between her teeth as she nodded.

"Then why did you run away?"

Dara raised her eyes once more to meet Kirsten's

sympathetic gaze and answered honestly, "It hurt too much to know he cared only for the coin he'd receive from my ransom." Dara glanced toward the tall granite walls of Morgan Keep and drew in a steadying breath. "Would Laird Morgan help me find passage back to my home? I need to reach France as soon as possible."

Kirsten ignored the question. "Did you tell Sir Wolf of your feelings?"

Dara pulled her hand free and came to her feet, too agitated by her memories to remain still any longer. Her hands balled into fists at her sides as she fought against the new wave of agony washing over her. She looked down at her friend, and her tone reflected her suffering as she said, "*Oui*, I told him of my love, but he said it was only an illusion."

"The beast," Kirsten said, her own heart hurting for her friend.

"Nay. Wolf is no beast. He is a man who still loves the woman who died giving birth to his daughter," Dara said. "He did not ask me to fall in love with him. He was honest about his feelings from the beginning. I was the fool who followed her heart's urgings. And I will be the one who pays the price for it." Dara didn't add that she believed she already carried the consequences of her love for Wolf within her womb. An innocent like Kirsten would never understand her perversity where Wolf was concerned. Dara knew no wrong or right when she was in his arms.

"You defend your captor well, Dara of Rochambeau," Kirsten said, intently watching her friend's expression. She had to know exactly how Dara felt before she could help her.

"I speak only the truth. Wolf is a good man, a true friend and loving father."

Her curiosity piqued, Kirsten sought to draw Dara out about the man who might be her half brother. " 'Tis said he is a bastard who has no family. 'Tis also said he is a mercenary who sells his sword to the highest bidder."

Dara nodded. " 'Tis true. But that does not make him less noble. He has gained his standing by the strength of his sword in battle and his honor upon the field. He knows little of courtly ways, but has earned the respect of his king and his men."

"If Wolf of Phelan is so noble, how can he claim what rightfully belongs to my father?" Kirsten said.

"Wolf claims what is his, nothing more. He earned Phelan with his sweat and blood. And he'll die defending it for his daughter."

Intrigued suddenly by the thought that she might have a niece, Kirsten asked, "What is the child like?"

Dara's gaze moved over Kirsten's features. "Ellice has eyes the same color as you and your father, as does Wolf." Dara frowned, suddenly puzzled by the resemblance of Wolf and his daughter to the Morgans. "Did I not know better, I would think you of the same blood. The resemblance is uncanny, especially between Laird Morgan and Wolf."

Kirsten's heart seemed to still breathlessly within the cage of her ribs. Then it began a rapid tattoo as excitement bubbled inside her like a newly opened flagon of sparkling wine. Dara's description of her captor had convinced her that she had to learn the truth about Wolf of Phelan. Somehow she had to make certain the man her father believed his enemy was not in truth his son.

Kirsten looked up at Dara and couldn't stop her question. "Does Sir Wolf wear a medallion about his neck with the symbols of a star, a thistle, and a sword engraved upon it?"

"He wears a medallion, but I know not what is carved upon it," Dara answered, wondering at Kirsten's sudden interest in Wolf. "Why do you ask?"

"One of my father's men mentioned it," Kirsten answered evasively. Until she knew exactly how to ascertain Wolf's identity, she didn't want to elaborate further. It wouldn't do for her father to learn of her intentions. For now, she would keep Dara's identity and her suspicions to herself.

"Will your father help me get back to France? I have vital information for King John," Dara said, abruptly turning the conversation back to the question Kirsten had avoided earlier.

"I do not know," Kirsten finally answered. "In time, perhaps. But for the moment, 'tis best for you to remain at Morgan Keep. You are safe from harm here."

Dara glanced toward the towering stone walls and then back to her friend. Kirsten believed the walls of Morgan Keep could protect them from anything. But she knew better. When Navarre learned of her escape, she feared nothing could save her from him. As Ox had made her aware, her cousin couldn't allow her to reveal what she knew of his intrigues. And had it not been for Wolf's constant protection, she seriously doubted that she'd be alive now to plan her return to France. Navarre was a viper whose venomous schemes reached far and wide.

Wolf's gaze shifted from the distant horizon to the base of the cliffs where the cold, gray-green waves of the North Sea ate relentlessly at the strip of narrow beach. He let out a low curse, venting his frustration at the lack of success he'd had locating his beautiful hostage. He'd traversed every inch of Phelan, seeking any sign of her passage. But no twig or footprint gave clue to the direction she'd traveled when she disappeared from Phelan.

Dark eyes reflecting his worry, deep lines edging his full-lipped mouth and brow, Wolf turned his destrier back in the direction of Castle Phelan. It had been nearly four days since he'd gone to Dara's bedchamber to find her missing, her bed undisturbed. After a night spent swilling down ale, it had taken most of the following morning for him to rid himself of the ache left in his head by the bitter brew. And another few hours to gain the courage to venture back into the lioness's den for another emotional mauling. He'd finally climbed up the stairs, determined not to allow Dara to go on sulking. She'd not come down the previous night for the evening meal, nor had she touched the tray he'd had sent up to the chamber. He'd been set to carry her downstairs if that was what it took to prevent her from making herself ill just to spite him. However, he'd not had the chance to prove anything to Dara. She had vanished, seemingly into thin air. No one had seen her leave the castle, and the guards had denied leaving their posts during the night, even for the call of nature.

Wolf glanced at the man riding at his side. "It would seem we just imagined the minx ever existed. No man or woman can travel without leaving at least some sign of passage."

"Aye. And in time we'll find the Lady Dara's trail," Ox said in an attempt to bolster his friend's flagging spirits. "Bull and some of the men are still scouring the forest north of Phelan."

Wolf pushed back his coif and wiped the sweat from his brow. Tiny lines creased the corners of his eyes as he turned his gaze north and squinted against the mid-afternoon sunlight bearing down upon them unmercifully. "I pray we do. The wench doesn't realize the danger she could find herself in should she fall into the wrong hands. 'Tis only a few miles to the border. Dara believed herself mistreated under my protection, but she knows nothing of ill use until she finds herself Morgan's prisoner. Her life would be of little value to the man. The bastard would readily ransom her to Navarre once he learned her identity."

A chill passed over Wolf at the thought of what would become of Dara should Navarre get his hands on her. Her death would be imminent, for the man could not let her live without jeopardizing his own life.

Ox studied his friend's weary, anxious face. Wolf had slept and eaten little since Lady Dara's disappearance. He'd been like a man possessed. When not out searching for her, he'd stalked about the hall, his mood as black as the night that prevented him from continuing his quest. He'd tried to hide his feelings by using every excuse under the sun for his combing the countryside. But Ox had seen through all the excuses; however, he feared Wolf had as yet to admit the truth to himself.

"You've allowed the wench to worm her way into your heart," Ox stated quietly, and watched Wolf flinch as if his words carried a physical punch to Wolf's gut.

Wolf's long, tapered fingers clenched about the reins, and his knuckles whitened from the pressure of his grip. He didn't look at Ox, but kept his gaze trained on the horizon as he nodded.

"I suspect the wench has finally trapped the Wolf," Ox said sympathetically. His heart went out to his friend. Dara considered Wolf her enemy.

"My feelings do not alter anything. Once I find Dara, I will ransom her as soon as it is safely feasible."

Puzzled, Ox's frown knit his dark brows. "Surely you jest?"

Wolf flashed Ox a pained look and slowly shook his head. The afternoon sun caught in the silken strands of his hair, gleaming a rich blue-black. "Nay. There is no future for me with the Lady Dara. I am a base-born bastard, and she is of noble birth."

Ox's frown deepened, and his sky-blue eyes seemed to kindle with annoyance at his friend's thickheadedness. The ghosts still haunting Wolf's self-esteem would make him send the woman he loved away. Ox had to find a way to stop Wolf before it was too late. "What in the devil does that have to do with anything if you two love each other?"

Wolf ignored Ox's question. "I've made my decision, and nothing anyone can say will change it. Dara and I came to an understanding. She knows there is no future for us, and she accepts it."

Ox's eyes widened in surprise. "You mean you told the Lady Dara the same nonsense that you've told me today?"

"Aye," Wolf answered, glancing at his friend.

Ox rolled his eyes heavenward and slowly shook his dark curly head in exasperation. "You and Bull make a pair. Thankfully you both are warriors, because you would ill serve our king as ambassadors."

Wolf's forehead wrinkled, and his brows lowered to shadow his ebony eyes. "I see little comparison. Bull has a tendency to put his foot into his mouth all the way to his hip."

Eyes sparkling with annoyance, Ox glowered at Wolf. He could complain about his brother's lack of tact, but he didn't like others doing so. Bull was just like him in face and form, and anyone who insulted his brother, also insulted him. A muscle twitched at the side of his mouth as he said, "Do you not oft' taste your own toes, Sir Wolf? Could your own lack of diplomacy be what made the Lady Dara take flight?"

A hand seemed to grasp Wolf's heart and squeeze. His breath froze in his lungs. He'd tried to avoid facing the truth, but Ox appeared determined to make him look into the mirror of his own deeds. Wolf pressed his lips into a thin line, stubbornly refusing to accept the blame. However, he couldn't hide from himself. In his heart he knew he'd intentionally hurt Dara to drive her away from him. He'd rejected the love she'd offered so innocently, fearing he couldn't hold on to it after the first flush of new love wore off. And in turn, his fear of being hurt had made Dara flee from him, and could end up costing her her life should he not find her before his enemies did.

Wolf flashed Ox a sheepish, apologetic look. "You are a good friend, Sean MacDonald. You've made me confront my own culpability. And I don't like what I see. I threw away the very thing I've sought all of my life, a woman who cares nothing about my heritage, a woman who accepts me as I am without the glory of titles and wealth."

Relieved, Ox grinned. "You are no pauper, Wolf of Phelan. And you have been knighted by King Edward the Third himself."

" 'Tis true that my purse does not lack for coin. My campaigns for Edward have assured my wealth, and in time I will see Phelan rebuilt to its former glory. But for now, all I need to make my life complete is the woman I love. And I pray we will find her safe and sound."

"We will find her, Wolf. You know Bull's tenaciousness won't let him leave a stone unturned. He's like a badger. If anyone can find Lady Dara, it will be my headstrong brother."

Wolf's lips twitched at the thought of his friend rooting about like a badger. Ox was right. Bull was too bullheaded to surrender to defeat. He fought, made love, and lived his life with the obstinacy of his namesake. Wolf glanced at his friend and mentally added, As did his brother.

Wolf saw Bull's tethered mount the moment they rode through Phelan's gates. Eager to hear his news, he reined his destrier to a halt, tossed the reins to the stable boy and quickly dismounted. Without a backward glance at Ox, he strode up the steps toward the castle doors, barely taking notice of the man in rags who lingered there.

"Alms, Sir Wolf. I ask for only a piece of bread to stave off my hunger," the beggar pleaded, sinking down in front of Wolf on the steps.

"Out of my way," Wolf growled, annoyed to find his path blocked by the ragged man. On any other day his own past would have made him take the time to question the beggar of his needs. As with all who came seeking food and rest at Wolf's door, the man would not be turned away. He'd be fed and clothed, as well as offered a haystack in the stable for use as his bed until he felt able to leave Phelan. However, today Wolf's thoughts were upon Dara and the man who might have information about her whereabouts.

"Please, I am willing to work for a few morsels of food to fill my stomach."

Wolf flashed an exasperated look over his shoulder to his friend. "Ox, take him to the kitchen and see that Cook gives him food. Once he's fed, tell Cook to put him to work." Without awaiting an answer, Wolf walked into the castle.

Ox looked at the beggar, wondering at the appraising look the man gave Wolf from shrewd, sapphire eyes. It piqued Ox's curiosity. Making a closer inspection, Ox's narrowed gaze swept over the beggar, taking note of the ragged garments he wore. A frown plowed a path across Ox's forehead. Though rent with holes, the beggar's tattered mantle was constructed from fine cloth and looked nearly new.

Ox's face darkened with suspicion. The man's skin, though smudged with dirt, lacked the sickly pallor of a pauper who suffered from hunger. Nor did his eyes possess the glazed, beaten look that often haunted the eyes of the hungry vagabonds who traversed the countryside in search of charity.

No, Ox thought. The man certainly didn't fit the mold of the beggars who had come to Phelan in the past. Ox gave a mental shrug. He didn't have the time to worry about a beggar at present, no matter how unusual he seemed. He had to be about his own business of helping his friend find Lady Dara. Putting aside his misgivings, Ox said, "Come. Cook will see you fed as Sir Wolf has ordered. When you've finished with your work, you may make your bed in the stables tonight."

"Thank you for your generosity, Sir Knight. The Lord has seen fit to bless me by leading me to this house," the beggar said, dropping easily into pace behind Ox.

" 'Tis Sir Wolf you owe your thanks. I just do his bidding, like all who serve him faithfully and well," Ox said, leading the way to the kitchens.

The beggar smiled as his calculating gaze came to rest on Ox's back. He'd heard of Wolf of Phelan's generosity to those who came hungry to his door. The man's weakness for those less fortunate than himself was becoming well known to the people who traveled the roads.

Paul Rochambeau suppressed the urge to laugh aloud. It had been so easy to gain entrance to Wolf's domain. God had been on his side when he'd had the idea to disguise himself as a beggar. And if his good fortune held, he and his sister would soon be on their way home to France.

Dara, I'll soon have you free, Paul thought as he glanced up at the tall, imposing walls that cast long shadows from the evening sun. He'd returned to Rochambeau to find his home in total disrepair and his sister taken to England for ransom only a few days earlier. He'd gone immediately to see King John to seek his help in rescuing Dara. However, he'd found no aid from France's monarch. King John had refused to loan him the ransom and had accused his sister of treason, swearing he'd have her executed if she ever returned to France. Destitute and left with no other recourse if he wanted to save his sister, Paul had come to England to try to help Dara escape her captor.

As Ox led the way into the kitchen, Paul slid his hand beneath his mantle to the sheathed dirk that lay hidden within the folds of his clothing. The razor-sharp edge of the blade he'd honed would be of little use against a great number of men, but it could be swift and silent if it became necessary to kill those who held his sister hostage.

Ox gave Wolf's orders to the cook and turned toward the passageway that led into the main hall. He paused at the entrance and glanced once more at the stranger. The man seemed a simple beggar, but Ox couldn't rid himself of the notion that he had come to Phelan for more than a few morsels of food and a bed made of hay.

Ox once more shrugged the thought aside. When the Lady Dara was again safely at home at Phelan, he could turn his attention to laying his suspicions about the beggar to rest.

"Sir Ox," the cook called before Ox could make his exit. "Has Sir Wolf found the Lady Dara?"

"Nay. But he will," Ox answered with far more confidence than he felt.

Cook nodded and turned to the loaf of bread the baker had just turned out onto the table. He sliced off a large chunk and handed it to the beggar, who had sidled onto the rough-hewn bench that the servants used when they took their meals.

Though his stomach had suddenly tied itself into knots, Paul took a large bite of the freshly baked bread, and then washed it down with a slurp of water from the cup Cook had set on the table for his use. It would not do to act as if he were not hungry. Beggars were always hungry. Paul took another bite of the bread, thoughtfully chewing the simple fair as he considered the cook's question. Dara was no longer being held at Phelan. Paul frowned. The news did him little good, for it seemed no one knew his sister's whereabouts. That concerned Paul. Dara had always managed to take care of herself at Rochambeau. This, however, was a foreign country, a country populated by enemies of France. Paul chewed off another piece of crusty brown bread and looked up at the cook, who stood slicing turnips into a huge black pot. He had to make sure that the cook found him enough work about Castle Phelan to give him time to learn what had happened to his sister.

Ox knew Bull had found no trace of Dara the moment he entered the great hall and saw Wolf's stance. Back turned to the hall, he stood with arm braced against the hood of the fireplace, staring moodily into the leaping flames.

Bull looked up at his brother's approach. He shook his head, confirming Ox's suspicions. Ox looked to Wolf. "What do we do now?"

Wolf didn't turn. "We ride out and search again. I won't give up until we find her."

Ox glanced once more at his brother. He'd expected no less from the man who had become obsessed with his beautiful hostage.

Chapter 14

"Damn me, brother, but I've never seen Wolf get so worked up over a woman before. I believe the man would give all he owns to get the wench back," Bull said, pushing back his coif and running his fingers through his sweat-dampened hair. He squatted down beside his twin at the edge of the stream. Using his cupped hands as a dipper, he splashed his hot face with cooling water. The heat of the late summer days was enough to wither the stoutest soul.

Ox nodded. "I fear you are right. The girl laid claim to his heart before she disappeared, and he'll not accept the fact that he'll never see her again."

"We've searched every inch of Phelan and more, but still have found nothing. I've sent men to the villages as far as Otterburn, but no one has seen hide or hair of the wench. 'Tis likely a reiver overtook her, and she's been taken far away. She may even be dead by now."

"Aye. But I'll not be the one to tell Wolf of our suspicions. In his present state of mind, I don't know exactly how he'd take such news. He's near exhaustion. During the past week I seriously doubt he's slept more than a few hours. His temper is volatile at the best of times. Should he believe what we do, he might take it into his head to ride north. Then we'd be at war with more than one Scottish laird."

A slow grin curled Bull's lips, and his thickly fringed

eyes twinkled with devilment. " 'Twould make things a little more interesting. 'Tis growing wearisome hunting the wench from daylight till dark, day in and day out. I could use a good fight to alleviate some of the tension."

"Aye, brother. I'm beginning to feel the strain myself. But for once we must think of Wolf, not our own pleasure. When our friend reclaims his woman, he'll be back to the Wolf we knew. And Edward will have more campaigns for us."

"I pray you are right, Ox," Bull said, coming to his feet. He wiped the excess moisture from his face and pulled his coif up over his raven curls. " 'Tis time to ride. We crossed the border into Morgan land several miles back, and 'twould be in our own best interest to head south unless we want to enjoy ourselves a wee bit and harry a few Scots at Morgan Keep."

"Nay, brother. We ride south. Wolf is expecting us back tonight."

Bull shrugged good-naturedly and grinned. "A man can hope, can't he?"

Ox and Bull climbed up the streambank and mounted the horses they'd left to graze on the thick clumps of sweet grass that greened the open fields. Intent upon their own destination, they failed to see the man crouched low in the underbrush.

Harlow Norton's eyes narrowed speculatively as he watched the Englishmen ride out of sight. The stupid Englishmen had unwittingly revealed the Wolf's weakness, and she now resided at Morgan Keep. Harlow climbed from his hiding place. Brushing away the leaves and sticks clinging to his green tunic, he made his way along the streambed to where he'd left his pony tethered earlier. Harlow smiled to himself as he mounted the small beast and kicked him in the side, setting him in the direction of Morgan Keep. Confident that he could give Laird Morgan the weapon he needed to regain Phelan without one man losing his life, Harlow whistled contentedly to himself as the pony's short legs ate up the distance to Morgan Keep.

Sitting with back stiff and hands tightly clasped in her lap, Dara listened as Harlow Norton repeated what he'd overheard to Laird Morgan.

" 'Tis true, Laird Morgan. The wench belongs to the Wolf," Harlow said.

Angus released a long breath and glanced toward the quiet young woman. She made no protest to Harlow's accusation. "Is it true?"

Dara swallowed uneasily. Norton had revealed the secret Kirsten had tried so valiantly to keep from her father. Dara raised her chin and looked Laird Morgan directly in the eye. "I am Dara of Rochambeau. I came to England as Sir Wolf's hostage, not his woman, as your man implies."

"But the Wolf loves her. I heard his men say so with my own ears," Harlow answered steadfastly. He flashed Dara a challenging look.

"I fear you misunderstood. Wolf does not love me," Dara quickly interjected. "I was nothing more to him than goods to be ransomed."

" 'Tis not what the Wolf's men said. They said he'd give everything he owned to get the wench back," Harlow replied smugly.

Angus Morgan appeared thoughtful. If what Harlow said was true, then Dara of Rochambeau was of far more importance than he'd first gleaned. She could well be the enticement Wolf needed to turn Phelan over to its rightful master without lifting a sword.

Angus flashed Harlow a calculating look and saw that his longtime friend had already come to the same conclusion. He smiled. "Take a message to Wolf of Phelan. Tell him I have the maid here at Morgan Keep and will assure her safety. Tell him also that she will be returned to him after he turns Phelan over to me."

A gasp from the doorway drew Laird Morgan's attention to his daughter. Kirsten shook her head. "Nay, Papa. You can't use Dara to force Wolf to do your bidding. She is my friend and a guest in your house."

"She is also the woman Wolf loves. He will freely surrender Phelan to me if he ever wants to see her alive again."

"Surely, you wouldn't harm Dara?" Kirsten said, astounded by her father's threat. She eyed Laird Morgan as if she'd never seen him before. And in truth, she hadn't. She'd been protected against the warrior Laird Morgan. She'd only seen her father's gentle side, his loving nature. She'd never been confronted with the man who fought fearlessly upon the battlefield, the man who risked all for victory, the man who never showed mercy to his enemies. That man was not the father she knew and loved. But that was the man she now faced.

"Kirsten, this is none of your affair."

"Nay, Papa. 'Tis my affair when you calmly threaten my friend. 'Tis also my affair when you think to use her as a weapon against a man who may be your own son and my brother."

"You speak foolishness, daughter. Now go to your chambers. I will handle the Morgan affairs as I've always done," Laird Morgan said.

Kirsten glanced toward Harlow Norton. "Even your own man suspects Wolf of Phelan to be of Morgan blood. He has seen the Morgan medallion for himself. Yet you keep denying it."

"I deny nothing. Harlow made a mistake. I told you what happened to the second medallion. Now desist from your harangue," Laird Morgan ordered, his expression darkening. He glanced back to Norton, who stood listening to their arguments. "Do as I bid. Carry my message to the man who now claims Phelan as his own. Tell him the price he'll have to pay for the Lady Dara's release."

"You send your man to his death," Dara said quietly, drawing all eyes to her. She came to her feet, regally raising her chin in the air. She eyed Laird Morgan with contempt. "You may think to use me against Wolf, but your man will lose his life. Wolf cares naught for me. He'll come to Morgan Keep, but it'll not be to give over Phelan. It will be to fight."

"Wolf will not risk your life," Laird Morgan answered confidently.

"You are wrong, Laird Morgan. I know Wolf of Phelan far better than most. And when I say he cares naught what happens to me, I speak the truth, because he told me of his feelings himself. I am but a means to raise coin to fill his purse, nothing more."

"A man says many things, Lady Dara. Especially when a woman does not return his regard," Harlow said, venturing into the conversation that had come close to becoming a family squabble.

Dara's eyes misted before she could stem the tears. She shook her head. "Perhaps that is true when a man believes a woman does not care for him. However, Wolf rejected me after I told him of my love." Dara drew in a steadying breath but couldn't stop the quiver that touched her lower lip as she said, "That is why I left Phelan. Had Wolf felt any warmth at all for me, I would have stayed with him until hell froze over." Unable to stay a new rush of hot tears, Dara swiped at her eyes and ran from the solar.

"How can you be so cruel?" Kirsten seethed through clenched teeth. For the first time in her life, she felt like throttling someone. And at that moment that someone was her father. Kirsten quickly followed Dara.

"The gel can be useful, Laird Morgan," Harlow said after a long moment.

Laird Morgan nodded. "Aye. If what you overheard his men say is true, then she's the weapon we need to bring Wolf to his knees."

"Do you intend to harm her if the Wolf doesn't surrender Phelan?" Harlow asked. He'd served Laird Morgan all of his life, but had as yet to see him intentionally harm a person innocent of any wrong. He didn't make war upon children and women.

Laird Morgan ran his long fingers through his salt-and-pepper hair and shrugged. "Not unless it becomes necessary." Angus turned to gaze out the narrow window. He didn't like the threats he'd made against his daughter's beautiful friend, but to regain Phelan he'd do whatever was necessary to succeed. Phelan rightfully belonged to him through his dead wife and son.

His frown deepened. Kirsten's words had resurrected the questions he'd tried to ignore during the past weeks about his son's death. He'd managed to keep himself from dwelling upon his conversation with his daughter after Harlow had seen the medallion. Now, however, he had to confront the possibility that his son had lived. The thought was nearly too overwhelming to contemplate. Angus glanced back to where Harlow stood. "Tell Wolf he is to come to Morgan Keep within the fortnight if he wants to see Lady Dara alive again."

"Ye want to see the medallion?" Harlow asked, understanding Laird Morgan's need to confront Sir Wolf.

Angus turned haunted eyes upon Harlow. He nodded. "I will see the medallion to satisfy myself that it is not the Morgan talisman. And it will also end Kirsten's delusion that she now has a brother."

Dara fled up the stairs and to the bedchamber she'd been given upon her arrival at Morgan Keep. She worked at the laces of her borrowed gown. The material slipped from her shoulders as the door opened. Clutching the bodice to her breasts like a shield, Dara spun around to find her friend watching her. She breathed a sigh of relief and let the garment fall to the floor at her feet. Unashamed of her nakedness in front of Kirsten, she reached for the tattered gown she'd worn from Phelan and tugged it over her head.

"Papa won't carry out his threat, Dara," Kirsten said, closing the door behind her.

"I fear your father may have no other recourse. That is why I must leave Morgan Keep immediately. I won't allow anyone to use me as a weapon against the man I love."

"You can't leave. You have no place to go," Kirsten said, hoping to bring some reason back into the explosive situation Harlow had created with his tales.

Dara jerked the laces tight and secured them before she said, "I will find a way to get back to France. My home is there."

"And the man you love is here," Kirsten said.

Pain flickered across Dara's face. "I can't deny my feelings for Wolf. And because of them, I'll not be used to hurt him."

" 'Twas merely a threat to bring Wolf here. Papa may not even be aware of his own reason for sending Harlow to Phelan, but I am. He wants to know if the man who claims Phelan is the son he's thought dead for over thirty years. He wants to see the medallion Wolf wears."

A thrill of excitement quivered up Dara's spine. "Do you believe Wolf your brother?"

Kirsten shrugged. "I know not. However, I'm willing to believe he is if the medallion turns out to be the one my father gave to his first wife."

Dara's face lit with comprehension. "That is why you

asked about the medallion. You think Wolf is of Morgan descent."

"I can only hope he is," Kirsten said. "I would love to have a brother and a niece. 'Tis lonely being an only child, even when you have the entire Morgan clan to consider as your family. And it would bring the hostilities between Papa and your Wolf to an end. We could all live in peace."

"I understand your reasoning, Kirsten. But you must understand mine as well. Should Wolf not be your brother, then your father will surely carry out his threat. I can't remain at Morgan Keep and allow that to happen."

" 'Tis far too dangerous for a woman to travel alone," Kirsten said, trying once again to convince Dara not to leave Morgan Keep.

" 'Tis too dangerous for me to stay. I will not see Wolf lose everything because of me."

"Willya not listen to reason?"

"Reason will not stop your father," Dara said, giving no ground in the argument.

Kirsten nodded, momentarily defeated. Since she could find no reason to make Dara stay at Morgan Keep, she would have to find another way. She couldn't allow Dara to flee back to France until she knew Wolf's answer to her father's message. Should Wolf agree to come to Morgan Keep to gain Dara's release, then she would know he loved her friend and the risk would be worthwhile. And should it prove otherwise, she'd find a way to help Dara leave Morgan Keep before her father could use her against Wolf.

However, that was in the future. She now had to keep Dara here, and there was only one sure way to accomplish it. Kirsten looked at Dara and wanted to apologize for what she intended to do.

"All right, Dara. I'll argue no more." Kirsten turned

toward the door. She paused with her hand on the latch and looked back at her friend. "And always believe that I never meant you any harm. You are my friend, Dara of Rochambeau, no matter what happens in the future."

Dara quickly crossed the chamber and hugged Kirsten. "I will never believe otherwise, Kirsten. I will never forget your kindness to me. When this war is over between England and France, I pray we will meet again."

Kirsten returned the hug. She gave Dara a wobbly smile and hurried out the door. She brushed at her tears as she fled down the stairs and to the solar where her father sat deep in thought. She had to tell him of Dara's escape to keep her friend from making the biggest mistake of her life.

Moments later several guards stormed up the stairs and forced open Dara's bedchamber door. Bewildered, she watched the burly-faced guards descend upon her. "Lady Dara, we come to escort you to the dungeon."

Dara heard only the last word and panicked. Blood roaring in her ears, her heart slamming against her rib cage, she dashed toward the door. Several strong pairs of hands grabbed her before she could make good her escape. Dara screamed as all her senses went into a frenzy of hysteria at the thought of being locked away in the dungeon. Maddened near the point of insanity, she thrashed about like a wild animal, fighting tooth and nail, biting and scratching her captors, to no avail.

Eager to be rid of the wild creature that was doing her damnedest to kill them with her bare hands, they hustled Dara down the narrow steps to the dungeon.

Wide-eyed with panic, Dara stiffened at the sight of the barred, iron-bound door. She sought to deter the inevitable by digging her heels in against the stone and shook her head violently from side to side. *Nay*, her mind cried as she tried to plead with her guards to have mercy and not put her in the black hole that she knew would consume her. Yet they paid no heed to the crazed moans that passed her stricken lips. The door gaped wide and menacing, like hardened lips opening upon a cavernous mouth, as the guards thrust their rebellious prisoner into the dank cell. One terrified shriek pierced the air as they took the torch and ascended the stairs to the main hall. They would report to Laird Morgan that his orders had been carried out.

Kirsten bit down on her knuckles to suppress her own shriek when she heard Dara's screams of sheer terror. She turned on her father, her fathomless black eyes full of rage. "How can you do such a thing? I told you of Dara's plans only so you could help me prevent her from leaving Morgan Keep before Wolf came to her rescue. I never meant for her to be treated in such a manner. I believed you'd have a guard set at her chamber door, not send her to the dungeon as if she were our enemy."

"I do what I must to ensure my victory, Kirsten. I could not allow the girl to remain like a guest under my roof when in truth she planned to thwart my attempt to regain what is mine by right of marriage. She is our enemy. She has proven that this very night."

"Nay, Father. Dara is no enemy to us. She did not plan to do us any harm. She only wanted to prevent you from harming the man she loves. Is that too much to ask? Would you not do the same in her place?"

Angus looked away from his daughter's taut, angry features. In all of her eighteen years, he'd never had to go against what she believed was right. However, this time was different. Too much lay in the balance for him to worry about a young chit's overly sensitive feelings. Dara of Rochambeau would abide in the dungeon until Wolf of Phelan arrived to bargain for her release. He'd not have her make him look a fool by allowing her to escape before he had his quarry well in hand.

Angus hardened his heart against the pleas he knew would follow Kirsten's bout of anger. They would be far harder to handle than her unusual display of temper. However, he had no other choice. Face set and eyes the color of steel at midnight, Angus looked back to his child. "Enough, daughter! I will not allow you or anyone else to undermine the decisions I have made to protect the Morgans. You may consider the girl your friend, but in my eyes she is only a weapon against a relentless enemy. Now go to your chamber. I will hear no more."

The Morgan stubbornness set Kirsten's oval chin at a pugnacious angle. A mutinous light danced in her stygian eyes as she stood with hands braced on hips and shoulders squared, giving not an inch. "I am no wee child to be ordered about, Papa. You canna send me to my chamber to make me forget that Dara is locked away in the dungeon. 'Tis not right, what you do. Your claim on Phelan has driven the heart out of you if you can use an innocent girl as your pawn to bring Wolf of Phelan down."

Surprise flickered over Angus's face before it flushed a deep red with annoyance. "Child, I've always been lenient with the rod where you're concerned. However, you're not too big to have your backside tanned. You are near full grown into womanhood, but that does not stop me from being your father. You will obey me, for I know what is best for you and those who reside on Morgan land!"

Startled to have his threats leveled at her, Kirsten's first taste for battle deflated before it was fully blown. Tears brimmed in her eyes and spilled over her thick lashes to run unheeded down her cheeks. "If anything happens to Dara, I will never forgive you. Nor will I ever forgive you if you do not set your grievances aside long enough to truly look at the man who claims Phelan. He could well be your son and the father of your grandchild."

Heartsick, Kirsten turned and fled up the stairs to her chamber. Like a small child, she threw herself upon her bed and wept into her arms. She'd learned much about her father today, as well as herself. The Laird of Morgan Keep wasn't truly a saint, as she'd believed all of her life, nor was she. Her burst of temper and her scheme to keep Dara at Morgan Keep evidenced her own duplicitous nature. The thought made Kirsten weep even harder.

A commotion at the door drew all eyes toward the entrance. Silence descended over the group seated at the long table as the guards shoved the red-haired Scot into the hall. Hands bound behind his back, Harlow Norton landed on his knees and tumbled headfirst into the rushes. He gave a growl of protest as his mouth filled with dust. Rooting himself to his knees, he struggled haphazardly to his feet and spat at the guards' feet.

"What is the meaning of this?" Wolf demanded, surging to his feet.

Harlow turned on Wolf, his freckled face livid with rage. "Is this how you treat a man who comes under the white flag of truce?"

Wolf's brow lowered, shadowing the expression in his eyes. His hands worked at his sides, itching for any excuse to tear the Scot to pieces. Like his friends, Ox and Bull, he felt a toll upon his patience from the tension of searching for Dara. "Truce, recreant? What would a fool like you know of truce? You sneak back across the border to spy, and then try to say you come under the white flag of truce."

Harlow squared his shoulders and glared at Wolf. "Aye. Ask your men if I did not come with the flag.

They will tell you I have come to bring a message from Laird Morgan."

"Laird Morgan must be even a greater fool than I believed to trust you to deliver his message to me."

"Save your barbed words for someone they can pierce. I come here under my laird's order, not to swap insults with a scurrilous knave who claims what belongs to another."

Fury singed a path through Wolf's blood. The veins in his temples stood taunt, pounding with anger like ancient war drums. He clenched his fists at his sides and growled, "You are a bigger fool than I first believed. You claim to come in peace, but your tongue will see your throat has a new mouth if you are not careful, Scot."

"I come here to deliver Laird Morgan's message. Should you not care to hear about the lovely young woman now in Morgan Keep's dungeon, then I will say no more."

Wolf suddenly felt light-headed. A white line formed about his lips as the blood slowly drained from his face, leaving his bronzed complexion pale. A giant hand seemed to grasp his insides and give an insidious twist. His fears had been realized. Laird Morgan had captured Dara, and he had locked her away in the dungeon. The thought of Dara's horror of being locked in the dungeon staggered Wolf's senses. He nearly groaned aloud at the terror his beautiful Dara would be feeling.

Wolf's eyes blazed with anger. In less than three strides he crossed the hall to Harlow. He clamped a large hand down on the front of the man's tunic and jerked him nearly off his feet. He glared at Harlow's paling features. The man's freckles stood out like tiny specks of dust against his pallor. "I should kill you here and now for what the bastard has done."

Harlow drew in a steadying breath as he looked up

into Wolf's furious face. He mentally made the sign of the cross. The man glaring down at him looked like the devil incarnate. Harlow moistened his lips. His voice was little more than a whisper as he said, "Laird Morgan said if you want the wench returned to you, you will come to Morgan Keep within the fortnight. He also told me to tell you that the price of the wench's release is Phelan."

Wolf released Harlow with a shove that sent him sprawling once more into the rushes. Breathing heavily, Harlow looked up at Wolf. He felt a tremble of true fear ripple down his spine. He'd met many men in battle, yet until this moment he hadn't truly contemplated death. Now he saw his own mortality in Wolf's black eyes. And he didn't doubt it would be a hard, agonizing death, for he'd trespassed against the legendary Wolf. Another shiver passed over Harlow. He easily recognized the look. He'd often seen it on Laird Morgan's face during battle. That look boded ill for anyone in his path.

Wolf took another step toward the man sprawled at his feet before he brought himself under control. A shudder seemed to pass over his lean frame as he stood looking down at the Scot. "Has he harmed the Lady Dara?"

Harlow shook his head. "Nay. But he bid me to tell you that if you want to see her alive again, you'd best make haste."

Wolf flashed Ox and Bull a tormented look before he reached down and pulled Harlow to his feet. He shoved him at the guard. "Lock him in the dungeon. I'll deal with him when I return."

"You bastard!" Harlow shouted as the guards began to lead him away. "I came under a flag of truce."

"Aye," Wolf agreed. "And you'll not be harmed unless I do not find the Lady Dara safe. Should that happen, then I'll take great pleasure in slitting your throat myself."

"Laird Morgan will demand my release before you get the wench," Harlow cried as the guards forced him into the stairwell that led to the dungeons.

"His demands make no difference to me," Wolf said as he turned back to the table where everyone had suddenly burst into rapid discussion over the Scot's message.

"What do you intend to do?" Ox ventured, pushing back the wooden plate that Dara had ordered the servants to use instead of bread trenchers.

"Exactly what my Laird Morgan wants of me," Wolf said, picking up his tankard. He lifted it to his lips and gulped down the bitter contents.

"Surely you don't intend to meekly surrender Phelan to that bastard?" Bull asked, puzzled that Wolf would acquiesce to the Scot's demands without a fight.

Wolf arched a raven brown. "Do you have a plan that would work better, one that will not get Dara killed?"

"We could lay siege to Morgan Keep. The bastards will starve in a few weeks."

"Aye. And so would Dara. I'll not risk her life for a crumbling fortress that was foisted off on me because my king didn't want to pay for my services with his precious coins."

Ox stood. "There must be another way, Wolf."

Wolf closed a hand over the medallion about his neck. Ada had promised that it would always see him safe. Now he prayed it would also protect the woman he loved. Wolf drew in a resigned breath. "Hopefully, if there is, it will come to me before I reach Morgan Keep."

"You ride tonight?"

Wolf nodded. "Aye. I'll not leave Dara in Morgan's dungeon any longer than necessary."

"But the men are not prepared to ride out tonight. We must wait until daybreak."

"Nay. I wait no longer. And I go alone. If Morgan plans to use Dara to bait his trap, then I'll not disappoint him. Should that be the situation, I expect you and Bull are capable of avenging me."

"Aye," Bull said. " 'Tis our duty."

Ox flashed his brother a quelling look before turning his attention back to Wolf. "There would be no need to avenge you if you would allow us to go with you. 'Twould be easy to take Morgan Keep. It is not that well defended. 'Tis nearly as ancient as Phelan."

"I've made my decision," Wolf said, and turned toward the stairs. However, before he reached them, a small figure dashed across the hall and grabbed him about his hard thighs, dragging him to a stumbling halt. He looked down to see his daughter, clinging desperately to him, her large velvet eyes filled with tears. Gently he lifted Ellice into his arms and tipped up her small oval chin so that she had to return his gaze. His words were soft and filled with all the love he felt for the child. "What has beset you, pet?"

Ellice's lower lip trembled as she gulped in a deep breath and said, "Are you going to bring Lady Dara back, Papa?"

Wolf nodded. "Aye. That is my intention."

A new rush of tears sent huge droplets over the edge of Ellice's thick lashes. They cascaded down her baby-smooth cheeks unheeded. "Oh, Papa. I'm so sorry. 'Tis all my fault for wishing Lady Dara would leave Phelan and never come back. I truly didn't mean it. I was just angry that you paid attention to her. I didn't mean her any harm. Will you forgive me?"

"Hush, little one," Wolf said, stroking her long hair. " 'Twas not you who made Lady Dara leave Phelan. 'Twas me and my foolish tongue."

Ellice's glistening eyes widened as she looked at her father. "Why did you want her to leave? I thought you liked Lady Dara."

"I didn't want her to leave, and I do like Lady Dara," Wolf said, smiling tenderly down at his daughter.

Ellice considered her father's words for a long moment before she said, " 'Tis strange to be a grown-up, isn't it, Papa?"

"Aye, sweeting. 'Tis most strange to have the feelings of a grown-up." Wolf set her on her feet. "Now I want you to go to your bed. 'Tis late, and I must be about bringing Lady Dara home."

"Will she be my new mother?" Ellice asked uncertainly.

"Would you like Lady Dara to be your mother?" Wolf asked, sensing his daughter had already considered the possibility long before he had.

At last Ellice nodded. "Aye, Papa. She is nicer than I thought at first. She can truly teach me how to be a lady when you decide to let me grow up."

"Go to your bed, minx," Wolf said, unable to contain his own smile as he turned Ellice toward the stairs and gave her a pat on her small rear.

Ellice paused on the landing and looked back down at Wolf. She lifted a small hand and touched her fingers to her lips before blowing him a kiss. "Good night, Papa. I love you."

"Good night, pet. Sweet dreams and I love you," Wolf said, and watched his daughter until she passed out of view.

"Will you leave the child an orphan?" Ox said, in another futile attempt to stop Wolf from going to Morgan Keep without reinforcements.

"Nay. I go to bring her home a mother."

Chapter 15

The horseman mounted on the white destrier came from the shadows of the forest. Illuminated by the light of the full moon, he rode forth, pale and ghostly. He came alone, his standard of the solitary wolf fluttering silently overhead. Though the sultry summer night's breeze still contained the day's warmth, the sight of the specter riding across the open field toward Morgan Keep sent chills down the spines of the guards on night duty. The sentry's voice quavered as he called out, "Halt! Who goes there?"

The apparition drew his snorting destrier to a standstill. The huge beast pawed at the earth with one large steel-shod hoof as its rider calmly removed his silver helm and answered, "I am Sir Wolf of Phelan. I have been summoned here by Laird Angus Morgan."

Having already received their orders from Laird Morgan himself, the guard nodded and called down to the late night visitor, "Laird Morgan bids you welcome, Sir Wolf."

Busily ordering the portcullis raised to allow Wolf to enter, the guards failed to hear Wolf's snort of doubt. The well-oiled gates opened easily, and within moments Wolf stood within his enemy's stronghold. Four armed guards fell into step with him, flanking him on either side as they escorted him up the steps and through the thick, iron-bound oak door of Morgan Keep. An uneasy hush fell over the assembly in the great hall as the guards led Wolf toward the dais where the ebony-eyed man sat enthroned like a king in his intricately carved chair.

Laird Angus Morgan watched his visitor cross the hall. Viewing the man Kirsten thought to be her brother, Laird Morgan's heart began to race within the cage of his ribs. When Wolf paused before him, his back straight, his black gaze blazing belligerently, the laird's breath froze in his throat. The face he looked upon was the face of his enemy, yet as he took note of the younger man's chiseled features—his piercing ebony eyes; his narrow, aristocratic nose; his full, shapely mouth; and the raven hair that had as yet to be touched by gray—Angus recognized the similarity to his own face. However, it wasn't until his gaze came to rest upon the tarnished medallion lying against the broad plain of Wolf's chest that Angus's blood slowly receded to his toes. There was no mistaking the emblem, though it had been over thirty years since he'd last laid eyes upon it.

Knees turning to jelly, Angus drew in a deep, steadying breath. He had to remain calm if he wanted to learn the truth, as Kirsten had urged. Clenching his jaw against the burning urgency to question the younger man whose very countenance bespoke Morgan blood, Angus waited for the Wolf of Phelan to speak.

Wolf's glare speared the older man with all the animosity boiling through him. His blood ran hot to throttle the Scot laird who had dared harm the woman he loved. He wanted to launch himself at Angus Morgan and choke the life out of him. However, Wolf was no fool. He was not known for his lack of caution. He was in the belly of the beast, surrounded by men who thirsted to spill his blood. He had to remain calm and in control of his emotions if he ever hoped to free Dara.

Realizing that Laird Morgan was not going to be the first one to speak, Wolf said simply, "I have come."

Angus nodded and cleared his throat. "Aye. And you are welcome, Sir Wolf."

Angus's attempt at congeniality went unnoted by Wolf. He had come to Morgan Keep for one reason. Wolf glanced about the hall, seeking any sign of Dara's presence. Finding none, he looked back to the Laird of Morgan Keep and found himself thinking there was something oddly familiar about the pair of ebony eyes that stared intently back at him. A frown creased Wolf's brow as he tried to recall where he could have encountered Laird Angus Morgan in the past.

Though Wolf couldn't retrieve any recollection of ever having met the Scottish laird, he couldn't rid himself of the sensation that he'd seen him somewhere. Perplexed, he searched Angus's features for a long, curious moment before his eyes widened in shock. He couldn't believe the memory his mind conjured up. He saw Laird Angus's image every morning in the reflection of his own metal mirror.

Wolf shook off the ridiculous thought. His only resemblance to Laird Morgan lay in the color of his eyes and hair. Drawing his mind back to the reason he'd come to Morgan Keep, Wolf said, "I have come for the Lady Dara of Rochambeau."

Incredulous to find his own likeness upon Wolf's face, Angus nodded again. "As I had thought."

Wolf flashed a scathing glance toward the men assembled in the great hall. "I come alone, so you can send your whelps back to their kennel. Or do you fear me so greatly that you must keep yourself well guarded?"

Unused to anyone speaking to him in such a manner, annoyance kindled in Angus's eyes. "Rest assured, Wolf of Phelan, I do not fear any Englishman."

"Oh? But I would not have thought you so brave, since you use women instead of battle to gain what you want."

Angus's fingers dug into the dark wood of the chair as he sought to maintain a calm demeanor. He'd not let Wolf make him lose control. " 'Tis far better to use a woman than to waste the lives of my men needlessly."

"Spoken like a true Scot," Wolf growled, his voice low and full of menace.

"Aye. We Scots are a wise lot who find no shame in retreat if it leaves us able to fight another day."

"Call it wise or call it cowardice. It means the same for a Scot," Wolf said.

Angus eyed the man who was the image of himself thirty years earlier and saw a veil of red fury descend to wipe out his self-control. He came to his feet, towering over Wolf from the dais. He no longer remembered Kirsten's suspicions. He saw only the enemy who claimed Phelan. "You should learn some wisdom, Englishman. You come here to seek the Lady Dara's release with a tongue as sharp as a lance. Let us see how well the dungeon makes it rust."

Before Wolf had time to draw his sword to defend himself, Angus's men swept down on him from all sides, their numbers easily subduing him. He continued to struggle against his captors until a blow from a wooden cudgel landed against the side of his head, staggering his senses and leaving him hanging limp between two burly men-at-arms.

Laird Morgan looked down at Wolf and found his gaze caught by the medallion swaying in the air. He bent and jerked the talisman from about Wolf's neck.

New pain welled in his heart as he cupped it in the palm of his hand. Harlow Norton had been right not to raise a hand against the man who wore it, for it was the Morgan medallion. Angus glanced back to his young enemy. He also no longer had any doubts about Wolf's true identity. The medallion as well as Wolf's face proclaimed him Angus's son.

However, Angus knew his acceptance of Wolf as his son didn't solve his problem with Wolf of Phelan. He was not a babe that Angus could take to his breast and tell of his love. He was a man grown, a man who knew nothing of the blood that bound them. A man who had been branded a bastard for over thirty years. It would not be easy to break through the barrier that time and misfortune had wrought. He needed time to think, time to explain to Wolf, time to make this man understand that it had been the lies of his grandfather that had separated them and nothing more.

Running a hand over his beard-stubbled jaw, Angus raised haggard eyes to find Kirsten, red-eyed from her earlier bout of crying, standing near the stairs. Releasing a resigned breath, he ordered, "Take him to the dungeon where his lady resides. Perhaps he'll cool off and be in a more amenable mood when his head quits pounding."

Kirsten's tear-blurred gaze shot to the Wolf and then back to her father. Unable to understand what had happened to make her gentle father turn into such a cruel man, she clamped a hand over her mouth to hold back her cry of anguish and fled back up the stairs. She had to find a way to help her friend and her brother before the madman downstairs had them slain. The slamming of her chamber door echoed throughout the keep and hit her father in the chest like a physical blow.

Angus sank back into the Morgan chair and wearily rubbed at his temples. As Kirsten had believed, he had found his son, but he feared too many years and too much hatred between their countries could well keep them separated just as surely as if Wolf had died at birth.

"Damn you, Phelan," Angus swore beneath his breath, cursing the man who had been his father-in-law as well as the nemesis who had ruined so many lives with his machinations. His lies had prevented Angus from being with Allyson during their short marriage, as well as keeping him from knowing the man who was his son and heir.

Angus glanced toward the stairs. After all these years, Lord Phelan's lies may have also cost him his daughter's love. The look on Kirsten's face had spoken more loudly than her accusations. She was bewildered by his actions, unable to correlate the father she knew to the man she'd seen that day.

"What should I do to set things right?" Angus muttered to himself, ignoring the odd looks flashed his way from his men. The voices that had stilled upon Wolf's arrival now excitedly began as a low rumble before bursting into a loud babble. Everyone talked at the same time, giving their opinions of the strange happenings taking place at Morgan Keep.

The keys rattled in the metal latch and the dungeon door swung open. Torchlight spilled inside, banishing the black shadows to the corners, making Dara blink and raise a hand to shield her eyes against the light that had been denied her since her incarceration. Instinctively she backed away, still too terrified to comprehend that an avenue of escape had been opened. She couldn't contain the trembling that beset her as the guards appeared with their burden. One chortled at the look upon her face and said, "Laird Morgan thought ye could use some company. 'Tis me understanding that there's no need of introductions. Yer already acquainted with the Wolf."

Wolf's name had the power to penetrate the terror that blanketed Dara's mind. Her sapphire gaze shot to the limp man as the guards released him and he sprawled onto his belly at her feet. He muttered a curse at the impact against the cold stone and rotting rushes. A moment later the guard took the torch from the cell, and the door clanged closed behind them.

Engulfed in the blackness once more, Dara felt the walls begin to close in about her. She couldn't breathe. Her chest rose and fell rapidly as she fought to draw life-giving air into her lungs. The hysteria that had governed her since Laird Morgan had ordered her locked in the dungeon now crept up her spine and threatened to overcome her again. Dara clutched her arms tightly about her but couldn't suppress the whimper of fear that escaped her as she struggled against the mind-blinding terror.

Wolf's moan momentarily jerked Dara out of the phobic morass. Drawing from a fortitude that she had thought long vanquished by her horror of being locked away, she managed to deter the panic invading every sinew of her body. She drew in a steadying breath and prayed for the willpower to help Wolf. He needed her. She couldn't allow herself to fall apart when the man she loved was in need.

Suddenly buoyed by the thought, Dara sank down on her knees upon the rotting rushes and flailed the darkness for Wolf. She held her breath when her hand came into contact with his shoulder. Using her hands to see, she anxiously searched him to ascertain that he'd not been seriously wounded. Finding only the lump at his temple, she breathed a sigh of relief.

Dara struggled to maneuver Wolf into a more comfortable position, but he was far too heavy. It took all of her strength to finally turn him enough to cradle his head in her lap. Unable to do or see more in the darkness, she sat soothing his brow and quietly talking to him. The sound of her own voice helped to stave off the fear that tightened every muscle in her body as she whispered, "I'm here, my love."

Unable to stop herself, Dara raised her head and stared into the black void surrounding her. She moistened her lips and quickly lowered her eyes back to Wolf. She concentrated all her attention upon him, fighting to keep the ebony monster from swallowing her once more.

"Dara," Wolf muttered, momentarily disoriented from the blow to his head as well as the darkness that blinded him.

"Yes, love. I'm here. Rest. You've been injured." Dara drew in a trembling breath.

The winds of memory banishing the cobwebs left in his mind, Wolf bolted upright with a growl of fury. "Damn the bastard to hell! When we get out of here, I will have Morgan Keep razed to the ground, and then the stones ground into dust. There will be no sign that a Morgan ever existed upon the face of the earth by the time I'm through."

Wolf reached up to take hold of the medallion to affirm his vow and found it missing. Another vicious growl escaped him. "And now I can also lay thievery at his door."

Too caught up in the horror seeping through her like a chilling mist, Dara cared little about Wolf's accusations against Laird Morgan. She reached out to Wolf, frantic for the security of his arms. Her voice reflecting her terror, she pleaded, "Don't leave me. Please, don't leave me."

Immediately contrite for thinking only of his own vendettas and not of the horror Dara must be suffering, Wolf took her into his arms, cradling her close against his chest. He smoothed the tangled hair back from her face and murmured comfortingly, "Hush, little one. I'm here. Nothing will harm you. 'Tis only you and I here. Nothing more."

Dara clutched at Wolf's chest for dear life, burying her face in the curve of his neck. Her voice quavered as she whispered brokenly, "I'm frightened."

"I know you are, sweeting," Wolf said, gently stroking the curve of her back. "But you mustn't allow your fear to control you. I am here with you, and I would die before I allowed anyone to hurt you."

Dara pressed her lips against the corded column of Wolf's throat, dropping tiny kisses against his skin as she suddenly wrapped her arms about his neck and murmured, "Love me, Wolf. Please, make me feel alive. Awaken my demons so they can drive away the terror before I go mad."

Before Wolf could answer, Dara claimed his mouth with her own. She thrust her tongue between his parted lips, challenging him, teasing him, until she felt his arms tighten about her. Dara pressed her breasts to his hard, muscular chest and rubbed provocatively against him. She heard him moan softly and shudder before he took command of their lovemaking. Within moments Wolf had undressed and lay Dara back against his velvet mantle. He stripped her of her clothing with the same urgency that she felt, before spreading her legs and driving into her satiny sheath.

Already wet with her own need, she opened to him, wrapping her legs about his waist to draw all of him deep within her. Together they soared out of the prison cell, away from the dark, dank, slimy walls that entombed them. They flew, upward into the summer's night sky, shooting like a comet across man's universe bedecked with jewels. Together they sought fulfillment; together they found it.

Dara gasped Wolf's name aloud as he spilled his seed into the moist haven awaiting it. Hips arched against

Wolf's, her belly spasmodic with the rapture that rippled through her entire being, she clung to his shoulders, savoring the emotions that bound them as one.

Suddenly secure in Wolf's feelings for her, she smiled and gently stroked the silken strands of hair back from his sweat-dampened brow. He could deny it all he wanted, but tonight Wolf of Phelan had proved his love without any words being spoken. The knowledge vanquished all of Dara's fear. Quietly, she said, "You love me, Wolf."

He drew in a deep breath and raised himself on his elbows above Dara. He couldn't see her face, but knew that her beautiful features were now soft with the wonder. Wolf's husky voice reflected all his pent-up emotions as he answered, "Aye, sweet Dara. I can deny it no longer. I've loved you since long before we left France. Only I was too big of a fool to admit it. Can you forgive me for the pain I've caused you?"

"There is nothing to forgive, my great Wolf. I can only rejoice that you have given me your heart and have come to take me back to Phelan."

He eased away from her. "Aye, I have come to take you back to Phelan, but I fear Laird Morgan doesn't intend for me to accomplish that feat."

Dara sat up and reached for her discarded clothing. She quickly pulled on the gown to keep the dungeon's chill at bay. "I'm sorry, Wolf. My foolishness has cost you dearly. I was too hurt to think. But I would have you know I would never do anything to intentionally harm you or those you love."

"Carry no blame upon your shoulders, Dara. 'Tis my fault that we have come to this pass. I came to Morgan Keep to free you, and only succeeded in getting myself thrown into the dungeon," Wolf said, leaning back against the slimy wall.

"Will Ox and Bull come for you?"

Wolf reached out and pulled Dara onto his lap. He cradled her against his chest, his chin resting against the silken pillow of her hair, his arms holding her close. "Aye. They will come, but I fear Morgan will never allow them to take us alive."

Dara shivered. She could find no words to refute Wolf's statement. From what she'd seen of Laird Angus Morgan, he was just as willfully stubborn as the man who held her in his arms. Dara squeezed her eyes closed against the wave of burning remorse that filled her. She would be responsible for Wolf's death. The thought settled sickeningly in the pit of her belly like tainted meat.

Silently, Wolf and Dara sat together in the dark, dank cell. Unable to speak of the future or the past, there was nothing to say, only to feel. As the minutes ticked by and lengthened into hours, the bond that they had discovered deepened until there was no need for words or gestures to express their feelings. Like faith, it lived in the very essence of their souls, needing none of the experience of the five senses to assure either of them that it existed.

In the wee hours of the morning the only sound coming from the cell was the soft breathing of the lovers who sat entwined while they slept.

The torch sending eerie shadows dancing along the walls of the passageway, Kirsten stealthfully made her way down the stairs toward the dungeon. Her eyes still red from her bout of weeping, she cast a furtive glance behind her to make sure no one followed. It wouldn't do for her father or any of his men to realize her intentions. She'd wept and cursed until an hour ago, when she'd suddenly come to the conclusion that it was left up to her to help her brother and the woman he loved to freedom. It hurt to go against her father's wishes, but she wouldn't let his anger over the past force him to harm Dara or Wolf.

Kirsten paused on the landing near the door that led to the main hall and listened intently to ensure that all were still abed. She breathed a sigh of relief when she heard only snoring and the usual noises that accompanied many men and women gathered in one place to sleep. Thankfully, it was still too early for even the servants to be about.

Kirsten wasted no more time. She quickly made her way past the hall landing and down the last flight of stairs to the dungeon. Placing the torch in the rusty iron wall bracket, she removed the key ring that she'd been given when she'd taken over as her father's chatelaine. Within her hand she held a key for every lock within the granite walls of Morgan Keep, including the dungeon. Careful to make no sound, she chose the right iron key and inserted it in the lock. The key grated loudly against the rusty latch, making Kirsten wince and flash another anxious look toward the stairs before she finished unlocking the door.

Fearing discovery, Kirsten quickly swung the door open and stepped inside the foul-smelling cell to find the two lovers staring groggily up at her, momentarily disoriented.

"Dara, 'tis I, Kirsten," she whispered. "I've come to help you leave Morgan Keep. Come, you must hurry before we are discovered."

Giving Dara no time to collect her sleepy wits, Wolf surged to his feet, bringing Dara with him. His height and girth seemed to shrink the dungeon in size. Kirsten took a step back, looking up into her brother's face for the first time. She couldn't suppress the smile of delight as she saw her father's image stamped upon the younger man's features. Momentarily forgetting the necessity for haste, she said, "Tis true that you are a Morgan."

Wolf's face darkened with annoyance at the mention of his enemy's name. "I am Wolf of Phelan."

The immediacy of her mission finally reasserting itself over the excitement of seeing her brother for the first time, Kirsten nodded. "Aye. You are Wolf of Phelan as well. Now make haste. We have little time. 'Tis nearly dawn, and soon it will be impossible to get you out the postern gate without being seen."

Wolf didn't argue. Capturing Dara's hand protectively within his own, they followed Kirsten up the stairs and through the narrow passages that led to the gardens. Understanding the vital need for stealth if they wanted to make good their escape, Dara struggled to keep pace with Wolf's long strides. When they reached the postern gate, Kirsten unlocked it and stepped aside to allow them to pass. She looked up at Wolf and said quietly, "Go with God, brother."

Wolf paused and looked down at Dara before looking once more at Kirsten. He asked the question that had been burning his tongue since Kirsten's sudden appearance in the dungeon. "Why are you helping us?"

"Though you may deny it, you are my brother, Wolf of Phelan. And I'm determined to assure that you and our father do not kill one another before you come to realize that we are a family. I canna stand by and allow the Morgan temperament to leave me an only child again when I've just discovered I have a brother and a niece."

" 'Tis foolishness that you speak. I have no Morgan blood in my veins. However, I am grateful for your help and hope you will forgive me for having to use your kindness against you."

Kirsten frowned up at Wolf. "I don't understand."

"You will," Wolf whispered. He moved so swiftly that Kirsten had no time to scream for help. Wolf clamped his hand down over her mouth and lifted her into his arms as if she weighed no more than a sack of flour. Kirsten struggled against him until she heard Wolf growl, "Give way, Lady. 'Tis no use to fight. I will not release you. Because of your kindness, I would not harm you unless you force me."

Kirsten's dark eyes reflected her dismay as she flashed Dara a helpless, beseeching look.

"You cannot mean to take Kirsten with us?" Dara whispered uneasily.

"That is exactly my intention. Morgan will now have to deal on my terms."

"But she is the one who freed us."

"Aye. And I'm grateful. However, 'tis time for Laird Morgan to learn how it feels to have someone he loves used against him."

"Wolf, please. Leave Kirsten here. No good can come of this. It will only add to the animosity between you and your father."

A muscle worked in Wolf's jaw as he looked down at Dara through narrowed lashes. "Morgan is not my father. Now make haste. We have only a few minutes to reach the forest under the cover of darkness."

Dara flashed Kirsten an apologetic look, but did not argue with Wolf further. She'd caused him enough trouble, and she'd not add more by barraging him with pleas. Her friend was in no danger from Wolf, and Dara was sure he'd release Kirsten once they were safely back in England. Once he accepted their kinship, she knew he'd protect her as fiercely as he'd protect anyone he loved.

Chapter 16

A squadron led by the MacDonald twins had just crossed the border on its way to Morgan Keep when Ox and Bull spied Wolf and his female entourage.

"Ho, Wolf," Bull called, relieved to see his friend alive. Urging his destrier into a gallop, his men followed suit, their mounts' hooves thundering against the earth as they raced across the open field toward their leader.

Welcoming the sight of his men, Wolf waved his greeting. In his present state, even Bull's call was gladly received.

Bull was the first to reach Wolf and his companions. He drew his mount to a snorting halt and raised the visor of his helmet. Relaxing in the saddle as much as his armor would allow, he crossed his arms over the pommel and briefly scrutinized the two females before calmly turning his gaze back to the man he'd come to rescue. Devilment twinkled in his pale eyes and a wry grin curled up the corners of his lips. " 'Twould seem you got more than you bargained for."

"Aye," Wolf said, releasing his hold upon Kirsten's wrist for the first time since leaving Morgan Keep. He'd had to keep a tight rein on the Lady Kirsten Morgan. Like her friend, she had a streak of perverseness that refused to let her meekly accept her capture. "I came

263

away with Laird Morgan's most prized possession: his daughter, the Lady Kirsten."

Bull's eyes widened in disbelief. "You managed to take the lady out of Morgan Keep without a fight?"

Wolf shrugged and rubbed at his chest where Kirsten had pounded her fists in her attempt to make him release her. "You might say that."

"And he also had help," Kirsten ground out, angrily eyeing her brother.

Bull arched a dark brow in question. "Someone helped you at Morgan Keep?"

"Aye," Kirsten cut in before her brother could speak. "I did."

Bewildered, Bull glanced at his brother to see if Ox had managed to understand the situation any better than he had. Seeing only bewilderment upon Ox's face, Bull looked once more at Wolf and voiced his confusion. "I don't understand."

"There's nothing to understand," Kirsten said, her Morgan temper stirred to the height by Wolf's treachery. "I helped save my brother's life, and in return for my kindness, he takes me hostage and forces me to come with him to England."

"Your brother?" Ox asked, speaking for the first time.

"Aye, my brother," Kirsten ground out, her ebony gaze shooting daggers at her newfound sibling. "Though he and my father are too stubborn to accept the truth."

"Cease this foolish talk," Wolf said. "I've heard enough. Ox, take Lady Kirsten up before you and try your best to keep her quiet." Wolf glanced at Bull. "I would ask to share your mount, but 'twould be too much a burden for the beast to carry the three of us."

Taking the unspoken hint, Bull dismounted and graciously offered his destrier to Wolf. "By your leave, Sir Wolf. I will ride back to Phelan with one of my fellow knights. You and your lady may have my horse."

" 'Tis a true friend who gives up his mount for another," Wolf said, smiling at Bull.

"Aye" was all Bull said, flashing an envious look at his brother. It would have been far more pleasant a ride back to Phelan with the beautiful Lady Morgan poised in front of him, instead of straddling a horse's hindquarters with the odor of his fellow knight's sweaty body blaring him in the face and assaulting his nostrils.

Without his armor, the deep cantle of the saddle left ample room for Dara to sit comfortably in front of Wolf. Exhausted mentally as well as physically from the past twenty-four hours, she leaned back against Wolf and soon slept. Guiding the well-trained animal with pressure from his knees, as he often did in battle, Wolf cradled Dara against him, savoring the feel of her, the smell of her, the sound of her breathing, the gentle beat of the pulse at the base of her throat.

It was hard to express the feelings this one woman aroused within him. His love for her brought every emotion vividly to life. There were no insouciant feelings within him concerning Dara of Rochambeau. She either enraged him to the point of madness or maddened him with such a fierce desire to possess her so thoroughly that nothing could ever come between them again. She had claimed his heart and soul with her beauty and spirit. And he realized that by denying or giving of her love, she could destroy him or make him invulnerable.

Experiencing a reverence that he'd never known before, Wolf glanced toward the clear blue heavens and smiled. He felt suddenly closer to the God he worshiped. His love for Dara had become as deep and sacred as the vows he'd taken when Edward had knighted him upon the battlefield. The God who had made the earth and all its wonders had also seen fit to bless him with the love of the beautiful and stubborn French-woman in his lap.

Wolf's arms tightened possessively about Dara. He would never allow anything or anyone to separate them again. Society could consider him a base-born bastard who was not fit to touch the hem of Dara's gown, but he'd be damned if he'd surrender the only woman he loved because of his lack of heritage. Neither king nor country could make him give her up. He'd fought to claim her, and he'd fight to keep her until the last drop of his blood seeped into England's soil.

To affirm his vow, Wolf absently reached up to touch the medallion before remembering its loss. Annoyed, he glanced over his shoulder to the young woman who sat straight and stiff in front of Ox. He'd have his medallion back from Laird Morgan before the man reclaimed his daughter. Wolf frowned. The thought of Laird Morgan once more roused the memory of the man. He'd admit that his own face held an uncanny resemblance to the Scottish laird's. However, he'd admit nothing more. What the girl and the Scot now resting in Phelan's dungeon claimed could not be true.

Or could it? The question rose in Wolf's mind to overshadow his staunch avowals to the contrary. He sought to push the thought aside but found himself slowing his destrier's pace to allow Ox's mount to come alongside. Before he could stop himself, he asked, "What do you hope to gain from your lies of my lineage?"

Kirsten forced herself to remain calm as she turned to look at the man who was her brother. Yet it took every ounce of her willpower to keep from screaming at him. In the past hours, her equanimity had been slowly deteriorating to the point of hysteria. She cleared her throat, drew in a deep, fortifying breath, and sought to keep her voice as even as possible as she said, "I tell no lies. And the only thing I have to gain is a brother."

"Then who told you this falsehood?"

Slowly Kirsten shook her head. "No one had to tell me that you are my father's son. His image is stamped upon your face. Did you not see it when you spoke with him?"

"I saw only a man set to destroy me and those I love."

"Then you are my father's son in all ways. For he, too, could not see the future for the past."

Wolf's brow puckered. "Speak no riddles, Lady. I am in no mood for games."

"I play no game, Sir Wolf. The past is what now drives my father to lay claim to Phelan. His first wife was the Lord of Phelan's daughter. She gave him a son, and I believe that son is you."

Wolf's frown didn't lessen. "Your ploy will not work, Lady. A bastard I may be, but I am no simpleton who can be convinced to turn over Phelan by some false claim of kinship. Even your own words belie your explanation, for had a man like your father had a son, he would have proclaimed it to the world the moment of his birth."

"Aye. No doubt my father would have done so had he known the child had lived. But the old lord refused to accept his daughter's marriage to a Scot, even when he learned she carried my father's heir. My father's first wife died soon after their child was born, and Lord Phelan sent word to Morgan Keep that the babe had also succumbed." Kirsten paused, giving her words time to penetrate the resistance she sensed in Wolf. Seeing a flicker of uncertainty pass over his face, she finished softly, "But Lord Phelan wasn't aware that when he ordered the babe sent away, his daughter had assured that my father's heir would be recognized one day from the

Morgan medallion that she had placed about his neck. It was the same medallion my father had given her upon their wedding day. The same medallion you wore about your neck when you arrived at Morgan Keep."

Never take off the medallion. 'Twill bring you luck. Ada's last words flashed disturbingly through Wolf's mind. Everything Lady Kirsten said seemed to follow the same path of Ada's story of his life. A premonitory chill traced a tingling path up Wolf's spine. He shook his head, denying that his enemy in fact could be his father. "The medallion is no proof of anything. 'Tis only a worthless piece of brass. There are probably thousands like it."

"Nay," Kirsten said. " 'Twere only two of the Morgan medallions struck. And until Harlow saw the one about your neck, it was believed only one still existed. The other had been lost thirty-two years ago, when my father's wife died."

Again Wolf shook his head. "Enough of this foolish talk."

" 'Tis not foolishness, brother," Kirsten said softly. " 'Tis something you and our father must accept so we can stop this war, before blood is shed and things have come to a pass that canna be mended with words. You and I are brother and sister. We share the same father, who is also the grandfather of your child. Let us have peace, Wolf. Phelan is rightfully yours through the blood of your mother, as is Morgan Keep through our father. As the Morgan heir, someday you will be the one who is laird of the Morgan clan."

Perturbed, Wolf kicked his mount in the side, distancing himself from the young woman who stirred the past to life with her stories of two young lovers and their child, separated by death and lies. He didn't want to think of such things. He didn't want to even contemplate the hopes such stories could rear from long dead ashes. The Lady Kirsten spoke of the very quintessence of his dreams. Dreams that still clung to the young boy within him like resin on a newly felled tree. He had tried to deny them, yet he knew that his every action over the past years had been governed by them. His need to be accepted, to carve a place in the world for himself, to force people to acknowledge that he existed even without knowing who had sired him, had all stemmed from the dictates of the small child that yearned for a family. He had achieved goals that few men in his position could claim, but nothing had filled the void within him.

Wolf glanced down at Dara. He had even denied his love for the beautiful woman he held because of the feelings of inferiority that he'd refused to recognize. He'd told himself that she would be like all the other noble females who had looked down upon the bastard mercenary after enjoying a few romps in his bed. And it had cost him dearly. He had nearly lost Dara forever.

Acceptance of his own vulnerability to the pain of his past seemed to rend the darkness that had shrouded his soul for so many years. The light of new birth, of new life, spilled through him, suddenly freeing Wolf to feel, to love, to acknowledge that the Lady Kirsten's explanation could in fact be true.

Wolf threw back his head and laughed aloud. Perhaps his enemy was his father. In time he would know; however, at the present moment all he wanted was to relish his liberation from a past that had haunted him for so long.

Dara stirred, Wolf's laughter awakening her. She blinked up at him, squinting against the piercing glare of the midday sun. Hiding a yawn behind her hand, she wondered what he found so amusing when she could find little to smile about in her awkward position in front of him. Her nap had left every muscle in her body screaming from being cramped between Wolf's hard body and the saddle pommel. Dara shifted her hips and regretted it instantly. An "ouch" escaped her before she could clamp her lips together. She heard Wolf chuckle. Piqued at his lack of sympathy, she flashed him a look that plainly indicated that he could go to a much hotter clime with her blessings.

Wolf's answer was a devastating grin that made Dara completely forget her annoyance. Her own lips curled up at the corners as she said, "Pray tell, Sir Knight. What has put you in such high spirits? It certainly can't be our accommodations from last night, nor can it be our early morning stroll."

Wolf's grin deepened and mischief twinkled in his ebony eyes. "I would not say all of last night was unpleasant. 'Twas worth getting bashed in the head and thrown into the dungeon to have you, my sweet love. I vow all men would willingly become prisoners to find the ecstasy I experienced in Morgan Keep last eve."

Dara's cheeks heated with a blush as she reached up and lay her hand against Wolf's beard-stubbled jaw. "I love you, Wolf."

Wolf placed his hand over Dara's and brought it to his lips before he said, "And I love you, my sweet Dara. Will you become my wife?"

Dara's eyes widened in amazement. "You're asking me to marry you?"

Wolf nodded. "Aye. If you will have a bastard mercenary."

"I will have you, my Wolf, be you bastard mercenary or King of France," Dara said, stretching her arms up to cradle his head in her hands.

"Or son of Laird Angus Morgan?" Wolf whispered against her hair.

Dara leaned back and looked up at Wolf. "Do you now believe what Kirsten said?"

Wolf shrugged. "I do not say I believe. But I am willing to acknowledge that there may be some truth to what she says. I will speak with Laird Morgan and hear his version of the story before I make my decision. 'Tis not easy to accept that your enemy might in truth be your father. Or that you have a family after over thirty years of believing yourself a bastard with no kin." Wolf arched a raven brow at Dara. "What do you believe to be true?"

" 'Tis not important what I believe. 'Tis what you think and feel. That is all that matters to me. I just want you to be happy, my love."

"Then you would be satisfied if I never learned who sired me? You could give life to my children without wondering of their heritage?"

Dara reached up and drew Wolf's hand down to her softly rounded belly. She smiled. "Nothing matters to me except the father of the child I now carry. You are my world, Wolf. Together we begin our own family, our own bloodline. Your seed now grows within me. It is the future, not the past. It has a heritage, a heritage you give it with your strength and love. That is all either of us will ever need."

Wolf gaped at Dara, momentarily stunned by her revelation that he was to be a father again. After what seemed an eternity to the woman who sat still and quiet, he threw back his dark head and once more his laughter spilled into the sunny afternoon. Tears brimmed in Wolf's eyes as he hugged Dara close and whispered, "Thank you, my love. Thank you."

The sun had already dipped behind the trees, ending the day with a brilliant pageantry of colors. Rose and gold, mauve and magenta, spread seductive fingers across the horizon, beckoning the night from its hiding place in the east. Only the distant rumble of thunder disturbed the peace that claimed the land between the setting of the sun and dusky twilight. The sound reverberated across the landscape, moving southward like a great wave.

Arms folded over his wide chest, eyes narrowed thoughtfully toward the north, Wolf waited patiently for his enemy to appear out of the woods. Though the sound of the approaching horses might be misconstrued by many as thunder, Wolf had not taken it for a show of nature's force, but that of man; precisely, his enemy, Laird Morgan. He knew the laird now rode posthaste toward Castle Phelan, Morgan's purposes similar to his own when he'd rode north. The man was set to rescue his daughter.

A grim smile curled up the corners of Wolf's mouth. He had expected no less of Laird Morgan once he realized his prisoners had escaped and had stolen his daughter. That was the reason Wolf had taken the Lady Kirsten as hostage.

Wolf glanced toward the young soldier standing guard at his post. "Go and tell Ox to have the Lady Kirsten brought to me here."

The young man obeyed without question, and within minutes Ox escorted Kirsten up the narrow steps to the parapet walk to where her brother awaited. Dara followed close upon their heels. Wolf frowned down at the woman who claimed his heart and asked, "Lady, what do you here? I did not request your presence."

Sensing Wolf's annoyance, Dara squared her shoulders and eyed Wolf levelly. "I come because Kirsten is my friend. She has done neither me nor you any ill. And I will not have her used as a pawn between you and your father."

Annoyance giving way to anger, Wolf's bronzed features turned to granite. His dark eyes hardened to cold, gleaming onyx as he looked down into Dara's small defiant face. "Your loyalty should belong to the man you claim to love."

"My loyalty to you is not in question here, Wolf. You hold my heart and soul. It is bound to you through eternity. Yet I cannot step aside and see my friend ill-used no matter how much I love you. She has risked much for us, and my own honor compels me to do everything within my power to protect her."

"You talk as if I intend to harm the Lady Kirsten," Wolf growled, unwilling to let go of his anger, though he couldn't stop himself from admiring Dara's spunk in standing up to him. He'd have her no other way. Her strength of character, her integrity, and her valiant spirit all combined to make him love her all the more.

"I do not believe you would intentionally harm her. But I know from personal experience that you are not a man who will surrender anything easily."

Wolf glanced to the young woman standing so quietly at Dara's side. "What say you, Lady Kirsten? Do you believe I will harm you?"

"I know not what to say," Kirsten answered. "During the past days I have become aware that people do many things under pressure that they would not otherwise do."

Wolf smiled. "I doubt I will be put in such a position. Your father loves you well, Lady. He rides now to your rescue, fast and hard."

"He would love you as well, had he the opportunity," Kirsten said quietly.

Wolf arched a dubious brow. "I seriously doubt Laird Morgan could hold any emotion for me beyond hatred."

Accepting the fact that she couldn't convince Wolf that their father was not the villain he believed, Kirsten glanced toward the distant trees where the thunder had grown louder. "What do you plan?"

Wolf considered her question for a long moment. "I

plan only to regain what is mine. Once that is done, you will be free to leave Phelan."

Kirsten glanced up at her brother. "Do you truly mean what you say? You will not kill Papa?"

"I don't plan to harm him unless he attacks Phelan."

"But he will attack if you don't free me."

"Then he and his men will suffer the consequences."

Kirsten reached out and lay her hand upon Wolf's arm. Her eyes pleaded with him, as did her words. "Please don't harm our father."

"Because of the debt I owe you, I would not seek Laird Morgan's death. I will do only what I must to ensure that he recognizes my sovereignty over Phelan."

The shadows beneath the distant trees suddenly came alive as Laird Morgan and his men reined their mounts to a halt at the edge of the clearing. A few moments later Laird Morgan himself rode forward, a white flag of truce waving in the breeze above his head. He drew his mount to a halt and raised the visor of his helm. For a long moment his ebony gaze moved over the tall granite wall, seeking out any sign of his offspring. Seeing Wolf, he called, "I have come for my daughter."

Wolf drew Kirsten into view. "So I surmised."

Laird Morgan breathed a sigh of relief at the sight of his daughter, unharmed. He'd feared Wolf had retaliated in kind because of the reception he'd received at Morgan Keep. "Release her and let us put an end to this game."

Wolf's thick lashes narrowed as he stared down at the man whom he unwillingly was beginning to believe was his father. "I play no games, Laird Morgan. Before I release the Lady Kirsten, I will have your pledge that you will give up your claim on Phelan and you will return the medallion that you stole from me."

"I stole nothing. The medallion is rightfully mine."

"Nay. My mother gave it to me, and I will see it returned or you'll not have your daughter back."

Laird Morgan removed his helmet and wiped the sweat from his brow. In the last few days he'd begun to feel his years. Wearily, he looked up at the young man who possessed his image as well as his daughter. It was time to lay the past to rest. He nodded. "All right. 'Twill be as you ask."

"Then you are welcome to Phelan," Wolf said, before ordering the gates opened to allow Laird Morgan to enter.

Kirsten stood beside Wolf and Dara as the laird rode into the bailey and dismounted. She threw herself into his arms and clung to him, relieved that no blood had been spilled between her father and brother.

Laird Morgan held his daughter close as he looked up at the man standing on the castle steps. Gently he stroked Kirsten's unbound hair. "I am grateful to you for not harming Kirsten. She is innocent of any trespass against you."

Wolf nodded.

Entranced by the mirror image of himself thirty years younger, Laird Morgan couldn't tear his eyes away from Wolf's face. "And you have my vow that I will never lay claim to Phelan again."

Again Wolf nodded, too bemused by his own resemblance to the man standing in front of him to speak. He had tried to deny any kinship with Laird Morgan, but it was growing more difficult by the moment to believe that it was by mere coincidence that he felt he was staring at his own countenance. Wolf cleared his throat and said, "Kirsten has told me of your claim to Phelan."

Laird Morgan's heart leapt within his chest at the opening Wolf had offered him. His ebony gaze locked with Wolf's. "Did she also tell you of her belief that the old lord lied about the death of my son?"

Unaware that his actions stemmed from his sudden need of security, Wolf draped an arm about Dara's shoulders, drawing her close, before he ventured into the shadowy realm of his unknown past. "Aye. She told me."

Laird Morgan's gaze didn't release Wolf's. "Do you believe it possible?"

A stillness seemed to settle over Phelan, leaving only the two men who now sought to sort out the mistakes of the past and confront one another. Dara and Kirsten, though still held close, no longer existed. Nor did the men-at-arms who watched from the distance, or Ox and Bull, who stood in the doorway behind Wolf. Laird Morgan and Wolf were alone battling all the lies, all the treachery, and all the pain that had come through the years.

The moments ticked by as Wolf looked at the man before him. Again he tried to deny kinship, but the small boy within him wouldn't allow it. He cleared his throat and said simply, "Aye."

Tears brimmed in Laird Morgan's eyes and a wobbly smile played upon his lips as he sought to restrain his own emotions. He set Kirsten away from him and swallowed hard to clear his throat of the tightness that had begun as he awaited Wolf's answer. He extended his hand to Wolf as he said, "I feel the same."

Wolf looked down at the hand proffered to him for a long, agonizing moment, then took his arm from Dara's shoulder, reached out and grasped the laird's hand firmly. His own smile was less than steady as he said, " 'Tis not an easy thing to accept."

"Aye. But given the time and opportunity, perhaps we can come to think of each other as friends instead of enemies."

"And as father and son," Kirsten interjected quietly. She glanced up at her father, her face radiant. "I believe 'tis time that you met your granddaughter. I have only been allowed a glimpse of her, but from what I saw as we passed through the hall, she has the look of the Morgans about her as well."

"Aye, she does that," Dara said, imitating Kirsten's Scottish brogue as she looked up at her handsome lover.

Wolf laughed and pulled Dara close, secure now in her love as well as his past. "Come. 'Tis time to tell Ellice that she has a grandfather and an aunt."

The celebration was still going strong in the hall as Dara made her way up the stairs. She paused on the landing and looked back at the scene below. It was hard to believe that only a few short hours ago Wolf had been enemies with the man who now sat at his table laughing and joking with him as if they had been friends for years. Dara smiled as her eyes swept over the sculpted features of the man she loved. The shadows had vanished. Wolf's face now looked serene. The knowledge of his paternity seemed to have given him an inner peace that until today had been denied him, no matter how hard he strived to achieve it.

Dara hid a yawn behind her hand and turned once more to the stairs, content to leave Wolf and his new family to get acquainted without her. She would have stayed to help Wolf celebrate with his family, but knew she now had to think of the welfare of their child. The day had been imbued with so much tension, so much emotion, that she felt drained mentally as well as physically. She knew it would do her babe no good to push herself further. Since returning to Phelan in the early afternoon, she'd had little time to rest and recoup from her ordeal at Morgan Keep.

Dara yawned again as she pushed her chamber door open and quietly closed it behind her. The small fire kindled to offset the evening chill did little to chase away the shadows that wrapped themselves about the chamber like grotesque creatures stretching out their tentacles to distort everything they touched.

Struggling to keep her eyes open, and far too weary to light a taper to give her a better view, Dara crossed the chamber to her bed. She sank down on the soft mattress and kicked off her slippers. She wiggled her toes, savoring the soothing freedom for her tired feet as she worked loose the laces on her gown. Dara stood and reached to pull the gown over her head. She did not hear the intruder, nor realize any danger until the hand clamped down over her mouth to stifle off a scream, and the arm encircled her waist, imprisoning her against a rock-hard body.

Fearing for her life and believing Navarre's henchmen had finally come to execute her, Dara began to struggle with every ounce of strength she possessed. She bit down on the fleshy palm covering her mouth at the same time she brought her elbow back into her captor's ribs. He grunted in pain and momentarily lessened his hold. Dara jerked her mouth free and screamed.

The scream ripped through the chamber, echoing down the stairs, silencing those assembled in the hall. Tankards stilled in the air, eyes locked, and forks clattered to the table as time seemed to freeze everyone in place except Wolf. He came to his feet before another scream unlocked the spell the first had wrought. Drawing his sword as he took the stairs two at a time, he rushed toward Dara's chamber. His father and the MacDonald twins followed close behind.

Wolf burst through the doorway, chest heaving, ebony gaze searching the dimly lit chamber. Spying Dara and the intruder, Wolf paused, cautiously aware that if he made the wrong move, it could well cost Dara her life. He lowered his blade as he eyed the stranger menacingly and said, "Release her if you care to keep your life."

"Nay, Sir Wolf. I come here to take the Lady Dara."

Dara stiffened, her eyes widening with recognition of the voice behind her. "Paul, is it truly you?"

"Aye, sister," Paul said quietly, his words for Dara's ears alone.

Tears of joy brimmed in her eyes, and her lower lip began to quiver. Misconstruing the look on her face as pain, Wolf's fury magnified tenfold. He took a step forward and ordered, "Release her or die."

Suddenly realizing the danger to her brother, Dara shook her head. "Nay, Wolf. 'Tis Paul, my brother. He will not harm me."

Wolf frowned. "Your brother?"

"*Oui,*" Dara said, glancing over her shoulder at the man who still held her.

Wolf's gaze locked upon Paul, searching the face of the man Dara claimed as brother. A brief memory flickered through Wolf's mind. At last he said, "You are the beggar."

Paul nodded. "*Oui.* I am also Paul Rochambeau. I came here to reclaim my sister."

Wolf glanced from Paul to Dara and then back to her brother. His face darkened. He'd allow no one to take Dara from him. "She is not yours to reclaim."

"She is my sister."

"Aye, and she is also to be the mother of my child," Wolf said.

Paul glanced uncertainly at his sister, shaken to hear of Dara's condition. Had he been wrong to come to her rescue? He shook the thought away. From everything that Renee had said, she had been taken against her will. Paul's sapphire gaze shot back to Wolf. Fury burned through him at the thought of the dishonor done his sister. "You bastard. You have sorely misused my sister and abused the Rochambeau name." Paul released Dara and stepped in front of her as he withdrew the dirk from beneath the folds of his mantle. "You will not go unpunished."

"No," Dara screamed, grabbing Paul's arm to stay him. "You don't understand. I love Wolf. I am proud that I carry his child."

Paul flashed Dara a withering look. "What say you? Have you lost all self-respect?"

Dara shook her head. "Nay. I have lost nothing from loving Wolf. I have only gained. He has given me life."

"Don't speak such foolishness. You had a life at Rochambeau."

Dara gave her brother a sad little smile and let her hand fall to her side. "Nay, brother. I lived your life. I took your place while you chased your dreams. I fought to preserve your birthright, not my own. And I learned that I am but a woman in a world where men like Navarre can use females as pawns in their evil schemes. I did my best for you, brother, but I will not sacrifice my happiness further. I love Wolf, and I will be his wife and bear his child."

Paul ran his fingers through his hair in exasperation. He didn't know what to do now. His plans to be the hero and rescue his sister had suddenly turned to dust with her announcement. Paul's spirits drooped as he glanced from his sister to the tall Englishman whom she claimed to love. He shrugged his surrender. "Then it would seem I have no more reason to remain at Phelan."

Dara's face fell.

Seeing her expression, Wolf quickly interjected, "I would think, as Dara's brother, you would remain here long enough to see her happily wed."

Accepting his future brother-in-law's unspoken offer of peace, Paul grinned. "*Oui*. I will remain long enough to see honor done. I will also remain long enough to learn more about my cousin's activities while I was gone. I am most anxious to know how Navarre figures into all this."

"And I am most anxious for you to hear it, brother," Dara said. "It will be up to you to see that Navarre pays for his treachery toward our family. He has impoverished Rochambeau with his schemes. It lays in ruin."

"*Oui*. I have seen the destruction to our home. It may take me years before Rochambeau is as it was before Navarre set his sights upon our wealth. However, I vow Cousin Charles will not go unpunished. Even if it takes me till my dying day to reclaim all we have lost."

" 'Twill not take as long as you believe," Wolf said quietly.

All eyes turned to the master of Phelan.

He smiled. "I have already begun Navarre's downfall." Wolf met Dara's curious gaze. "As I have often said, no one threatens those I love without suffering the consequences."

Paul chuckled. "I see I will be leaving my sister in good hands."

Wolf nodded sagely.

Paul glanced at the men crowding the doorway behind Wolf and arched a curious brow. "It would seem, brother-in-law, that you must make your men realize that we are soon to become kin."

Wolf burst into laughter as he closed the space between himself and Dara. He pulled her to him, draping a strong arm about her shoulders. He eyed the group who stood awaiting his orders. " 'Tis strange how quickly a family grows once it's rooted. Since this morn I have become a groom-to-be, a son, a brother, a brother-in-law, and an expectant father. It makes one wonder what will come on the morrow."

Dara's glance moved over the grinning Laird Morgan,

Ox, Bull, her own brother Paul, and then to the small wide-eyed child who peeped from behind her new grandfather's legs. She held out her arms to Ellice, who quickly came into them and hugged her tightly about the neck. Dara looked up at Wolf and quietly said, "More of my love, my great Wolf. Much more of my love."

Wonderful historical romances by

Cordia Byers

Published by Fawcett Books.
Available in your local bookstore.